An Ogham Magic Series

Wild Hunt

Julie G. Murphy

ACKNOWLEDGMENTS

Thanks very much to Catherine O'Connell who helped me find Bitty's cottage, holy wells and dolmans throughout Ireland. It was a great trip with good company. A shout out to Tadhg who drove me up to the Spring Hill Halting Site but wouldn't let me get out, and to the doorstep of Cork Prison where I wasn't allowed to take pictures. A great big thanks to Nancy Schumacher, my publisher, whose attention to detail helped take this book to the next level.

Ogham Alphabet

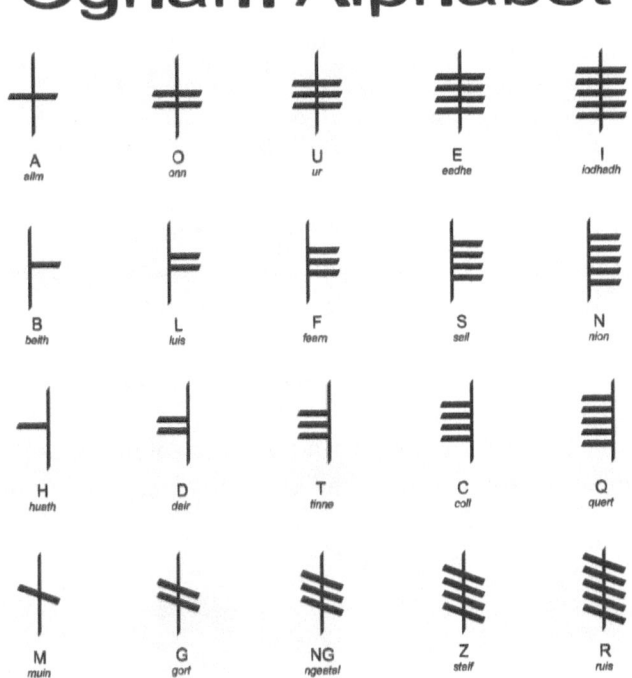

'Kindred Spirits' Sculpture
A tribute to the incredible generosity the Choctaw Nation
showed the Irish people during the Great Famine.

Brother and kin to all the twilit gods'
Living, forgot, long dead: sad Shadow of pale hopes
Forgotten dreams and madness of men'
Outcast among the gods and called the Fool, the *Amadan*
Yet dreaded even by those immortal eyes....

CHAPTER
ONE

Magic
Draoideachta

F og to start, with the odd bright spell, and then lashing
rain is the shite Irish weather of the day. Really...of
yesterday, probably tomorrow and the day after that.
I'm just saying that the heavy damp is complicating my already
less-than-brilliant mental outlook. My excuse. It's June. The
Tuatha Dé Dannan, the Irish Gods...cute hoors that they are
anyway...are especially active in the month of solstice.

So I'm soaked through but also sweating from the quivering
suspense of it all. A sort of baptism without a river. The thought
of where are they, the hoor-gods, is followed hard on its heels
by where is it? I search through the pockets of low fog for the
bell tower of Saint Peter's Catholic Church. I'm peering down
the distance of "*An Phríomhshráid*" in old Gaelic, or North Main
Street, Cork not just because it's a shockin' Irish evening with
the rain making me blind in two eyes and that churches are
solid, without leaks, and offer free rest for the weary.

1

Er, yeah, but not only...those ARE all good. I am weary... babbling-weary in the pissing rain and coming sunset. I wipe my vision clearer to scrutinize between wattle and timber houses. I squint into the light-sucking voids of narrow lanes. I keep walking. There is one thing about a good rain in Cork. At least the smell of shite and smoke is less pungent.

I'm trying to find this church because the best treat about Catholic churches is that they have only THE ONE GOD in them. One joyful, singular, cracking, ALMIGHTY God. It's spiritual genius. Everyday day I say to myself...too shiteing bad it's not true.

Because there are at least three thousand gods in the world, one for each type of animal and plant, plus more. Two thousand, nine hundred, and ninety-nine, too many. For a bit more perspective, here in Ireland, the Dagda and his large-as-life relatives are a full cart of nutcases. They are a rain-shower of shites, a daily dose of our Lady of Perpetual arse kicking. The men and women of Ireland sang when Saint Patrick came along with a magic staff, a mission, and some simplification. 'Twas Himself, the Big P, who sealed the gods, large and small, underground. They were the real banished snakes. He hunted them down and tucked away the key. And then he cornered the market on all things magic.

"Almost...feckin' almost heaven." A bit of joy perks me up when I can see the bell tower in a break of the clouds, and then the iron gates surrounding the courtyard of the church.

It's the "almost" I'm concerned with in June. Almost sealed; almost stripped of magic; almost gone. That and it's the second week of the month; that shower-of-shite time, the summer solstice when magic is at its most powerful and the veil is thin. Harvest time for the *Tuatha Dé Dannan*. Cutting hay on the longest day when magic is strong and the veil thin. They think of me as free labor and/or dead. No preference.

I'm almost through the blessed door. As the sun is almost setting.

Consider the immortal gods of Ireland. The Milesians were

the first to get them underground. Patrick's power from the Roman church sewed them up and reduced them to fairy status. Eventually, they became only powerful enough to harass the housewives who forget to leave out the daily offering of milk on their steps, or to curse the poor farmers for plowing under their fairy forts.

With all the believers turning Catholic, I expected that finally the Irish Gods wouldn't exist to anyone anymore.

What a load of bollocks. They absolutely exist, especially at night when the seal weakens and at the solstice when all magic strengthens through the ramped-up residual faith of humans. The pressure of the growing magic is making my nose bleed and my joints ache. Nearly there. My hand is on the latch of the priests' door. A black bird flies at my head. I brain it with my blackthorn club. It is just a bird in the end, but I'm twitchy.

No other country hailed Catholicism more than the Irish. They fell hook, line, and sinker. One God seemed marvelous, extraordinary, and wonderful to this God-exhausted country. But just because people didn't believe in the *Tuatha*, didn't make their jolly non-existence true.

The Catholic Church controls the magic in Ireland. The *Tuatha* may screech my name, but inside a church, they can't touch me. Just a few more steps through the door to my sanctuary for the night from the great triple-goddess of ill-humor, malice and envy, the Morrigan, Babd, and Macha and all the other vengeance-seeking *unseelies*. My fingers are tingling. I glance over my shoulder.

The Good People, yeah, no. They've got unending notions of Themselves, and they're all half mad with inbreeding, like the British Monarchy. Other than that, they're feckin' lovely altogether.

After I slam the priests' door behind me, I lean onto it. You never know if you've come too close. A church on every corner, lads. Get on it.

I have my wool *brate* around me cocoon-like. It's been a

normal, inhospitable, damp day. That's turned into a foul, soaking, blustery night, when an ale and a fire is the only cure.

Sure, what fire…what ale?

I'm inclining to feel sorry for myself tucked into a small room with only stone benches lining the walls. Not warmer in, but at least dryer. My leather shoes squelch on the black flagstone floor. All of me is dripping, and my feet are waterlogged.

Ok. It's good enough to feel safe. I unwind my cloak, drop my bag, and put my feet up. Sure, I need sleep. My eyes are scratchy like. The rain and pressure of trying to see through the dark and fog has thinned them.

From the nave, the central part of the church, the smell of incense from a late evening vigil circles the alcove. Myrrh is seeping under the pointed stone archway through the drawn red-velvet curtains that hang there, voices as well. There is a low hum of prayer.

I focus on its fragrance. I inhale its sweet aroma and taste its sweetness on my tongue. I feel my muscles relax. I place my blackthorn club on the stone bench and then spread a piece of gray cloth. On it I place my sustenance, a roll, and cheese, water. The cheese is moldy around the edges and the bread stale. My tongue searches for swirls of flavor as I chew and relax. I plump my bag on the bench and tuck my *brate,* cloak, around me. As I finish with a long drink of water, I listen to the murmur of the devout and the rain on the roof. I'm warming. The voices comfort me. I am not alone. Satiated and with the roof of the church over my head, I can let my eyelids close.

June is trouble. There isn't a civil word for the month that has Saint John's Eve in it, AND me sister's birthday. She was born on Saint John's Eve. When magic is at its most powerful, she came into the world. She'll curse me, literally, if I don't bring her something. To get there, I have to travel church to church.

Anyway, she'll have to get in line curse-wise. How old is she now,

anyway? Born thirteen hundred and thirty-three. Thirteen-seventy now. Three and forty years. I can remind her of that when I see her. Jaysus, I'm getting too old for this shite.

As if to clear me of that notion, of being too old, or used up...or possibly just for the craic of it (knowing the *Tuatha*) vertigo triggers inside my skull, a brain tornado. I feel my eyes bouncing. My head has invited in the storm outside like.

"Feck off."

I try to stand. Maybe I'm not far enough inside the church. Get to the altar. Bracing against the wall at my back as I reach out to a lateral wall, my hand lands on the nose of the stone effigy of the used-to-be mayor of Cork City.

I throw up. Brutal.

Coughing and spitting, I steady myself. Can't hear a thing with the superstorm in my ears. The red curtains...not even a fluttering hem. The stone effigy begins to disintegrate to sand under my hand like the feel of an ocean wave at the shore pulling beach out from under my feet.

I stare through the vertigo as the rolling, sharp edges of the carved face deteriorates. First the nose and then the eyes, like melting stone. Sand bunches under my hand and falls to the floor through my fingers. The script erases like a hand brushing away letters written in dirt.

It stops as it started. Nausea lingers. I collapse onto the bench. I can hear.

For a split second.

Next there's a pressure of being pulled, lengthened on an invisible torture rack. My joints ache, my muscles bind and unbind, my sight blurs. It's hard to catch a breath from the pain and the squeeze on my vital organs.

I'm in Catholic Church for feck sake.

Celtic magic. Power over the weather, the elements, incantations, magical objects, invisibility, raising aloft, sounds, shapeshifting...shite! I scrutinize my hands.

Eejit, they don't shapeshite others.

The magic ends with me on the chilly floor, breathing in and breathing out. I am mince, masticated and spat out. I smell my vomit in my clothes, in the room. There's always a sense of fight or flight, mostly flight when magic has grabbed me by the balls. I don't know what this is, but my balls are in agony, probably bleeding.

Gods only know what's next. Instinct says run.

You run.

I make myself sit up. With the help of a stone bench and a wall, I stand. The movement is by degrees like an aged man shifting bit by bit upward. Can't say it was done without a lot of swearing. If swearing could be an incantation, there'd be some gods who felt it.

I glance around the alcove. The sharp stone floor is rounded-like as if centuries of human feet have walked it. It's worn. The mayor of Cork has no nose. That singular proboscis is now an anthill of granulated dust.

In all fairness, I have to say whatever that was, it was epic.

I walk like a drunken peasant to the pointed stone archway that connects the alcove to the nave. I peer out through the red, velvet curtains. If I'd been hard-slapped, the effect would be the same. The body of the church is a gutted, hollow of a room with a concrete floor, movable walls, and metal stairs to a glass-balconied loft. Golden stained windows gone, pews gone, altar gone, priest gone, parishioners gone. Maybe I whiffed too much incense.

I smell coffee. "Coffee?" What the hell? I ask myself, not to mention "metal stairs" and "glass-balconied loft."

There are single-post café tables and plastic folding chairs.

"Plastic, folding chairs?" Head trauma is what I'm thinking. My mind is talking shite. What there is not. There is not a single Christ-suffering cross. Gone is the altar piece of fluted Corinthian pilasters. Gone is the painted surround of a dove with flames of glory on the wall behind it. Gone is the

mayor's gallery over which the king's arms were carved and painted.

I back into the alcove and drop onto the stone bench. And then the migraine begins. My mind is filling with information of this new coffee-and-plastic-filled time, historical gaps of knowledge. The pressure of new facts, words, cities, places pushes on my brain, and expands it at the same time. I growl in pain. Feckin', low-life, devious fairies.

How can they be doing this with their low magic? Even in the high-magic of June?

They live in all ages simultaneously. Time is fluid to immortals, but this is heavy-hitting magic. More than they've got between them. "I'm feckin' mortal," I roar into the pain. They are always forgetting that. They'd steal your eye and come back for the lashes. When the pain ends, I slump into myself. I feel like shite-faced roadkill.

"Jaysus, my blackthorn club." My eyes pop open. I see it. It's not dust. Relief is not enough of a word. I pick it up and inspect the Celtic Ogham letters carved into it. The potent five; *Beith*, the birch tree, for release and regeneration, *Luis*, the rowan tree, associated with Brigid for protection against enchantment, *Duir*, the mighty oak for masculine strength, resilience, *Tinne*, the holly, plant of warriors, and *Straith*, the blackthorn tree, associated with the *Cailleach*. This letter works against the dark side of magic. They are all as if carved just yesterday. Which means this...I'm gonna need the club and the magic the carved letters hold within it.

Side thought, and this hits me hard. What's up with the magic of the Catholic Church?

Feckin' fairies. I breathe out a long breath as the half-life of their magic eases my discomfort. Still, there isn't a bone in my body that wants to move, ever. My brain is wanting a nap for a thousand years like, but an unquiet shifts under my skin, making me restless, pressing for action. A fear of what this is. An immanency so strong I stand, even through the pain and

imbalance. I try the pointed-top, priests' exterior door that I came in through, but it is now locked and no key.

Only option…to stroll through that red curtain into the non-church where there are people, people who are not tatooed, blackthorn club-carrying, *brate*-wearing persons. Once again, cute hoors these fairies.

A woman with dark medium-length hair tucked behind her ears sees me first. Her once over is, er, yeah, stinging. Also, her nostrils flare meaning stink. Her hands hold pieces of a solid multi-colored plastic mat that come apart in squares like a piece of a puzzle. "Oh! Where did you come from," she says smooth like, and then, "I'm very sorry but you're going to have to leave now. The event is over. We're just cleaning up."

"Great craic then?" I ask as I walk away, with the left-over aura of vertigo leaning me like I'm a boozing man who has been sleeping it off on a church stone bench. Which is what she thinks. Lady, I wish. The four additional women taking down the event stare at me, and I at them as I make my way across the gray cement floor in my red, *léine,* belted tunic, which hangs to my knees and its slack hanging over that belt like a fat-sagging stomach. I suddenly panic-remember my Ogma's knife. I pat at my waist. It's there. Steel is indestructible, the leather sheath feels whole.

A stout lady with painfully short, color-deficient, dark hair, and wearing what my strained brain is calling, baggy blue jeans, and an aran sweater, and holding a cane says, "Thanks for coming," like she's seen everything in life, and a long-haired, *léine*-wearing, knife-toting man leaning on a blackthorn club with lime-coated spiky hair and a blue woad-tattooed cheek is an everyday occurrence for her. Not to mention the torc around my neck. Pretty sure it's not, and I have to admire her smoothness.

I leave the church by the front door. The entrance area is still recognizable, solid-built like for the ages. I step into the low-light of a rainy, late evening.

Couldn't I be in nice, sunny, southern France?

Outside. Gone is the clip-clop of horses or rumbling carts. Mostly it's a harsh, hoarse constant hum of movement and voices and engines. A metal conveyance whizzes by. My mind says, "car." I'm standing in the courtyard by two solid, old-growth oak trees that were saplings, what, an hour ago. Now strings of small lights climb round and round their massive trunks. A man gathering plastic trash asks me if I was the entertainment for the wedding, maybe the pipes player. Good to see the Irish are still in there taking the mick out of everyone.

"Feck off!"

The man laughs.

Nothing for it. I arrange my brown *brate*, over my shoulders to cover my clothes. I square up and walk nearer to the road. I'm standing by the street looking, most likely, like my brain is slow. I'm orienting, from a whistle-stop journey from the fourteenth century, and fighting pain and leftover vertigo, and panic when someone yells, "The nurse is looking for ye," and from another, "Did ya mean to wear those clothes, or did they take the rest? Where's yer Leprechaun?"

"Up ye'r arse," I call. I might be a bit grouchy from the trip.

I glance up and down the street. My brain tells me what things are, magically updating like, but my experience of these things is new. Lights like. From lamps along the street popping on, also the occasional car headlamps. Light glows through the windows of open establishments. Across from me, on the corner, is a gaming shop named Kaiju that has a monster logo in an orange circle.

The line of compact, street-front shops are all painted in saturated, primary colors. The "Scotts for Tools,' signage is deep red with white letters. "Idea Pet Shop," next to it is mustard yellow with back letters. 'Spice Inn' signage is white on red. The small shops or restaurants are linked elbow to elbow in a long line on either side of North Main Street. The living quarters above are various designs of brick work with

large, airy Georgian windows, many of which are covered with plywood.

Sure, Cork is still a tip.

Under a red awning is the store front to Minihane's Jewelers, next to that, in light green and blue, Vincent's Charity Shop, then The Kiddie Zone in puce yellow and red. Also, a 'Puff 'N' Stuff, CBD' shop, which my mind tells me to try out sometime. I step outside the wrought-iron, eight-foot fence onto a cement footpath. Next to Saint Peter's defunct Church is a Gorta charity shop (open late on Fridays) that has a green book cover in the window saying, 'Keep Calm, Sure it'll all be Grand.'

Sure, it will.

I'm half torn to just find another real church. This is Ireland. There must be more. I have no idea where to go or what to do, or why this has happened. All my intuition is saying duck. I only know that if I get any of those collective Goddesses within my grip, I'll squeeze so hard their collective eyes will pop out. I know it's the women because men are less inventive. As to the why any of it? It will come or is here. I glance around.

On a black road, a fast-moving metal vehicle blares at me as if I'm going to step down in front of it. It douses me with a spray of black gutter water.

Effin' rich. Maybe this is hell.

Perfect. I can't just stand here like a gob. Anyway, this is Ireland. I relegate the anxiety to the usual area in my brain and commit right to walk in search of drink. North Gate Castle used to be down this way, always hospitable. Definitely, probably gone, but it's a direction and then I'm slammed into from behind. I twist and land on me arse.

"I'm so sorry. Are you hurt?" this rushed woman exclaims, and then she takes in my clothes. "It's you. God, it must be. Phew. I thought I'd missed you. The plane was late. Two hours."

Never mind I'm on the street like.

She's still babbling on, and then boom, right across her

stream of words, an explosion punches through the veil. Magical pressurized waves throw the woman onto me. I smell the singe of high energy. Windows blow. Alarms from the cars parked on the narrow street pierce the air. More significant is something roars. The heat of its projected breath warms the air. Out of the dust-gloom, a Kaiju monster, in full fury, emerges.

Shows how any bad situation can turn for the worse.

TWO

Téigh go cac
It's all going to *$#!!

A feckin' Kaiju. They don't breathe fire but still, they are damned impossible to kill, and it's looking straight at the pile of me and the woman. So it's me, on my arse, with my arms and legs wrapped in my wringing-wet cape, and not to mention the flailing woman. There are not words strong enough.

I glance around, not a single bazooka or tank. What?

The Kaiju is a theropod from the late Cretaceous Period. It comes out of the sea, normally. This one erupted from the orange circle drawn on a shop sign. As in a magic circle. As in a magical creature. The monster is not a demon. He's just an enchanted sucker someone has trapped in and then broken out of a closed circle. We are all suckers of someone evil and powerful in magic.

It has dark green skin, a tan belly, and glowing, red, angry eyes. It's designed to create paralytic horror, and it's doing a spectacular job. It's angry and roaring.

The woman gets to her feet. I unwrap myself from my clothing while thinking, *seriously an effin' Kaiju.* I just want to end myself laughing.

The thorns in my blackthorn my club are four inches long and as strong as nails, but I'm not sure they will pierce the rough, plated hide of the creature from a long-range toss. Normally a blackthorn tree's thorn puncture, with a blood-letting penetration, creates serious wounds, allergic reactions, and intense pain. I'm talking sepsis…organ failure, septic shock, blood clots here. Only if you can pierce the thing. It's like someone knew this, knew me, and had it all planned.

Along with this bad boy's gigantic, rigid, impossible-to-pierce-plates that grow out of its skin, other things I have to consider are his large powerful hands with nails like the fangs of an ancient saber-tooth tiger.

If I'm lucky, I might be able to miraculously slash the groin area where the plating thins. If I can get close enough, and then it can eat me in the time it takes the septicemia to kill it.

Not to mention…I have to be ready for my *geasa,* my curse, to kick in with an adrenaline spike like an energy injection

The *geasa* begins sending out poisonous desires. Within the compulsion to do battle, my heart engorges with blood. It pumps the liquid like a tidal wave to my limbs and brain. My veins stretch with the overflow. Shock pain radiates through every part of my body. A plus, the electrification cures migraines.

The neurons in my brain are reconfiguring to the mental state of a berserker. Unless I control the craving to fight, each meet-up will be my last, as the Morrigan intended. The *geasa* does not allow for intelligence, just the overwhelming desire to kill. This one is designed to kill the recipient, not to protect me.

A cute little trick conjured up by the Morrigan Herself. I'm pretty sure the curse includes a violent struggle with a truculent Kaiju.

I force my brain to slow, to observe. I've gotten better at it over the years, pressing through the noise in my head to a solution that won't get me killed. I am compelled to fight, but I have managed to control how. I've never by nature been one to choose exertion anyway. I'm more inclined to the very easy number.

The Morrigan hates it.

Next to a shop door by me, my updating-by-magic brain says, is a three feet, plastic ice cream cone with a large, plastic, chocolate flake bar sticking out. There is an iron pole there up the middle of it for stability, useful for impaling through a large eye socket and into a small brain. Now I'm sucking diesel.

"Ice cream and chocolate," I wave the giant cone in his face. "Come and get it."

Dumb sod doesn't deserve this. It just doesn't.

Lactose intolerant, I think as its spiked tail, like a whip, sends me and the cone crashing into a building.

The window gives and so do my puny ribs. A fresh cut bleeds into my eye. Blood is very viscous and hard to see through. My nose is broken, and I can't breathe through it. I suck in the pain. Just another day under *Tuatha* magic.

Through all this, the woman is not in a panic and has not run. What's wrong with her like? I always get the mental ones.

I have hung onto the cone/spear, and I stagger onto my feet for a javelin throw before it goes for her.

The woman is staring at the magical creature. They are like a pair of strangers who have discovered in each other a mutual attraction. It's all there but the slow-mo run and the lift.

Away with the fairies. She is laughing and swearing alternately. Standing large, she outstares the thing. Her eyes are wide with fear and the incredible, but she's standing her ground. Her lips are moving with surety, or at least intensity. I can't hear her. Praying most like. I smell its breath like drying seaweed on a beach. It's that close, and her eyes are closed now. Aye, closed. Her lips are working away, though. Nutcase.

I stretch back my arm to begin the throw. It's a one-shot deal. I consider the distance. In a long vertical toss, the pole must retain enough power to pierce the eyeball and the small brain. I've got to get to the brain wherever it's hiding in that massive skull. For extreme force, I reach into the *geasa*, and I hold the spear with the Ogma's hand.

The Kaiju wakes from its momentary enchantment and steps down the road. The tarmac cracks under its weight. It's like an above ground earthquake in sound and destruction.

Unceasingly, she calls her insanity towards the creature, even as the damn monster pounds down on us like a swinging wrecking ball with long nails and bad breath. If I miss, it's all balls. But I don't get the forward motion in play before the Kaiju sways, like a drunk on a walk outside to piss. Like something in his small brain popped. And then, her an immobile statue or not, I grab the woman's arm and run like blazes.

The creature sways again, takes a step, then another. It falls like a sawn tree, only it's not fir boughs that are coming down, but legs, arms, tail and head. The wrought iron fence spikes in front of Saint Peter's church pierces the monster's chest in several places. The Kaiju's head takes out the oldest once-upon-a-time church in Cork. Luckily, it's closed. The creature farts like it was constipated.

That works. I slide down the front wall of an Indian take-out and sit against it in the litter of fast-food wrappers, cans and gum.

"NO!" she screams. I grab at her, but we're both slick with biliverdin, reptile blood.

She runs, *runs*, towards the Kaiju. Towards it. After crawling over the rubble, she is next to it, hand reaching forward. She's frightened and not quite touching the hard scales...still. Off the end of her fingers a thorough dousing of Kaiju blood drips. It's dripping from her hair and clothes as she stands. What in mourning? In guilt? In compassion? Like her old dog has been put down. She'd take its head in her lap if she could; it's that intense, Herself standing next to the body.

"No." She is still crying. It's all bollocks, for her, for the creature. Feckin' fairies.

Even though there's Kaiju blood all over my head, mantel, and shoes, I make myself pick up a bottle from the cement path, and I scoop into it as much biliverdin as I can from the pools around the beast. My head's not completely screwed on either. Also, I'm wondering if I just can leave the carcass here as someone else's problem.

She's now moved on from her keening to staring at the Kaiju like she wants to kick the tires to see if it's real, to see if any of this is real. And maybe in that, a swift kick of pique for biliverdin'ing her. I don't blame her. Through the years, I've wanted to kick a few damn things myself.

The hard scales are turning to a brown, full-bodied wine-looking liquid, leaving the inside organs naked for less time than a man needs to comb a balding head. I pull her back as the rest of the magical organism follows. We slip and fall in a soupy mess that is running down the road and into drains. From the warmth of it, a fog rises in the area. Fog, nothing the Irish haven't seen before. Or deep, dark puddles on back streets.

"Liquification...Jesus Murphy," she says. And finally, there she goes. She does the, my-knees-are-giving-out, shite-this-is-real, slow slide down the wall to the gum incrusted sidewalk. Shock setting in probably, as her legs turn to jelly.

"Head between your legs. Keeping breathing, deep breaths."

She does keep her head down and breathes.

The Kaiju is gone. Not much we can do about the blown windows, the flattened cars, or the cracks in the road, or the church. "Probably should get out of here." But I don't move. I'm that exhausted and disoriented.

The woman, her head is still in her hands, but the biliverdin bath has evaporated. Steam's coming off her as she throws up. She raises her head as if it's heavy or fragile. She does that arm thing that women do to sweep a lot of long hair out of their face and behind their back. She inhales and says, "Way to go with that ice cream cone."

With that crack, in the face of all this, I decide I like her.

"There was a deadly chocolate flake sticking out of it. What were you doing back there, for Christ's sake?" That must be me moaning as I stand and offer a hand to her. Fortunately, the Kaiju was a bit of a buzzkill for the evening pedestrians. No one about for now. They'll come back. "Up you come."

"Clothes," she says. "Clean clothes." She pulls at her extra-long sleeved, tight-fitting pullover sweatshirt that has been cut and then laced at the sides. The sweatshirt is long over her hips and thighs and leggings. The leggings have an artistic pattern of feathers, white half-moons, and golden suns in the fabric. There are lace patches at the knees. Suddenly, I don't feel half bad about my own clothes.

+++

The Gorta Charity Shop next to the church is just past closing time, but the cashier must have hit the road, out the back, when the Kaiju passed her window.

"What's that you've got on anyway?" she asks as she pushes on the door and finds it unlocked.

"Did I ask you that?" I say as I walk over the threshold of the shop.

"Dibs on the bathroom."

I take scissors I find on the counter to cut off my clothing. Better that than the shite-pain of raising my arms. I stuff the rags into a small rubbish bin. I find the sliding hangers full of clothes along a rack strangely tranquilizing, and the choice surprising. If I've been pressed to a new fight of cosmic whatever this is, I'm looking for proper attire. Projection of fierceness begins with clothes.

"Whoa, put something on," says Herself, as she comes out of the toilet.

"I want something cool."

Clothes fly at me from every direction. "Jeans, a white button-up shirt and a merino wool, gray, knit jumper, and ya baby, a Hard Traders trench coat, from SNS. It's even black and not worn at all. All you need now is a black skinny tie," she says as she throws. Underwear hit my face. "Now use the bathroom."

I pump hand soap onto paper towels to clean up, including my hair under the faucet. The flare of my *geasa* has cleaned my pipes on the inside. Nothing like snaking out my pipes still blocked with the past with a push of pure adrenaline. I like jeans; my arse looks. Good jacket. After looking at her previous clothing choices, I'm surprised at her good taste. The mirror is remarkably clear in showing the firework of bruising around my nose. It used to be a good nose. Well-shaped and strong. I've worked hard to protect it. I'm going to rip the piss out of someone. "Feckin' fairies," I recite to the mirror as I pop my nose back into place. Same again while putting my arms into the sleeves of the shirt and coat. Dammit.

I keep my wool mantle. It's good and warm.

The woman changes into really tight jeans and a North Face, orange jacket, which I tell her makes her target-ready. She scoffs and changes into a worn, silver-blue, Antora jacket with hood. Her black hair is wet and braided down the length of her back. In fairness, she cleans up well. "Got any money?" she asks.

"Skint."

"Typical." She throws money on the counter, and we're back on the street. "You can't tell your blue eyes from the bruising."

I'm just that vain that I note she has noticed my eyes. Really,

I look like resurrected dogshite, while she looks thriving. I rub my hands together and glance around. "That drink I was after is now called for." I spy the first possibility, the Black Dog Saloon and Mexcaleria. In better days it was a shop with living area above that had airy bay windows on two levels, place of pride. The bay windows are still there, but now it has a long, wide plastic signboard attached across a decaying stone front. The sign reads, 'Chemically Speaking, Alcohol is a Solution.' No finer words ever written.

I head towards it, she redirects me. "Seriously?" She gives out to me. A lot of censure in that voice of hers for having about died just minutes ago. Possibly used to getting in and out of binds this one. I'd bet good money she's never seen a real-life Kaiju before, though. She hasn't given herself a blinking moment to process.

"My money, my pick, and it's not going to be a Mexcaleria dive."

A few more blocks down, Ryan's Bar looks a finer place with its five window panels that advertise "Beamish" and "Murphy's Irish Stout." Inside is dark, but the smell is exactly what I am thinking about. Ale. I'm there. At the bar, next to an old punter, his cap on the stainless-steel top, a dark ale in front of him, I say, "I'll have what he's drinking."

She asks the same and we are walking towards the back, drinks in hand. We pass two more punters sitting on a button-upholstered, red, vinyl sofa that backs the long wall. In front of them are low tables that have heavy, wrought iron legs. The men are like mannequins of themselves. Only their arms move to reach for their pints, and they hardly speak. It's all been said, and so they are watching us. We are incomers. If they heard the roar of the attack of the Kaiju, they either thought it was a car wreck, or just couldn't be bothered.

I inhale the imprinted, heavy, malted smell as I head to the peat fire. I'm chilling down from the sudden drop of magical energy, kind of like a fever breaking. I ease myself into a padded chair in front of the flames. As I knock back the beer, it occurs to me that Saint Peter's isn't a church anymore because it was closed for business.

I'm thinking of three, the time jump, the Kaiju, the defunct church. Three in magic is a catalyst. Usually for things that can kill you.

The woman is staring at me. At *me*, for feck's sake. I should be staring at her, mourning a magical monster...like she killed it.

"Are you *Padraic O'Duibh*?" She's got my full name and in Irish. "I'm supposed to give you this," my companion in near-death says, while sitting across from me with her pint already empty. Only she doesn't give me anything, but caves inward. She won't cry again, but wants to, that's clear. "What is going on?" Her hands are fisted, trying to be strong and all that. Join the party. I'm amazed she's made it this long. Not weak willed. The fairies know what they want.

"That wasn't a dream," she streams on. "I'm not hallucinating." She studies her hands to see what, if they're really attached like? "It didn't deserve that. Oh god, I'm going to throw up." And she's gone, but her bag is still here. I feel myself grin. Facing me is her name burned into the side, Mealla. Only the first name, though. The bag was tossed without consequence onto the dirty floor...well-used bag means easy-going or low funds, or both. That she left it alone means way too trusting.

I note as she strides back from the toilet that she's got Herself back. She takes back her seat. She's a contender. Leaning over towards the floor, she lifts the scratched open-topped, brown leather bag with fringe and colorful beading that could easily hold in it a man's head. She plops it onto her lap.

"On this day, in this country, in this city, in that church to who has to be you," she finishes, glances at me again, shrugs, and drops a golden envelope onto the table. "I googled your name. It means Patrick the Black in Gaelic."

I down my pint. Waving my glass at her, I ask, "Ye?"

She takes the empties and comes back with two more pints. That's pure class, after I saved her life. I raise my glass, and tip it towards hers. "Thanks very much. *Sláinte*, health."

"Open it," she said as she pushes the envelope across the table. "I didn't want to know before, and maybe I still don't want to know, but what the hell is in it?"

Get the job done type. Trying to extricate from the situation as fast as she can. Like that's going to work with fairies. "What were you doing back then? Chatting the Kaiju to death."

"That makes her mad. What the hell were *you* doing? Open this."

"Do you believe in fairies?"

"Sure. So does Disney." Her impatient eyes are boring holes through me.

I study her. She really hasn't caught on. So why her, this innocent? Capable but witless. Well, not witless. Maybe instinctual. I prefer trained.

"From British Columbia, to Ireland, to Cork, to Saint Peters, that's been my red-eye." She pushes the envelope closer. "Just for this envelope. Open it." She's gone to more sipping her pint now.

"What? There's no mail service these days?" I quip. No go. She leans back and waits. No blather. A little grinding of teeth, but no fault finding. She took the stupid job, she'll finish it. Sure, that's exactly what she's thinking.

"So what's in this, then?" I take the envelope. Less interested in it than I am in her. I know the fairies. They didn't send me an envelope. They sent me a person. She's ordinary at first glance. Good looking in a dark way, but not glamourous. Very striking the bright blue eyes within their almond shape, in a round face of darker skin, framed by black hair straight as pouring Guiness. I pass the envelope under my nose. It hasn't even a faint ozone odor of chemical changes that alter the atmosphere with an energy zap of magic. I tear into the back flap and dump the contents on the table. Whoa in spades. "Appears like I can pay for the next round."

"What! That's it. All the way here to deliver money. Why didn't she just download Venmo?"

That's cleared her sinuses.

I take my eyes from her indignant face and peer inside and pull out a greeting card in yet another "envelope," smaller, white. I pull out a card with a fluffy, white dog, with sun goggles over his eyes, with his head out a car window, and his tongue sticking out. Inside is written: 'Hope you have a sun-in-your face, wind-in your-hair sort of day.'

That's rich, as I hear a squall of rain on the roof of the pub. "Who gave this to you?"

"A woman came into my shop."

"Was she beautiful beyond reason or reality? Just a touch off?"

"Nope. Over sixty, a little dried-out looking, long black hair and cheap wire rim rectangular glasses. Great breasts, though. Must have been fake."

"There you go. In a trusting form, an old hag, but she couldn't go all the way to ugly. Long hair and great breasts have always been her vanity. They weren't fake. A deal was struck?"

The bartender lady comes by to collect dead glasses. She stares at the pile of Euros. "Fake," I say. "We're in a play. It's a prop." I shove it all back into the envelope.

The horror must be coming together for Mealla sitting there across from me. Her blue eyes have a lot of white showing anyway. Sure, an edge of fear has finally crept in. Like all her nightmares have come alive.

"*Ná déileálann le sióga*," I say knocking back the rest of my pint.

"What's that mean? I'm screwed?" All the bar patrons glance at the raised voice of a foreigner.

"Something like that." I feel sorry for her. She didn't know. The Goddess Hoors are slick.

At this point we both need a things-are-never-going-to-be-the-same whiskey, and another where-the-Gods-tread-humans-are-torn-arse-to-limb pint, except I'm hurting and need to find a holy well for healing.

"I'm going—" she begins.

"To go back? Yeah, no. You took payment from a fairy. I don't know what this is, but you're in."

"—to the bathroom." She walks away, then pauses and looks over her shoulder back at me. "You are *Padraic O'Duibh*?"

"Em, you know my name and in ancient Gaelic."

"Shit!"

"Yeah."

CHAPTER

THREE

Pog mo thóin
Kiss my...

The River Lee which flows around the center of Cork hasn't improved with time. It's wreaking my head that the river's now a quiet drift of dirty water through mossy concrete walls. It's a fouler, all the wildlife gone along the unnatural bank. Sort of stunned, I can't stop looking.

"It's a river."

"Not really."

"Come on."

I study Mealla's back as we cross the river on a plain, flat-topped, stone, dual-lane bridge. She's something or why send her? She might be a magnet for magical monsters. I can't quite get over that she isn't like buzzing about all this. Though, it's true, she has two quick pints in her.

"This area was once open ground with hedge rows of gorse, ferns, and blackberries. And birds, deer."

"Ya? A thousand years ago?"

About. No bird-song. Just roaring and beeping. I stop short. *And no feckin' Abbey.*

"A thousand years ago there was an entire Franciscan abbey here. Stone hall, a kitchen, a cloister, six large dormitories, six cellars, a water mill, a fishing place for salmon, and a salmon weir on the River Lee there. The monks owned plots of land that had on them a dole house for the poor of Cork and another chapel in the Northern Hills called *Cilleen Na Gurranaigh*, 'The Little Church.' The abbey that was once here, Shandon Abbey, and 'The Little Church,' were connected by a tunnel."

I feel a loss and a fear that what I'm looking for, what I need is not here anymore, either. I look at the name over the arch, what's left of the original abbey, and read, "'Franciscan Well Brew Pub. I laugh. Feckin' narky ballocks."

"Why are we at another pub?"

"Because there's a holy well in there. The Shandon Holy Well." I guess, if the monks could have chosen what was to come next, this would have been it.

She follows me as I walk down a narrow lane. Fairy lights hanging from the ceiling. Fairy lights, what shite I think as I walk the lane under them. There are topiary trees in grey pots and hanging baskets with red and white flowers. The floor is a weave pattern of two-tone bricks. The double-doored entrance is framed in panels of square sheets of copper riveted around the frame. To the side is hanging signage with a monk on it and a lager in his hand. Perfect.

According to stickers on the door, the pub was Bar of the Year for twenty-nineteen (twenty-nineteen!!) and is the best tourist bar in Ireland. It's number five on a list for the top five most haunted places in Cork City. Because its lager garden sits on a thirteenth century monastic graveyard, I do believe it's haunted. In twelve, ninety-one, sixteen friars were killed, and others wounded when a fight broke out between Irish and English Franciscan brothers during a provincial chapter meeting. Ghosts here seem reasonable.

Through inner, glass-paned doors and to the left in the low light is a well-lit bar with abbey-like appointments of pointed window architecture. The multiple taps shine. The place is all copper and wood.

Through more glass doors is the outdoor lager garden with hanging flowerpots of pink petunias, a fake grass floor and scattered old tables. I smell baking cheese and sausage from Pompeii Pizza Bar. Its Italian-style tiled front takes up a corner of the lager garden.

"I like this place, and I'm starving," Mealla says as she gets in line.

"Yeah, good idea. I'll be right back." I walk straight to the kegs in the back to a stone wall built against a hill. Definitely original to the abbey. The holy well is there, a t-shaped opening in the wall.

Holy wells in Ireland number by the thousands. They are located by roads, by churches, in fields. Pre-Patrick they were portals to the other side of the veil. Bathing in or drinking from a holy well could give you wisdom, healing, insight. The druids visited them when the gates of the other world opened on Imbolc, Beltaine, Lughnasa, and Samhain. Holy wells are still power sites, but Patrick closed them as portals and opened them as healing centers.

It's not great that the bar is lively, but pain has altered my breathing. I'll tell anyone who asks what I'm doing that I'm mad keen on holy wells.

On cue, a drinker says as I nip around the bench. "They probably don't let people just go down there."

"Oh this," I say. "I'm writing a book about wells in Ireland."

The sound 'ahhh' ruffles through the group.

"Sure, I wouldn't mind." I point to my nose. "Some healing."

And shite if they don't watch me descend the heavily worn steps to the bottom. "He's writing a book," I hear one say to a newcomer. "He's after a cure," says another. Then laughter. It's all craic in Ireland.

I step around some fake plants and up to my ankle in cold, clear water.

The act of writing itself is magic. Ogham writing is primitive letters etched onto stones in Ireland. Each letter and its sound has active magical properties. I bend to make the Ogham symbol for "B" in the thin layer of green algae on the stone bottom of the nearly dry well. It is a vertical line with a horizontal line that is drawn from the middle of the vertical to the right. These lines, pronounced *Beith*, are associated with the birch tree. The letter controls, new beginnings, change, release, rebirth, purification. It is not literally for healing like the holy well, but a backup. Overlapping magic has worked for me before.

To activate the well, I circle five times around the small space while reciting the prayer to Saint Francis. Then "Beith," I say with serious appeal.

I wait for the pain to stop. I collapse against the rough stone of the side of the well when it does.

"Well?" a woman calls down. The group laughs again.

I climb out. "Hilarious." I smile. "May I use that?"

"Go for it." She glances at her mates. Her eyebrows raise.

I give her a thumbs up. "'Holy Wells, Not Just a Puddle of Water,' is the title. Look for it next year."

"Mental," I hear from behind, and then more laughter.

"Go, ok?" asks Mealla. She's been waiting for me at the till to pay for the pizza.

"Jerks."

"Just tell them to get a life."

Back inside, the ale taps have a shiny brass core selection European of beer. In addition, there is the Franciscan Well core range of lager, Rebel Red, Chieftain IPA, Friar Weisse, Shandon Stout. Great stuff and I'm floundering here looking at it all, or just beginning to feel chloroformed from the last hours.

Mealla side-glances me. "What do you like? Pale lager, Irish red ale, a bock, a porter, stout, pilsner, IPA's." Women always try to fill in the gaps when things are getting sticky. "Two pints of your Rebel Red." She orders and then waits for me to pay.

"There," I say to her as I walk towards the snug, a private, enclosed area next to the front door away from the crowds.

The pizza smells spicy delicious. The stout chases it down my throat fine. I'm back to whistling a bit in my head. Sure the fairies found me. I'm not buzzing about it to be honest, but this all, ye ken, all of it is an improvement, and I'm going with it.

"What's your name?" I ask in between slices. "I can't keep calling you, she-who-takes-money-from fairies." That's what's in my head plus the name on the bag. But I want to know if she'll tell me her full name. How smart or dumb is she? The fairies caught her out.

She keeps chewing and then belts down her drink. She's obviously deciding whether or not to tell me. Right, so. She's getting more careful. She's aware, so, of *fiodhrádh,* that her true name is her binding name. "You already have mine. Fair play."

"That's what they all say."

"How many 'they' have you been associating with?" She startles a bit at that. Still, overall, she's being solid. Too solid, maybe. There's more to her than a witless mundane tricked to fly to Ireland by the fairies. They've gone to a lot of trouble over her.

"What about you? Look at you and that blue tattoo on your face. And talking weird about things in the past."

"Blue woad. You know my name."

A little shrug to her shoulders.

"I asked you if you believe in fairies.

"I don't..." she buys time, "...or didn't," that's under her breath. "I have a website, Trainingintotemism dot com. It's also for Wicca. So I've always said I do believe. I sell peace pipes, dreamcatchers, herbs, candles, books on spells. I teach seminars. I sell at powwows and Wicca conventions. My book is a bestseller. *Shamanic Magic.* I do shamanic certification online. You can buy my book on Amazon."

Way too much present day to process. Part of me is wondering if she is piss-taking.

"Er, you do then."

"It's a business. My business, and I'm good at it."

"Sure, what you're saying then is you didn't believe a word you've written."

"What I teach is correct. Belief is not important to content."

"Until you stared down a Kaiju monster."

"Yes. Until I stared down a magical creature." This whole bravado stick of hers crashes. Thoughts of sadness and loss, shrink her, again. "I was trying to help it.'

I feel like shite for being smug. "What were you doing? You were there in the moment," I ask kinder, like.

"I don't know...saving us." And she rallies. "You were kinda useless."

"I was not useless."

"I didn't get my ribs broken."

"I took all the hits. It was dead on you."

"I know. It didn't work." She didn't explain. I didn't ask just yet.

We both finish our drinks, and she volunteers to get more, but not before holding her hand out for more money. "I know how much you have. If you want to know," she adds as she walks. "I think I put it to sleep."

Cool as ice. She's there all right.

I'm feeling no pain, the pizza is eaten, and another pint is on its way. In my life, enjoying the moment is very important. I drink the next pint, savoring the taste, the variation from what I'm used to. I let time tick over because I need the reset and probably Mealla does too, but also because of the monks' graveyard we are sitting on top of. These men were at the least pure arseholes, at the worst minging pricks. Haunted. I'm counting on it.

Maybe Mealla is also a mind reader because she says, "So this is the most haunted place in Cork." She is a tourist in some aspects. "Do you know, the excavation of monastic cemeteries showed that monks suffered from degenerative bone disease caused by obesity? They dropped dead in early middle age from heart failure, stroke, diabetes. They weren't a healthy bunch."

"Yeah. I know that."

As I feel the cold promise of deathly hallows, I'm looking at her looking at me. "No," she squeaks out. Maybe she is psychic, or she feels it too. "You've been waiting for this," she accuses. "And you didn't warn me."

"You're there. You know enough. And anyway, we need answers to a lot of questions."

"I'm still processing."

"Sure, you are."

A bogle with a long forehead, made longer by the bald, shiny pate on the top of its head does duly materialize. The ghost's small eyes, nearly covered over by his aging, sagging lids are as canny and disdainful as ever. I know him. A total ball-ache of a monk. His lips are as thin as his nose is long. It's substantial and pink-veined. I hoped that this one at least would have gone to hell, chained to a rock in great thirst, and with a pint of lager just out of reach, and a naked woman laughing.

"Padraic," he says jolly like. His paunch vibrates from the hilarity. "Sight for sore eyes; the sight of ye makes me eyes sore." He becomes as material, as life-like as when I had last seen him. Only he is dead now, so there is that bit of good news about him.

"It was you who came with the time bend then?"

"Did you feel it?"

"Did I feel it?" He says like I'm the most stupid person he's ever laid eyes on.

"Do you know why?"

He looks hard at me. I feel him. He's in command of a fair amount of magical energy to keep him corporal. "I can't believe the time and energy used to bring you of all choices forward," he sneers at me. "Won't help them. My pecker was more useful than you are."

"No doubt."

"And Herself as well," the ghost says in a purring voice, like he's the cat and she's the mouse, "The snake oil saleswoman."

"Takes one to know one." She tosses back.

Not sure we want to anger this nearly one-hundred percent corporal, magically wrapped ghost-monk.

"I like what they've done with the place," I say to change the subject and redirect the flatulent old man's attention to me.

"Tolerable. Still, it's not like the old days, is it? I miss a good *neallta fola.*"

"Yup lovely stuff the old clouds of blood invocation of slaughter."

"Today's priests today can't bother their arses with the Celtic magic of the church. Don't know it. Can't perform a decent *cia póg—*"

"Magically induced confusion or delusion," I translate.

"—or *creadair or dicheadal di cheannaibh,* or even a half-arsed farc."

"Power object...incantation, ward to restrain."

"There's not a one who can do a *feath fiadha* or can even to pronounce it."

"Magic mists of invisibility." A thought startles me. The old magic could be coming back. *Fógairt,* ward to compel, *fiodthnais,* feat of harmful magic, *millteorracht,* magical attack...the lot. The old Celts knew magic. Now, no clue, and I'm glimpsing why I'm here. The priests are trying to resurrect that skill set for themselves. The gods want it back.

As the monk rambled on about *neart inár lámha, fírinnear áv dteahger, glaine inár gcroí*...strength in our arms, truth in our tongue, clarity in our heart, an old *fianna,* warriors of Ireland, honor code, I feel hot energy come off him. His presence is becoming even more solid, engorging on magic power.

Shiiiite.

His gray-tinged ghostly eyes eat her. She holds his stare.

Ah, feck. Why does she do that?

The look on his face turns to shock and then to hatred. He's sensed what's in her, who she is. I don't even know that.

I sail the metal pizza plate at him. Turns out corporal is good because he actually takes it on the bridge of his nose and reacts, breaking the bond between them. Enough time to pick up my blackthorn club. I jump the table and swing at his ghost-liness. "*Luis*," I yell. I need the apotropaic magic of the Ogham letter to shift his attention and bore it into me. Kinetic magical energy explodes from him, and I'm thrown to the wall. Feckin' ouch.

Before I can get back, she is coughing and then choking. Large as life he is, and she is clawing at the hands at her neck. I swing hard at him with the blackthorn, invoking *Luis*. He alters the corporality in his chest and the swing passes through him. Using one hand, the other still around her throat, he rips the club from my hand and rams it through the floor and into the ground. Her eyes protrude from her head.

"A kaiju was waiting for my arrival," I try to control his attention. "It burst from a magic circle."

"And it nearly bested you."

"How do you know?"

"You invoked the holy well."

Ogma's knife in hand I try to think where for a lethal stab on a ghost, corporal or not. Instead of exsanguination, I think more of injection. I call again for the power of the Ogham and carve the letter deep into the bogle, cutting deep to take the power inside him.

He's roaring now, shaking the place. Glasses falling off shelves. Wouldn't I just love to send this arsehole to Hell? She passes out. He swings at me with one arm. It's easy to avoid as he is anchored in place by the woman he is trying to kill. He hides in invisibility. The hands remain to finish her. The magic he takes from this place is monumental. Years of ancient priests.

I press the knife into the air where his body should be, slashing vertical lines with two horizontal lines. The sound of sizzling is heartening, only she could be already dead. Finally, the hands spring open and dissolve. There's hope here that the whole damn bogle is away to the devil. Yeah, no, this dirty bastard has survived this long. He's not going that easily.

I dive to her and begin resuscitation. A spectral laugh, and then the remains of my pint float across the snug. It disappears into a wall where once was an opening to an underground passage to the *Gurranabraher* neighborhood where the monks owned a second church. This monk has ridden rings around us.

Mouth to mouth, I'm not giving up and am thinking of throwing her into the holy well when she opens her eyes and gasps a breath in. We are on the ground, again, a bit traumatized, again. I, for one, have never been this flat-footed. She, maybe, finally, all this is beginning to wreak her head.

"A fit," I say to those around me.

"Need an ambulance?"

"She's good. I'll get her home."

I help her to a chair. "What the hell." Her voice is a whisper and hoarse. Her hand shakes as she pushes back hair from her face. "This place needs exorcizing."

God if she isn't class.

The monk responds, a voice without a body. "They tried. Dogshole hucksters. Milklivered. The church isn't what it used to be in my day."

In his day, the demon Azâzêl taught monks to make swords, knives, bracelets, Armârôs. They taught enchantments. What I'm saying is, in the vernacular, this monk has demon friends. We are lucky to be alive. Again.

FOUR

Fiothnais
Feat of harmful magic

We escape the Franciscan Well Brewery with our lives, or her life, and I'm like, what the feck just happened.

"We're even," she says in a raspy voice. "That was a surprise. Another one." She laughs, and it sounds as hysterical as it should. And then she coughs all the way back across the bridge.

"How are you? Are you ok? Damn nutter. He didn't expect us, but he made the most of the moment." She notices me staring at her for a beat too long for comfort.

"What?"

"The monk was there at your throat. Not my throat, your throat. Like he recognized you and was after your soul as in the life and soul of this party."

"Don't be ridiculous."

"He was startled to see you. His dead eyes nearly popped out of his skull when he realized what he had in front of him. What does he know?"

"I don't know," she roars at me. And then, like she's trying to hold in a nervous breakdown, she stops walking and wraps her arms around herself.

I've never in my life comforted a woman. Woman normally tell me to puff off. I've been impressed when this one was getting on with it. I end up patting her shoulder and saying, "We'll sort this." To my relief it seems to work.

"Yeah, we'll sort this," I say again as she smiles.

"It's Mealla, Mealla O'Conner."

"That's a fierce name. It means 'holy woman" in Irish."

"I thought it meant 'lightening.'"

So it does. So it is.

She shakes herself out and is looking less like a horse with fright. She starts walking again. She's there and then she's not. It is a lot of shite to take in.

"Number one in sorting this all out is to stop by the Kaiju Gaming Lounge to see what's inside."

"Why there?"

"When I walked out of the church, I saw what I thought was a painted Kaiju only it was a real Kaiju trapped in a magic circle in the signage over the shop front. I saw a light in the upper window. It's all we've got."

We stare at the gaming shop with its broken sign.

The shop is diagonal to Saint Peter's Church. The Kaiju hadn't far to go. Someone knew I'd be blurry from the trip. Someone was tracing Mealla's every step. Two for one discount. There are still two flattened cars, a red Focus and a tan Corolla, blown out shop windows and now some *Garda*, cars with their flashing red lights. The men in uniform are looking perplexed. The street is one way and narrow. A diagonal section of pavement has a green mark from the evaporation of the beast.

A mobile phone lookup of the Kaiju Gaming Lounge lets us

know that the place shuttered as of December twenty-second. So not open, but someone was in it. And that person was doing more than deciding what to do with some gaming consoles that line both walls in the narrow, dark room, making the inside look like a submarine for tourists. From the online pictures, they used to have great birthday parties there, cake, pizza and video games.

Leeside Leisure casino next to it is up and running with a pair of lit, bright red cherries in the window. "North Main Street is derelict enough to draw in dark magic," Mealla observes in a dead-pan voice. "Saint Peter's Church is now the Cork Vision Centre. You'd think it's a place to buy eyeglasses,"

"We need to get inside the gaming centre."

I notice Mealla gesturing towards something behind me. She isn't startled, so I turn without alarm to see a nun flying down the path hailing us with her handkerchief. She's not of a recent issue. She's old and wide and wrapped in navy blue, but for a white blouse. On her head is a whiff of equally blue fabric that is also waving like a flag from the pin-point in her salt and pepper hair. Her skin sags at the jowls as does her neck, but her skin is wrinkle-free and fair and downy-soft looking, like buttermilk. No sun in Ireland. Figuring her age and weight, I'd place a bet at two to one whether she'll stick the last twenty yards. Still, the old dear is mad keen to catch us.

"Here ye are back, thank God. We need to talk with youse two. We know who youse are and what ye're about. We know a Kaiju was released." Now she is winded. "Come with me," she says after an intermission and when she's within talking distance.

"You knew the monster was to be released?" I say at the nun like she's hard of hearing.

"Shhhh, no…" still a bit breathless, wheezing. "Haven't ye ears? I said we'd heard one had been released. Sister Constance got knocked by it and taken to the hospital. I've replaced her to bring youse two to the convent, and I had to wait here hours on my bunions to see if ye'd return. Where have ye been?"

"You were supposed to meet us. But missed us."

"Jaysus, Mary, and Joseph, ye are deaf. *She* was supposed to meet ye and got taken out. No one expected it, the total twats. Just come with me now, and no arguing." Her tongue is sprite enough when she needs it to be. The antique nun leads down South Main Street. When we don't immediately follow step, she vigorously waves us forward. "Get a shift on," she commands. "I need to put up my feet."

Must be an ex-schoolteacher.

"Is she for real?" Mealla asks with enough tart in her voice that I can tell a nun or two has been in her face.

"She is, barely. And not mythological. And she has been on her bunions waiting for us."

"There's things ye need to know." The nun's there talking over her shoulder towards us trailing behind. She looks like she'd rather eat shite than bother herself to tell us the things we need to know. She's smart enough to realize that we may eat her if we knew.

+++

Saint Brigid of the Isle Convent is at four Sharman Crawford Street near a smaller, lower branch of the River Lee west of center of Cork. It is an ancient, imposing three story red brick building with rows and rows of grey, stone-trimmed, pointed windows and a hip and valley pitched roof. Much of the brick is now darkened from the exhaust of motor vehicles. The structure is only back from the street by a cement path. The red and gray stone fence is reinforced on top with pointed, wrought-iron points. The neighborhood is rough like, but this place could see itself through a siege.

The receiving room we're put into is ultra-modern off-white with brown leather arm chairs and a polished mahogany coffee table that shines beautifully. No tat or clutter. The table, an acre of unadorned, unbroken surface. Not even an ornamental, leather-bound bible.

It should have had a fireplace at one time, but that is gone, unnecessary with internal heating systems. The room is warm. No expense spared in the decor, right down to the plush, feet-friendly burgundy wall-to-wall carpet. Nuns have always had the money to move with the times. It used to be patronage. They may have to work for it now. That and property value increases over decades.

The door to the room opens without sound as a different nun, who buys her clothes from the same store as Buttermilk, enters the room. This one is thinner and youngish with still brown hair that is streaked with gray. Her eyes are small in her head. With her enters gravitas and authority.

Buttermilk begins without preamble. "Got them as they came back to the gaming shop." She settles back more comfortably in her chair, like this is going to be good, like this is what she expected, and she's in a comfy chair. Her eyes are sharp with intelligence in the way of all old people that still have their wits about them, a sharpness of having seen it all, lived it all. Life holds them no surprises.

"Sister Mary, it must be time for your medications."

"Took 'em." Delighted with herself, she chuckles as she sits deeper into the singular floral-tapestry, winged chair. "We hear ye were fighting the monster with an ice cream cone. Not much there to recommend ye."

"Sister Mary."

This time Buttermilk stiffly rises. "An ice cream cone," she says to me as she passes my chair.

"*Cailleach searbh*," I say.

"Old woman, is it? *"Leathcheann."*

"Thank you, Mary," the nun in charge says it like she has this problem with this particular nun a lot. Then she stern-glances me.

She waits until Buttermilk closes the door. She long sighs then carries on. "Will you have some tea?" There is a pinched inevitableness to her face. Her eyes are flat like she knows that this chat, this meeting is only the beginning. "I'm Sister Rose." She continues with the preliminaries as she waits for the tea cart to be wheeled in. It arrives and smells like a bakery. She pours and offers around the milk and sugar.

Cool as the clotted cream for the scones, she then passes around the baked goods, like tea and treats will ease in anything. She waits for the ceremony to end, bites to be taken, like we haven't been buzzing on the edge of our seats over what this thing is. Only then when Mealla has just about got a strop on, then Sister Rose arranges herself with her cuppa and begins. Pure control. "I'm sure that, at this juncture, you're both looking for answers."

"We are…" She glances at me with a don't-take-the-piss sort of expression, and I finish anyway "…not just looking for answers."

That slows the nun down. She was expecting maybe fear, panic, a-what-the-hell explosion, but not thinly veiled disagree-ment. The nun smiles like so-that's-how-it's-going-to-be. It's a painful, little smile and there's sorrow there as well, but also some impatience. What she's got to say is big, kaiju big, get-over-it big, yeah-that-was-very-bad-but-this-is-worse big.

The nun waits a heartbeat. "I'm sure you are, so I'll get to the point, but some history first."

"Maybe the point first," I growl. "I've saved Mealla's life twice."

"Once." Mealla pipes in.

"Ok fine. Once for you and once for me. The point is I was time bended, and we've had our lives threatened twice."

"Twice? What was the other time?" Sister Rose's unnaturally calm voice both breaks and melts ice. She may not be real happy inside either with all the goings on.

"Father Laurent's scut-ghost."

"Franciscan Well? What were you doing there?"

"Invoking the well and eating pizza."

"We just don't have enough people. You both made it though I'm heartened to see."

"It's all been lovely stuff," I say. "Cracking."

The nun scoffs. "You are here with the help of the *Tuatha* to supplement for the weakness of the Catholic Church in controlling magic."

Mealla starts laughing.

"Cork Vision Centre!" I'm startled to the depth of the obvious. Another obvious that hits me is that this convent isn't exactly buzzing with inmates. "Sure you know yourself that that's trouble."

"Trouble is an understatement. So here you both are."

Not laughing now, Mealla explodes, "You're joking, right?"

"I assure you I'm not. You, Mealla, are a Metís of both European and Native American extraction. You are a unique combination of shaman/witch, descended from a native tribe of Canada and Biddy O'Conner of Ireland."

"I'm what!" Mealla's eyes are popping out. She is copping onto the depth of the obvious.

"What we were not told, though," continues Sister Rose as her voice increases to cut through the next interruption she sees brewing on Mealla's face, "and what we see now is that you are a hidden sorcerer. Unexperienced, untried." Under her breath, Sister Rose adds, "unbelievably." She inhales deeply, for strength and patience and grit and bravery. "And that you were not told anything."

She pauses waiting for that strength she's praying for to kick in.

"All of this, you both here, stems from The Third Secret of

Fatima. Do you know Fatima, Our Lady of Fatima, the place in Portugal where three children received apocalyptic visions and prophecies in six visits by the Virgin Mary in the year nineteen-seventeen?"

Sister Rose took in what must have been my blank face and Mealla's not blank face. Mealla must have been brought up Catholic…sure Irish mother.

"The prophesy states basically that the church would weaken from the inside out," Rose adds.

"We don't need a prophecy to tell us that," Mealla says like it's now become her purpose in life to hold up that mirror, the sins of the church.

"A reckoning? Is that what you're asking for?" Sister Rose is still calm. "This is it, then, the beginning of the reckoning. This convent is trying to…" she closes her eyes…"make things right. Please, let's proceed. Have some more tea." Her voice is strong with conviction. She knows what she knows, the expanse of realms and beings and magic.

"There were three secrets given out by the Virgin Mary, you see. No one today believes or even knows about them. The first and third are the most applicable today. In the first vision to the children, Our Lady showed us a great sea of fire under the earth. In it were demons and souls in human form. They each burned like charcoal, the means of the fire, the flames coming from them. The demons resembled unknown animals and were black and transparent."

She sips again from her floral china cup as if she were talking about flowers in a lush garden and not burning demons like sparks in the dense and smoking, enraged fire of hell.

"The third secret was published on June twenty-six, two-thousand; eighty-three years after the first apparition of Our Lady. It told of the pope, bishops, priests, men and women religious going up a steep mountain. At the top, they were fired upon with bullets and arrows and killed. Beneath a cross, an angel gathered up the spilled blood into an aspersorium and sprinkled it on the people still coming up the mountain. The pope explained this secret by saying that the suffering inside the church didn't come from enemies from the outside, but from the inside, evidence that Hell would be winning."

I finish for her, "The end of the church, with that the free-for-all release of the very potent magic locked within it and controlled by it." I whistle. Never thought I'd see the day.

"The release of all magic," she says slowly word by word.

"I'm an indentured lad from the competitors, Sister. I've been in Hell, but I don't have any experience doing battle with it."

"Don't be coy, *Padraic O'Duibh*. It's not helpful." Rose pushes back deeper into her wing-backed chair. "You're a priest." She'd been waiting to drop that into the conversation. The desired effect, Mealla gets whiplash in her neck turning towards me.

Sister Rose carries on like there's no time for anything. There isn't, but feckin' nuns. "Here excommunicated priests are insiders and making the first play for control. The prophecy is the destruction of the church from within. That is happening." She takes us in and shakes her head. She's swearing like a soldier inside. I know she is. "This is a fine mess. We have been planning, mobilizing. We didn't think you'd arrive clueless. Or unwilling."

Two more nuns quietly arrive like slippered specters, and I'm suddenly thinking that "coven" and "convent" sound similar. It's becoming clear that a battle to the death with the Morrigan might be preferable to this.

"The Goddess your *geasa* is owed to—"

"The Morrigan?"

"Worthless woman," Sister Rose spits out.

"Singing to the choir. You thought with a *geasa* I'd be willing?"

"I was told there would be arrangements." She takes in the

wide-open shock in my face. "They didn't tell you anything at all."

A new nun steps through the door. "She may not have told them anything, but she did get them here," the woman points out as she glides to a chair.

Rose nods her head. "So, there it is. We're here because the Third Secret of Fatima is in play, and it is beginning here in Ireland."

The new nun smiles at us and says, "The end of faith, cardinals opposing cardinals, bishops against bishops, a wholesale abandonment of God among clerics, the throne of Christ into the antichrist."

I want to say it all sounds ridiculous, but there's a dread in me that thinks otherwise.

Sure for Mealla too, though she's trying. "The antichrist? Are you kidding me?" Her traumatized glance bounces from nun to nun to me. She's half rising from her chair. Only she's not asking them what they're smoking. She's trying to turn her world back to right side up. She's come to know that it's real. It's hitting her hard.

Rose looks to me to do something.

Yeah, no. Mealla and I've been set up. So the church can't do its job of holding back magic, black magic any longer, and we're here to plug that hole? If *I'm* feeling the cold as I think it. Ice is cutting away at Mealla's vital organs.

Magic is up for grabs, and sure, I can think of a multitude of powerful back-benchers who'd love to get their hands on it.

"A vacuum of faith is creating an immortal hour, a redistribution," says Rose her voice for the first time a bit pleading.

The nun has sucked all the air out of the room.

Mealla standing and pacing says, "Holding back black magic? The two of us. That is the point of this speech?"

The nun pinches her nose under her glasses. "One step at a time. Maybe I've given out too much all at once."

Ya think. Massive migraine scenario. I know my head is

beginning to hurt, and it seems like Mealla's too. She gone from snake oil saleswoman to completely bagged up in less than three hours.

"Let me explain better why you two, in particular." She drinks a lot of tea as if her throat is very dry. "Mealla, your great-great-great grandmother on your father's side was a shaman. Her magic blood, of course, has the possibility of being passed down the generations. I think you also had a great grandfather who was a well-known and revered shaman."

"My mother never let me visit my father or grandfather on the reservation after they left me alone at age ten, a full night on a mountain to find my spirit animal. I grew up without the spiritualism of the tribe."

"Please sit down, Mealla. And yet you certify shamans."

"Those who can't, teach," she says, and she gives up and sits.

"But you can, and you are, and the certifications are valid. You have her blood-power, that's what I'm saying. Specifically, through your shamanic ancestry your specialty is magical creatures. You can commune with spirits and magical creatures. And, let me emphasis, all this is crossed with your Irish ancestry and the bindings between the Native Americans and the Irish historically. Your mother is Irish. She is descended from the White Witch, Biddy Early."

"I sell shaman magic potions, both pipe and liquid. I teach people about shamanism and give out certificates...for money...to give people peace and harmony. I write books on WICCA. I'm a Métis, mixed native and Irish. Grandfather said the famous family blood would never to flow through me." That's what Mealla says but her eyes glaze as her thoughts move inward probably to the Kaiju.

In a pause for reflection, there is no sound of a fire in the grate. I feel the need for some relaxing sound. The warmth and cheer of a roaring fire would have been good for the atmosphere in the room.

Rose puts her cup and saucer down on the cart. Within the ceremony of afternoon tea, fine china, dainty sandwiches and scones, and chocolate cake, we should have been talking about the weather, or the lavender in the garden, or about dresses or shoes. But Sister Rose keeps on burning our souls with the blunt knowledge of ourselves.

"Biddy was accused of witchcraft as late as the year eighteen, sixty-five. She had a blue bottle given to her by the fairies. She looked into the dark liquid in the bottle for answers, and for cures, a sort of apotropaic magic. She was not popular with the priests. At the time, it was said that she cut into the priest's five shillings per customer profit. So you have the blood of a dragon through your family's shaman ancestry, and the magic of a witch, through your Irish ancestry and the woman Biddy Early." Rose signals the crockery to be taken away. "Obviously, the magic hasn't been expressed," she mutters as she stacks cups on a tray.

Sister Rose finishes gathering used cups to the tray. I grab more scones before they leave. Suicide makes me hungry, and I'm ravenous, and the nuns can bake.

"Ok, then." Mealla is trying to adjust and wants to turn the spotlight from her. So gesturing towards me she asks, "Who's he, then? Just a priest?" She gets into my face. "Really, a priest?"

"I hear he's very touchy about who he is," warns Rose.

"For good reason," I growl from my chair.

"Actually, he is a mortal son of the Irish God, Ogma, *and* a once-upon-a-time a priest."

"To protect me from the Irish Gods, which obviously hasn't helped and didn't help."

"So clearly you're a bastard. I can guess how that came about. Ogma's the swarthy God." Mealla pats my knee and says. "Could be worse." I'm scowling inside at her. "Ah, come on. Isn't he the inventor of Ogham writing and also isn't his passion for battle so intense that he has to be chained to hold him back, strategy-wise?" She leans forward into the description. "He was Nuadu's, and also Lugh's champion in the battle against the Fomorians. His is a *trí dée dána*, the three gods of skill with Lugh and the Dagda. That's your dad...so weird that all this might actually be real. It can't be real. This isn't real."

"It is all very real I assure you," Rose says.

"What's all this about a curse? Hum? Mealla tips her head and raises her eyebrows.

"When he was five—"

"Enough," I say.

Sister Rose reconsiders her words. "Enough said that the goddess Scathach trained him for combat on the Isle of Skye. During training, in a fight with the Morrigan's son, his hand was cut off. One–handed, Padraic still killed the brute. Ogma restored your hand with his own hand, the hand of the mighty Ogma. Padraic wields the Ogma's knife in that hand, and from that hand he has the powers of the Ogham letters."

I see Mealla glance at the scars on my wrist. "He had snakes in his heart. He was trying to kill me. The feckin' Morrigan laid a curse on me as a blood price. I will never be free of that damned Goddess because I refuse to die."

"Sister Joan, the whiskey, I think."

Sister Rose watches me. "We hoped together you would be somewhat invincible. Well, so far, you're both not dead."

"So the nuns are working with the *Tuatha*, a foot in each camp. How's that going?"

She pauses. Her shoulders slump forward a bit. Her eyes dull. Fair dues. I get it. She didn't think that an agreement with the gods would be so one sided with her doing all of the actual work. "The religious world is vast," is all she says.

"The church has controlled magic for a long time to the point the mundane don't know it exists." I say.

Sister Rose straightens back up and has a face on her that ye get when you'd murder for a drink like. "It's about keeping magic out of the wrong hands."

"We talking about any other wrong hands? Anyone else besides the priests out shopping?" Mealla pushes back.

"One step at a time. For now, a group of priests who have abandoned their vows are massing together—"

"Massing together," Mealla snorts.

Sister Rose ignores her. "In order to take over the throne of Christ, they have to empty it."

"You know, the throne of Christ has had many antichrists on it already. Popes with mistresses, popes who have murdered, thieved, whored."

"Clearly the problem." Finally Sister Rose snaps.

"Why would the *Tuatha* care about the throne of Christ?" asks Mealla.

"Payback." I inject.

"I don't think we need to call these men "priests" anymore. They are practitioners. They are using their power from becoming priests in the church for selfish reasons, and they are no longer a part of the church."

"Who's not in on this to get the magic for themselves?" Mealla asks.

"You aren't. He isn't. I'm not," says Sister Rose.

A new 'trí dée dána.'

The door bursts open. A younger-older nun calls over to Sister Rose as she walks. "Sister Vianney says she heard something going on at the bishop's house, loud voices, and a loud bangs like fireworks. So she looked in. There's been another one."

Rose turns to me and Mealla, "Another one meaning, a priest's skin has reached its melting point."

FIVE

Tuathhaid

Male person with supernatural powers

The look on Mealla's Métis face is pure bombshell. I know, what with her change of perspective. Seeing a magical creature pop out of nowhere is an eye-opening reality that could blow your orbs out, a huge monster at that. She's correct and between the two of us, me getting used to modern times and her getting used to the world of the Grand-Other; she's got the worst of it.

"Come on *trí dée dána*." I take her arm. Actually, saving ordinary people from gods has been a private calling of mine for some time. "I want a motor vehicle," I say to Sister Rose, "'cause they are fierce."

If we are going to get killed in all this, my mind tells me I want to try out a Porche, minimum.

"I have no idea what to do," Mealla says as I pull her towards the door.

"You can put magical creatures to sleep. Which, if you ask

me, is a fair enough gift. Above that you've got to find that bit of magic in yourself, a glow, a levitation of an object, a spell gone right and expand on it."

"I've never———"

"Bullshite. You have. Even if it was an accident."

"There's a car out back. Sister Constance will drive," calls Sister Rose, bloodlessly, really.

+++

"Not what you had in mind?" Mealla asks, leaning forward from the back seat of the car, as Constance takes a corner shifting down like a pro. So why is she driving a state-of-the-art-convent-clown car?

It's a black Fiat 5000L, a box on wheels. At the least, it could have been red and without dents, or the long crack in the windscreen, or one that's ignition works on the first go. No, yeah, I get it; this is what happened the last time they pushed back on the furies of hell.

Sister Constance pushes through the yellow lights, weaves through traffic into any tiny openings available. She is using the clutch and stick to accelerate and decelerate like a super spy trying to lose the bad guy. She has her strop on. We stop on a pebble driveway at a fast skid. That's my girl. To think what she could do with a Porsche.

The headlights of the car highlight a super white, modern house that is angular and blocky. It overlooks the River Lee, and it's been an uphill unpaved road to get to it. It is not a middle-class house. This is a bishop in Ireland's trophy house of a bygone day. The freshly painted white exterior expands the light from a waxing gibbous moon.

"Coming on to a full moon," says Mealla.

"I've been noticing."

As much as she knows, she's been an unbeliever for too long. 'Coming onto a full moon,' isn't very witchy. I know she's got the lingo, but not on the tip of her tongue. And rituals at the time of different phases of the moon are witching entry-level. The problem with weak practitioners using big magic is the lack of control.

Magic is mind and physical control of the flow of energy through space and time. Energy has no beginning and has no end, like the One God, and there's no circuit breakers or fuses. And it produces heat. When there is energy overload there is lots of heat. Where there's heat, there's fire.

Sister Rose's stakeout nun meets us at the door. She already has picked the lock, her tools of the trade in her hand. Nuns everywhere should be proud.

"The noise was from the back, upstairs, and a flash of bright light. It's not pretty."

Inside, the carpet is plush. My eyes follow the rise of stairs and the white wrought-iron banister. The house is ultra-modern. No Georgian doors here. The modern Irish now drink more wine than lager. They are a part of the European Union and a trip to France is to load up the car with cheap wine.

I smell the blood, and the sear of energy from downstairs. Mealla sneezes. "Why isn't the place up in flames?"

"The practitioner had some control. He melted and charred things instead of blasting them," explains the lock-pick nun.

The destruction is in the in-house chapel. The practitioner is on the ground in front of the altar. Skin cannot really melt. Under excessive heat, say one-hundred and eighteen degrees, it begins to burn. At a hundred and thirty-one degrees, second-degree burns. Its chemical arrangement has changed for good. Skin, at one sixty-two degrees, is destroyed. This man's skin is destroyed, and the fat underneath has melted. Caught face-first in a failed spell. He was bleeding from a cut to his forearm until his heart stopped.

Grand. Lovely.

"A blood rite," says Constance. "He was using his own blood to fuel the spell."

"There's the cup...or chalice I should say," says Mealla. "A blood libation in it to draw in a demon, for it to drink."

"Having some trouble, I'd guess, by the state of things."

"More and more blood, more and more recitations to fill in the gaps," Mealla fills in. "Like a failed orgasm."

That's great stuff.

Mealla's all in as she eases closer to the corpse. A number of expletives from her make the air feel bluer. I follow her. Shite, he does look bad, the anticipated third-degree burns, and under that, melted fat that has disfigured the underlying structure. His eyes are not level. His jowls have run off his face like globs of excess glue.

I sigh-swear and walk around the altar. What a tool, I think as I consider the man...totally jeepers-effin' thick. What was in it for this guy that he'd put it all out there, his face a thermal mess? What glory?

For that matter, we are all tools, him, Mealla, me. Fighting for somebody else's glory. The *Tuatha* in league with nuns. Ye can't make this stuff up.

The room is...was Spartan clean and without clutter. A closet with burn marks on the door has protected some vestments. I pocket vials of holy water. The Roman Missal book for the Mass is there. I run my fingers through some loose, unconsecrated, unleavened hosts in a bowl. In the Catholic Mass, the ritual is to shift Jesus's purpose and energy into white thin wafers and into wine, so a magic summoning so to speak.

"Weirdly, there is grape juice here instead of wine," I mumble. So going for unfermented. Wine is fermented. Grape juice is unfermented. The hosts are unleavened. Historically, practitioners of necromancy ate unleavened and unfermented foods before a summoning. Only this guy got it wrong. It's supposed to be unleavened black bread. And usually, the ritual goes on for days, even weeks. So he's trying for a short-cut. Time is pressing on them.

Looks like the knife used to cut himself came from the kitchen, not an athame. The fella couldn't quite bring the demon or bogle forward. Maybe the thing got angry. It could see the cup of blood waiting for it, feel the fresh air of this world on its face. Frustration pushed forth its own blast of energy before the way through closed.

I've only been time bended for one evening, I think as I roam around the room taking in the char patterns on the floor and the heat patterns on the walls. *How much farther will we all be in this mess before this darkness sees daylight?* Blind in one eye and can't see with the other.

The smell is twisting my nostrils, like a burned-out rubbish tip.

"This sort of summoning isn't easy to do." Mealla's voice is tight. It's hitting her in waves, a realization so profound that it's staggering. Even though shamanism and WICCA have been a part of her life for a while, she's never seen the results. She's being enlightened.

She is clearly battling an inner disturbance. Hell, I'm battling an inner disturbance. The smell of thermal energy residue is rank. The nuns are walking around like they've seen it all. Which is suspicious.

Mealla's mind is zipping over a lot of ground, and the nuns should give her credit that she's staying on this side of going mental. This man's face got too close to the kettle on the boil. Is the Morrigan part of this? Absolutely. I don't know how, but absofeckinlutely.

Mealla braids her so-black hair into a long plat down her back to keep it behind her. It's her all business-look. She's realizing she has to reverse herself from those-who-cannot-do-teach to the opposite of that, by yesterday like. "Bet you don't know that early necromancy evolved from shamanism. They both practice communicating with the dead. A shaman uses the trance-state to enter the spirit world to bring help to the outside world. They go there to question an ancestor or petition for some intervention. Priests were the medieval necromancers. They wanted four things: manipulation, illusion, knowledge, and control."

Nerve control chatter as she walks around the floor. "There's no circle here. It's a conjuring. And here is the payment." She looks down into the chalice resting on the altar. "Question is, is this straightforward or with a side of theurgy? Is this a simple evoking or is the goal henosis?"

"She *does* have the vocabulary. "No idea what you're talking about."

"Theurgy is asking a god to do something or not do something. Henosis is uniting with god."

"Like becoming a god?"

"I don't know about becoming, but what is he trying to unite with or ask a favor of? Will I see it running at me with a big set of teeth anytime soon?" She points down at the blood-filled cup on the altar. "If the blood of this practitioner has been imprinted within the demon, it is craving his blood. We can use it. We can find out the 'what.'"

"You want to call it? That's insane. Look at this space. Have you ever done this before?"

"No but I do know how, in theory."

"Is that like in theory that I know I must swing a sword in battle and that it cuts people to kill them, but I've never actually done it?"

"Exactly."

I feel my knickers up my bum.

"And we have to do it right here, right now before the craving fades." Mealla walks to the cabinet, takes out and unfolds a white, linen, twelve-inches-square cloth. She lays it on the ground.

"That's not a circle." I say that, not because I think she doesn't know what she is doing, but maybe just a little. She draws a circle around the cloth using the blood. She's going for it. Jaysus.

"It's a holy cloth," she said as she sprinkles holy water on it for good measure. "We don't know what we are dealing with. I've never done this. I want back up. It will burn the demon and keep him from fully entering the circle, I hope. I think we all just want to see it."

Still, with knickers up bum, I say, "How about a nice shamanic trance-walk in the spirit world to ask around? Less danger, less heat, and I hear it comes with great drugs."

"Not always, besides, if you want to walk about in the spirit world with the blood-smell on you that a demon is craving, be my guest. I can make it happen." At the same time Mealla is talking, she is typing on her phone and reading the screen. We wait, the nuns and me.

"What are you doing?" I finally ask.

"Googling the procedure."

"Jaysus be to God...for magic circles?"

"I just want to be sure I haven't forgotten anything." She recites as she reads. "Say the quarter call, circle casting, or invocation...slowly...visualization...understanding...energy flow and control...visualize what is to be coming."

"Mealla—"

She squares her shoulders. "We're doing this. I saw a nice Glenfiddich Grand Cru on a sideboard in the dining room. If this goes right, you pour."

"If this goes right, the whole bottle is ours."

She closes her eyes, and her lips move in a dialogue with her energy, her desires and intention. I feel the draw of power, the willpower to summon. The weight of the air in the room changes. My ears ache, and I'm sweating. Her will against its will. The blood. Heat energy expands from that point. It rushes across the floor in all directions. The right side of the circle forms, lifts, then descends down the left side until a perfect orb of energy throbs as a heart. I feel the rhythm at my core.

She's deadly.

The cup of the priest's blood sits on the center-edge of the altar, just out of the perimeter of the circle.

The sound of her words change. The crystal-clear circle-orb develops a blackness at its center, and then things get scary. Cacophony of war-like sound begins. A claw rips open the roiling black gloom.

Red sprays against the boundaries of the orb. Mealla startles like she feels the spray. Her words stop. Her energy wavers. The circle thins. I want to take control, but I can't. I reassess places of escape. But Mealla is standing taller. Her chanting resumes.

The heat is mounting. It's a sauna in where we are all fully dressed, with rivulets of sweat tracking down our cheeks. It's hard to breathe. The room is lung-scorching like. I'm edgy from the tension of energy.

A hand pushes through the rip, silky, white skin, but cut and bleeding. Ok. Then a snarl and an arm pushes through the opening, like the GrandOther giving birth.

Feck. It's roaring.

Mealla's face is reddening. The exertion is too much. She's banjaxing. She's used herself up too fast. Her words are getting weaker. The edges of the circle are thinning again.

"Shut it down," I yell in the deepening chaos of sound and energy in the room.

Unrelenting, she stands more erect.

Tools. Effin tools.

I get ready to call on the Ogham letter *Nion,* the ash tree, a connection between worlds to maybe reverse this transition between worlds. But there is nothing I can do until her circle fails. My hand is on the Ogma's knife as well.

Another rip, another hand startles me, both reaching towards the blood-filled chalice. Either the circle or the anointed cloth burns it, and it screams. It punches against the wall of the magic circle. Mealla reacts as if she's taken a body blow. It strikes again and again, bouncing Mealla's body back with each hit.

Her eyes spring open. She glares at the bulging blackness. Her words quicken and increase in volume as she step-by-steps towards it. She is reaching into herself, into her anger and pushing all that is her towards the circle. She is not a person that will be beaten. Like high-voltage wires, the circle buzzes with excess energy, overload.

"Close it, effin close it," I scream at her.

I don't know if in her state she can hear me.

"Shite. Get out of here," I yell to the nuns. I back-swing the Blackthorn, and in a single twisted movement follow through the stroke towards and through the circle. I'm chanting *Nion*. Stupid way of going on, breaking the circle. Desperate needs. The Ogham, *Nion,* uses the magic of the sacred Ash tree as a portal. I'm hoping to open a new transition between worlds to shift the demon through it as the circle is breaking.

After I swing, breaking the circle and invoking the magic of Ogham, I go for Mealla. At the same time as we are falling, I'm shifting us both to behind the altar. My mind and body antici-pates the next move, maybe a knife fight with a demon. What happens though, the whole thing, the circle and its content, explodes from a release of thermal energy. Bits soaring every-where, the holy altar cracks but holds. Behind it, I shelter her with my body and keep my own head down. The intense light brightens my closed eyelids.

It's possible I have accomplished what the practitioner didn't, burning the house down.

CHAPTER
SIX

Nar chuire Dias ar do leas thú,
Gods will never grant you peace.

No good ever came from taking money from a fairy or killing her son. I rise from the debris. I'm not dead, so there's that. Then I remember, and anticipation shoves me to my feet, ready for the bastard whatever, whoever it is. I nearly pee myself in relief that there's nothing. Sort of nothing. The room *is* on fire.

I lift the brain-addled Mealla. She is trying to move in weird, uncoordinated movements like a blind kitten just out of the womb. "I have you." She's making small mulling sounds. I could play knock knock on her brain and it's nobody home. Exhaustion…or I might have created a magically connected backlash in her body. Sort that shite out later.

As I am carrying her to the door, I kick a big object. I glance down…at the back of the head of the demon-thing. Has to be. It must have stuck out its head just at the blast. Present in both worlds when the door closed. He couldn't get out fast enough. We got its head on this side.

The nun's head pops into the room. "You've got to get out."

No kidding.

"Grab that!" I say to her as I nod my head towards *the* head. Next, I'm rushing out and telling Constance to grab the Glenfiddich. Mealla got her demon. The nun joins us with the head wrapped in the priest's vestment pilfered from the closet, or as I like to say, saved from the fire.

Don't effin stop raining now.

"In you get." I stuff Mealla into the back seat, then jog over to the front passenger seat. The head joyfully is at my feet, and the two nuns finish up in the back like the clown-act the Fiat was built for. Constance spins the wheels on the white pea-sized gravel and guns it down the narrow lane, hurrying before something we don't want to have to shove over for, like a *Garda* car with its light flashing, comes up the narrow lane.

Once on a main road, we breathe a little bit. The green vestment has shifted off the head. I recognize the face. I shove the head with my foot. "You right prick."

Constance says, "Language," as she shoves the gear up to fifth and finds her openings down the motorway.

"You can't do this job with these shites on a sanitized vocabulary, Sister."

╫╫

At the convent, Rose sees the state of Mealla and hustles her to a room. They call in the local doctor just in case.

"You look like warmed over dead. We've neglected your sleep. So we'll talk about it all in the morning," says Rose as she guides me to a bedroom. I'll send up some food.

"The head?"

"Will be put into the refrigerator."

"The vault refrigerator?"

She actually rolls her eyes.

"That's me being serious," I call to her as she walks down the hallway. I just know she wants to flip me off.

My bed is in a small, sparse cell, but it is comfortable with a fluffy down comforter and pajamas. I'm tempted to take down the cross over my bed. I'm beginning to have had enough of religion. I need all the help I can get, though. Besides, it can make a grand weapon.

In the morning Rose sees me getting breakfast, she says, "Mealla is awake. Right as rain, she must have just depleted herself."

"I'll take her up food."

"I'll have a sister do it. You eat."

"No, I need to."

I find Mealla sitting on the edge of the bed, dressed and taking in the weather, which is washing her windowpane. "Does it ever stop raining here?"

"Here's how much it rains here. If you're driving by a beach and the sun comes out on a summer's day, you don't go get your swim togs. You park and strip down to bra and shorts. You spread whatever you have in the car to sit on, on the sand. For if you go home, the weather will have turned by the time you get back. It does stop, though, in between game days."

"I blew it."

I laugh. "Eat some of this." I put the tray next to her. "The sausage is lovely." I lift the plate lid and pass the wafting smell under her nose. "I broke the circle. The energy buildup was heading toward nuclear." I hand her a sausage.

"I walked away from *this*, all of *this*, when I was a kid." Those blue eyes regard me as she finishes with, "I knew when I first encountered *this* that I wouldn't be normal; my life would be hell, and probably very short."

"So you knew…"

"Oh yeah. It was riveting at the age of ten that night on the mountain. Either no one would believe me, or I'd be like those freaks who see ghosts. I can see ghosts."

"So at ten your fierce little self told the spirit world to take a flying leap, and then you just cracked on with life, only you merchandised your talent."

"Whatever. I convinced myself it was all a bad dream, which it was. Twenty years I've said that to myself."

"Wait. If your grandfather was a great shaman—"

"He wasn't, much to his disappointment. It was my great-grandfather. Even if grandfather sensed it in me, he would have ignored it because I am a half-blood."

The rain had eased up to delicate patters.

"You don't like the catholic religious I sense."

"The clergy in Canada were not very good to the indigenous children throughout history. Also, I went to a catholic school. Nuns are intense. How do we know they're really on our side?"

"Seems like they are, but they all have crafty eyes. All ten of them and including the old ones."

"The place is kind of echo'y. What can ten old dears and ourselves do against a magical ordeal by gods?"

"Finish up that food. You'll need your energy."

+++

In spite of a recent full-out renovation of the convent, the dining room has a utilitarian, cafeteria-like feel with stainless steel counter tops in the adjoining kitchen and multiple simple round tables and chairs. We sit down, the nuns and Mealla and me. "Have you ever read, *The Tragic Deaths of the Children of Tuireann?*" is my opening.

Tea all round is brought, of course.

"Yes," says Sister Rose and Mealla together.

"So you'd agree, Brian, the son of the God Tuireann is the ancient example of a psychopath. He's the god that said, 'I think less of killing a man than a pig.'"

"We have his head?" asks Mealla.

"He has three brothers. Three stupid brothers who are the issue of the father Tuireann and his daughter." The head—" I shove a chocolate digestive into my mouth and chase it with tea. "—is one of those brother's."

"That's better, isn't it? It's in storage and safe," Rose says without a beat, as if having a dead *Tuatha's* head in her refrigerator is a common daily occurrence. Maybe it is. I don't know what these Sisters of Saint Brigid have been up to. There are sayings for times like these...whiskey is the only cure.

"All three brothers are dead," I clarify. "But still seems they are available for work. It's Luchar."

"Just what the Irish gods are worried about. Magic is releasing in an uncontrolled way." Sister Rose wipes her mouth and refreshes her tea.

Buttermilk enters and lights up when she sees me. "With youse two being the best we could find, they're *still* worried."

"Talk to them often?" I ask her. That's what I like about Buttermilk, she's always so positive.

Rose pinches the bridge of her nose like another headache is beginning. "Thank you, Mary. If you'd just listen now. We are all working hard to stop the prophesy."

"Yeah, with youse two." Buttermilk almost cackles.

Nice to have a fan base.

"Mary, isn't it time to...em...to check the...fountain for algae?" Rose says.

"Not a bit of it," says Buttermilk as she hobbles over to flick on the hot water kettle.

"Maybe Butter—Sister Mary has a point. Just Mealla and I and even with Constance's excellent driving, it seems—"

"Severely understaffed," calls out Buttermilk.

"They're struggling, the practitioners," says Constance.

"They'll get better," I say. "They would steal the eye out of your head and come back for the eyelashes. What about Brigid, Lug, The Ogma himself?" I say. "How about some heavy-weights joining in?"

"Ogma can bring both his hands," says Buttermilk.

I gesture towards Buttermilk with a sweeping arm gesture. She's right though, two hands are better than one. Ten are even better.

"The Irish gods can't do anything overt. All the other gods...that would start hostilities." Rose regards Mealla. "First bit of magic yesterday?" she asks her. "Big time magic too."

"It was frightening...over-whelming," Mealla says with conviction.

I cough. "She was intentionally driving back Luchar with a truckload of anger-management magic." I pat her hand. "You did have spit in your eye."

"Yeah, well."

"What would you do differently?" asks Rose.

"Keep the power consistent. Don't exhaust myself. I've been thinking." Mealla glances at each one of us a twinkle in her eye.

Uh oh.

"We should get the head to talk." She laughs into our stressed faces. "No seriously, the Celts were headhunters, and they kept the heads of their enemies as trophies. They used severed heads as oracles. The Welsh have Bran the Blessed whose head, after death, ate and drank with his friends in a cave until the cave was opened."

"Do you know how?" asks Rose.

"I've been googling all the ethnic groups that did this. Native Americans did it. The Persians, Romans. The Germans used their dead enemies' skulls as drinking mugs. I searched for their magic systems to see if I could get the right components, to make the head talk. A good compound is about the components. Like chemistry."

"Like a potion?" asks Constance.

Mealla scoffs. "It's not a "potion" anymore. It's an "elevated component." It's elevated with will and intent. It's alchemy, elevated chemistry. Making something ordinary differently and elevating it. I mean "potion" give me a break. So witches, pointy hats, and warts."

"Have you, personally, ever elevated a compound?"

She shrugs her shoulders. "Haven't needed to. I teach others how to."

"And have the students?"

"I'm sure. They think so. It's so hard to measure outcomes."

My-what-the-feck mind scramble, Buttermilk says out loud for us all, "That's a load of bunk."

That punched some air out of her for a second. Mealla comes back with something about mental health, and ta-da, observe the last few days; she is not bunk. You can't be a sham shaman who isn't a sham without moxy.

"Bran the Blessed is associated with the Ogham, *Fearn*. The symbol for the alder tree."

"The alder…" and Mealla glances at Buttermilk, a little fear in those bright eyes, "…is smoked by indigenous tribes blended with KinniKinnick in ceremonies. 'Kinnikinnick' actually means to mix something animate with something inanimate. Maybe we can smoke him out."

Constance laughs, a real-life laugh, a life-is-absurd laugh. It is when you think about it.

The nuns collect the alder leaves. We toil and boil it in a stainless-steel pot. I cut through the water and leaves the symbol of *Fearn* with Ogma's hand and Ogma's knife.

"I sell pre-rolled herbal smokes called Bear Blend. No tobacco. My best seller has red raspberry leaf, mullein, lavender, mugwort, calamus, passion flower, calendula, lobelia, clove and vanilla bean. Kinnikinnick makes you drowsy." Mealla is selling it. "That's why it's good for ceremonial smokes. I put that in my Bear Blend Dream Herbal Roll along with valerian root. As the smoke rises to heaven, we call out to the spirit. Maybe we should burn some alder leaves as well. For backup."

So there's two Mealla's. One is the internal, prepossessing, introvert, survivor. I say survivor because she's tough, young and that doesn't come with an easy life. The other is pure snake-oil salesman.

"He's not in heaven," I point out.

When we are ready, I have to go get him out of the refrigerator. Mealla makes it clear that I am the ancient Celtic warrior. Stuff people say when they aren't going to be the ones who are going to clean a public toilet. Escape-the-hell-out-of-it things.

"I'm not *that* ancient. Not head-of-my-enemies-keeping ancient." Doesn't matter. I'm still the dogs-body that gets to take the head out of the refrigerator. That's what I'm here for. The grunt work.

"Don't look so sore. The nuns have been looking at it each time they take out the milk for tea, at least eight times in the day."

The women are arguing about where to put it as I hold the head in my arms. I'm really glad it's fluid-free, its body being dead before decapitation.

"We just had the dining room repainted," says Constance. She's thinking about our last attempt with the spiritual world at the bishop's house.

"Got to be outside," says Buttermilk.

"People can look in," says Rose.

They lead me to a cell-like bedroom, and I finally get to drop the thing onto a desk. Mealla is looking up how to call watchtowers to the four corners of the room for protection.

Google-magic, it's a slow process.

"No protective circle?" I ask.

"I'm going to have watchmen guard the four corners of the room. How can we blow the alder at it, and pour the compound into its mouth if it's in a circle? We have to be in the circle. We just want to get it to talk."

"Words of the moment. Crack on."

"I'd like to try for my tribal ancestors for the watchmen. Not sure it will work. We're in Ireland. I guess can't call one of the the *Tuatha*, you know which is pretty standard in these things."

"Madness."

Mealla gathers herself. She's owning this. She starts loud and strong. Blah, blah, blah blah blah, "…to protect this sacred space and all in it." She opens her eyes and looks to the four corners. No watchmen. She shakes her head and goes directly to plan "B" whatever that is, which ends with the same chant, "…to protect this sacred space and all in it."

From the four corners, energy hums and pushes out waves of heat. A mirage forms and undulates as it clarifies into four *giant* salamanders.

Ok then. Fire elementals. Related to dragons, they are blotched purple with thick heads and bodies. They have poisonous glands with an alkaloid toxin. They cause muscle convulsions and hyperventilation. They are born of fire and are not consumed by it. Dropped in water, they poison the drink. It's said they are not devils, but humans with no soul. Mealla is all about over-kill, but then the salamanders shrink to their normal four-inch selves. Not as brilliant or convincing.

The burning, dried alder makes me cough, as I walk forward to open the god's gob, so Mealla can pour the compound on his tongue.

"Is there a tongue?" I step up to the putrid thing resembling a head. "Drink this, ye bastard," I say as I stick my finger into Luchar's nose. Give me strength. I lift to open his mouth. The tongue is a molding mass of swollen, gray matter. My fingers in his nostrils, I remember how much I dislike this guy. Mealla pours the potion into his mouth cavity.

"*Fearn*," I call out, and carve the Ogham letter into his tongue. I'm jacked as the head spits and gargles, like it's clearing its voice box. Getting there. I don't like that he's not contained in a circle, but also relieved that he's not contained in a circle. I glance low to the salamander watchmen. They seem alert enough.

Mealla calls Luchar's name, and then blows the smoke and the breath of the word towards his head.

When the ball-ache sputters and my old enemy Luchar son of Tuireann animates his head, my hand wants to smite him dead again. When you finally get guys like this dead, you pray, beg, blackmail, use any currency to make sure they stay that way.

CHAPTER

SEVEN

Piseog
Superstition

L uchar's head hacks. In all his glory. It's disgusting to watch as the tongue is limbering up. His eyes are opaque and sunken, with black veins shooting from the middle. Even though I've been listening and staring, I still startle when words burst from it like a speaker punched on at full volume. It's not like the words are clear what with the tongue about as flexible as a stuffed sausage.

"*Losca...los...ca...dh is dó or..t. Mal...mallacht Go d...tit... fidh...an o...o...í...che ort...*"

What a feckin' treat. "What's that slabber, you bastard? Can't quite make it out."

"*Thu fecker.*"

I catch that.

"Padraic O Duibh, *tha mi gad fhaicinn...*"

"He's warming up."

"*Agus duilich a bhith a ciohead gu bheil thy cuideachd.*"

"Not as sorry looking as you I guarantee. *Shan eil e cho duilich a bhith a coimhead.*"

"*Loscalocadh is dó ort. Malmallacht go dtitfidhan oíche ort.*"

"What is he saying?" Mealla shoots at me.

"I'm cursed and going to die a fiery death. Expected stuff. Why were you being summoned by the practitioner you *carson a bha an sagart gad ghairm*?"

The big gaping hole in the head called a mouth opens and possibly laughs. The stink, worse than a yearly-cleaned men's toilet. Add to that smoke, perspiration, alder potion... compound in the room, it's all lovely stuff.

"Is that laughing?" Mealla asks.

"He knows we are desperate," I grunt. "Go ahead, laugh. Ye'er the one without teeth."

"Were you being summoned or are you the guy that showed up?" Mealla asks in the same general tone as the teeth comment. The eyes slosh from clear to a creamy milk color and back. The voice becomes more powerful and high pitched. His sound reverberates off walls and presses in on my eardrum. When Mealla drops to her knees, her hands over her ears, I'm half torn to drop kick the head across the room, but then the great gob of a mouth opens and blasts out a *sí gaoithé*, a fairy blast. A salamander absorbs the razor-sharp wind into their enlarged mouths. Well played.

The head is not done. The tongue ejects out of the mouth like a cast spear, with Mealla as the target. The three salamanders race me to it. A watchman catches it in its teeth, rolls and spits it to the floor. It lights the tongue on fire like a petroleum-soaked rag.

Shite. The smoke alarm goes off. A mattress corner catches fire on the way to consuming the whole bed before a nun pops in with a fire extinguisher. We are all hacking. Nothing like it, smoke from polyester and foam. I wipe at my burning eyes and then attend to my dripping nose. I can tell you this for nothing; magic is rarely graceful, and definitely never pretty. Its detritus is always damaging and mostly environmentally unfriendly in a toxic-to-humans kind of way.

His sound, set at a decibel to make ears bleed, has gone blessedly silent. The magic invigorating it has weakened. Mealla thanks the fire salamanders before sinking to the floor. She passes out. We're flying now.

What's left of the tongue is smoldering. A nun uses a jam jar for its storage. The glass is made to be resilient to high temperatures such as boiling fruit and sugar. She takes charge of the head…in a Dunns Store bag.

I pick up Mealla. Her ears are bleeding. Shite, eardrums bursting is almost worse than migraines.

Rose is in the hallway. She actually rolls her eyes when she sees the state of Mealla. "Profitable?" she asks. It's an economy of words from stern lips, with no hope in its tone, like Mealla is slagging off or something.

I could eat the nun's head off. I just say, "She's giving it her all. She's flah'ed out. And if you didn't notice, she got it to talk. It didn't have much to say. But that's Luchar in total."

✝✝✝

A less bloody Mealla comes into the dining room complaining about how destructive magic is. "I'm constantly washing off soot, or blood, or body parts."

"You must be hungry," Rose waves her forward.

"Starving and I'd murder for a beer."

"Sister Vianney, would you please bring that?" A change of tone here. Not that Mealla is beginning to care one way or the other.

"There must be a mastermind to all this melting," Rose continues as she glances round the table in the dining room at me and three other nuns. None of these women like their holes being kicked.

There are crosses here and there on the walls. The religious ornamentation is sparse in the convent either from good taste or from religious-tat exhaustion. There is one statue of Saint Brigid. I gesture towards it every time I walk by.

Rose is laying it out for us. "One thing everyone at this table knows is that whatever these practitioners are doing, whatever they want, whatever they are summoning, it's in three days on Saint John's Eve."

The nuns all nod.

Who are these women?

"We must improve. We can't find a lead. We haven't been able to discover what exactly they're planning."

"Now, now there's no shame in failure," I contribute. Yeah, no, I can be like that, but Rose refuses to rise to it. On the other hand, she does look like she's tortured by hernias. I admit, I've always had an authority figure problem.

I let the front two legs of my chair hit the floor. "I suggest that someone put the Kaiju in the sign at the gaming center, someone skillful. It's a short stroll to North Main Street to see if anything was left behind."

The walk back to north Main Street is recess like.

"Salamanders?" I ask Mealla as we stroll under a threatening gray sky.

"Good story. So that overnight on my own on the mountain top for my spirit animal...turns out it's the fire salamander. Small but able to squirt toxic fluid and walk through fire. Related to dragons. I didn't know *that* connection until Sister Rose. So there you go."

"Quite the night."

"It was."

We take in the busted sign at the gaming center. There is a roll-down, metal door protector in the front, so we head to the back. The shops are connected, and we have to go out of our way to find a lane that takes us there. Once medieval, the lane is narrow, dirty with trash blown up against the walls. Turns out that the back door of the gaming center is stout and has a padlock as well as a deadbolt. I swing my blackthorn club, a single enhanced blow, and the padlock breaks.

The deadbolt is another issue.

"Almost got 'er done," Mealla says. "Hang on." She rummages through her beaded bag. "That's an easy pick."

"You too?"

"All smart women have them."

We let ourselves in, and I close the door behind us as we enter the main room where a continuous, single-piece shelf/desk lines the length of both black walls. At the top of the room, we walk by two sets of gray, vinyl loveseats with a black coffee table in between. Pausing in back of the white front door, I glance at the tall counter to the side. Here the walls are orange. The floor is a fake, grey stone linoleum. It's like they decorated with sale items from a going-out-of-business second-hand store.

Mealla picks up a package of 'On the Go' Belgian waffle cookies with a chocolate-flavored coating and waves it at the Pot Noodle Styrofoam cups. "Food provisions for obsessive gamers. Keep 'em full. Keep 'em from leaving."

"All this needs two locks and a roll-down metal door?"

"Go figure. The computers are gone. Let's go upstairs," says Mealla.

I smell The Damp first. The spaces upstairs haven't been fully aired for a long time. There's a lack of a paint, a well-tread carpeted floor, and filthy Georgian windows. Beyond the pervasive mold, the air smells funny. The ozone of used energy is obvious. A desk, a chair, a stained floral sofa have been pushed to the walls.

"I saw someone in here that evening. A light was on." I stride to the desk in the corner. I open drawer after drawer as I rummage through the clutter of the Kaiju Gaming Center, the pencils and paperclips, sales slips, birthday party reservations, until I find the electrics bill.

"Eoin Hurley."

"Does he own the building?" asks Mealla.

"Sounds reasonable. Could he be our practitioner?"

She shrugs. "No one has broken into the place. They would have had to have drawn the circle from the outside, drawn it and said the evocation. That could be done without entry."

"But I saw a person in here." I walk to the windows and gaze out. I imagine us on the sidewalk in front of Saint Peter's Church. The view is unobstructed. I look around me. On the floor are a couple of bags of the Belgian waffle cookies. The practitioner waits here, watching, eating. Comfortable. He sees me come out. He waits for Mealla. He breaks the circle.

Mealla gasps, "Maybe, a visualized circle from the inside to the outside. He'd be a pro's pro to do that. You have to visualize the blue light of energy and use your hand as the instrument to control it. The circle is cast, you maintain its visualization, summon a Kaiju, and hold it."

"All while eating a Belgian waffle. Yeah, no, he's good. And he knew the time and place." I stare out the window. The busted up church still there. "So, as I'm standing there waiting for my head to get off a carousel ride, he waits. This yoke is not thick, so he doesn't want to give me time for my head to clear. I'm standing there for like five minutes, but he doesn't break the circle. He's waiting."

Never, ever take anything from a fairy.

I don't feel sorry for many people, hardly any. Most get what they give. But money talks to those who are skint or Mealla'd never been suckered. Doesn't matter. They'd never have accepted a "no" answer from her. There's now a terrible thirst for magic.

"For me? Just because I have a distant, and I mean way back there, blood line with a dragon lady? And Biddy's close relationship to the fairies?" Mealla pats my shoulder. "I could take comfort in it wasn't only me he wanted. Nice not being alone."

"Let's figure this out sooner rather than later."

"What are we, sitting at the pub?"

"We don't know how he did it, but we know he was here. He had a key, and either the key was given to him, or he had it already. We know he drinks at the Fran-Well. How else is a dead monk of eight-hundred years, who can't leave the bar-restaurant, to know what's going on? That *gobshite* went for you not me."

"What is this, a contest? If they get me, they get you by proximity." She glances away in a typical female give-me-strength pause. She might leave it at that, but yeah, no, then she says, "If they come after me, you're in front."

I carry on like the patient man I am. "There's these unpaid electrics bills, in the name of Eoin Hurley. Obvious why the place closed. He could be either the building owner or the gaming center manager. Either have a key. Or a friend of a friend or the key could have been five-fingered."

"Clear as muck."

"Well, let's tuck into Eoin. See where it leads us. It's all we've got."

The old stairs creek under our weight as we descend. We search the ground floor more. "Look at this." Mealla rips off a sheet of paper that was taped to the window face out. On it a monster Kaiju is baying to a yellow sunset. White words are centered across the top of the page. "Last day of business, twenty-second of December. Thank you for your support, Eoin Hurley," she reads. "That's two strikes for Eoin."

She types the name into her phone. "He lives on Westgate Road, Bishopstown, six miles from here. He used to be a monk, surprise."

<hr />

. . .

In front of the courthouse on Washington Street, we get on the number two-zero-eight bus to Bishopstown, a suburb of Cork. On the way down The Western Road, I take in neighborhoods of different eras. North Main Street is shoulder-to-shoulder, small shops built over time beginning with the Vikings and burning down a number of times with Saint Peter's church, the only building left from my time, finally taken out. A few miles down Western Road begins three story Victorian semi-detached homes of once elegant but now petrol-exhaust stained brick The homes are tall, with short iron fences at the footpaths and stamp-sized patches of unkempt grass and garden in front. The widened, four-lane street now laps at their front porches, and the money has moved farther out still to more quiet places. Ireland has always been simply built, no huge extravagances in architecture. It's always been an outpost country without huge slushes of money.

We get off the bus at the corner of Westgate and Curraheen Road with the Viscount Pub on one side of the street and Dunnes Department Store on the other. As we knock shoulders walking up Westgate Road, she says, "I get you don't want to be here. Isn't this what you do, though?"

"First off, all of the not-mental ones get out of this business. Second, I didn't choose it. What about you? First magical dream in and you're out."

"I was ten."

"I was five."

"It's not a contest. Let's get this done, and we'll all be on our way home."

"You're joking, right? This is mighty. This won't end with the rogue practitioners."

Galtemoor sits near the street on a rise with a short driveway on a vertical slope. A low plastered stone wall circles the plot. The grass inside the perimeter is tall, the garden full of weeds. All the attached houses on the street look close enough to the same with a wide front window, a door, some brick and a garage. Simple.

We are in front of it, standing on the footpath, and staring at Mealla's phone. A video begins on the screen with the heart-shaped face of a lad with an already receding, black hairline. He stares into the camera with dark eyes as he calls the ex-monk Eoin Hurley a scum-bag and a bunch of other bad things. He puts a newspaper picture of Eoin up to the camera and says that this boyo should have horns on his head. The video is five years old. Mealla freezes the screen.

"Only nine-hundred and fifty views," she comments.

No horns, just a bald top on a round face. He's a man of a later age with stretched lips, bags under the eyes, and eyebrows that have thinned at the inner corners. He was talking when the newspaper photographer snapped the picture.

"I look closer. "Well, now, would ye look at that? Interesting a photo would pick it up."

"What?"

"Right there." I point with my finger. "See that bright spot, that sort of glow? That could be a familiar hovering just at the man's shoulder."

"Or a reflection of something."

"I'd say sure bet in a horse race."

Mealla gets her nose closer to the screen. "I can't tell." She proceeds to scroll down different sites with Hurley's name on them. "Anyway, *this* house, interestingly enough, is going to be exorcised, tomorrow." She studies the house not ten feet from us, probably expecting it to sprout horns. "If we're going into the house, you'd better get your ice cream cone," Mealla says as she opens the gate to the front walk.

"Going into a house that's about to be exorcized. Aren't we just off our heads?"

Mealla replies, "Aren't we just." Full stop.

EIGHT

Feath fiadha
Magic mists of invisibility

I f someone asks for aid from the power of a demon, while using dark magic, he's the bad guy. If someone prays for an angel to smite someone, and then have that someone eaten by worms until that someone breathes his last, he's the good guy. The use of magic is a matter of perception. Either of the perceptions can double back on you in a heartbeat.

The reception room in the house is long, with an aspect window at each end and a bowling-alley-like wood floor. The white brick fireplace has smoke stains. The windows have full length gold-satin curtains. The walls, watercolors of Ireland and Africa. There are no religious artifacts, no pentagrams, no rugs hiding a permanent circle. Only the basics in furniture. There's no compound residue in the pots or vapor stains in the particle-board kitchen cabinets.

There is a stink of death. Stronger as we start up the stairs. A stench that always has me holding tighter to my club.

The first pool of blood on the carpet is at the landing, like the person heard something, walked to the banister to check, then sinew-tearing violence. The white door at the end of the hall isn't much more than a splinter of wood, and a path of blood to it. I request Mealla to stay. She doesn't.

As I near the opening, the smell of sulphur burns my nose and brings tears to my eyes. If I don't walk into that room and see a burned, skinless corpse, I'll be surprised.

Shite. I tell Mealla that she probably doesn't want to look.

She walks in on my heels, into a room that is a battle site. Blood has sprayed on the walls like an art form. As far as I can see, there is no body. The window is closed.

I edge in to position myself to see over the edge of an upturned bed. "Jaysus, it's a *Cwn Annwn*."

"What? A hellhound? Are you sure? Let me see."

"Stay back. I don't know if it's dead." Her head immediately is peering over my right shoulder.

"A soul hunter. Pure white coat, emaciated rib cage, ribbed back and bright red ears. Can't see them, but it should have red eyes. The rest is pretty clear. Is it breathing? Maybe they don't breathe."

"You're the magical creature expert."

"Do they die?"

"Only an angel blade between its bony shoulders kills them. Pretty hard to do, impressive."

"Then where's the angel blade?"

"Brilliant question. Jaysus a hellhound. Even a practitioner getting the best of it is something I never thought I'd say."

"Attached bathroom." Mealla indicates with her head.

"Get behind me." She's too absorbed in the hound anyway.

I hit the doorknob to break the lock. From the blood everywhere, the hound did its job before dying. Eoin I assume crawled in, locked up, and died. He is slumped on the floor in a pool of the rest of his blood. Exsanguination can take less than five minutes if the neck or groin are involved. The hellhound got both. And more, ouch.

There is a blade on the cool tile floor, but it's not an angel blade. "Impossible," the word injects from me. A Hound of the Hunt is impossible to kill. That this nutter got lucky without angle blade doesn't sit well with me. That's along the lines of miracle stuff. Yeah, no, not this guy. Not without help.

Mealla yells my name. From the tone, something shite-hot is happening. I'm thinking the hound wasn't dead.

From the bathroom door she is not more than ten feet from me, still I can only just make out a flailing arm, or a flash of a hand. A gray fog cloaks her entirely. Not uncommon outdoors in Ireland, but not indoors. A fecking *Slúagh* a host of souls. That's why the hellhound is here.

I swing through the cloud with my blackthorn club. "*Straith*," of the blackthorn tree. I yell the Ogham letter, initiating the raw power of the club. Its energy and movement do nothing more than shift the cloud, which reforms. I brandish the club again, over and over to at least interrupt their focus. If given the chance they will transport her by air far away and alone to die, but most victims don't survive the trip.

Sluagh are the army of the unforgiven dead. They are a diet gone mad, thin, haggard, fatless, skin-clinging souls. They fly bird-like with leathery, cape-like wings. And they are most active at solstice.

The dark cloud moves with her as she writhes and throws herself all over the room. I hear her go from screaming to chanting, but the words are broken, ineffective. Jaysus though, she's trying.

Shite. I keep swinging, keep parting the swarm, and keep putting holes in the walls. I need to pull deeper from within. From the strength of Ogma and the *Cailleach*, "*Straith*," I bellow, calling into the darker side of Ogham magic. I've never used the club with such intent. Never, and shite it begins to vibrate hard, up my arms and rattling my head. My vision is blurred. I have to double fist it as a cyclone generates from its end. "Drop," I yell at Mealla. God, for once she listens, throwing herself to the floor.

I aim a thin razor level above where I think her body is, hoping to miss her but not them. That it's possibly too near; I'll have to live with, or she won't.

A fairy blast, like a divine-powered leaf blower, explodes from my club, and the souls hit the wall, and then break through it. I follow the mass, obliterating their tenuous corporal formation. The pressure explodes through their cavities, and then they burn until they are ash on the carpet.

Mealla's clothes are shredded. She's bleeding and dazed. She tries to stand but drops down again.

"See why I don't want this job?" I ask as I step over charred, skeletal souls to help her up.

"Admit it. You love it."

I force open a broken cabinet that still has in its grasp a heavy gallon of water labeled "Holy." I pour it over her, and into her gashes to kill the residue of dark magic. And then I make her drink some. "We don't want fairy fever."

"Is that really a thing?"

"Yes, but I made up the name."

Wind from a broken window disperses the ash. You can't kill a *Sluagh*. They're already dead.

Mealla is sitting on the floor in a puddle of water. She leans back against the wall. As she recovers, I thank the *Cailleach*, the old crone of winter who commands storms through her own blackthorn club, and the Ogma. I've never had such power available to me. Not even when I'm the one death is closing in on.

"Shit, I like this shirt," she utters.

"That was a *Sluagh* by the way."

"I thought *Sluagh* are a group of *Unseelie* fairy, monster-like, that ride in the Wild Hunt, and make you crazy when you look at them," she says in a tired voice.

"And souls of the rotten dead."

"If hellhounds guard entrances to the world of the dead, hunt rotten, lost souls and evil fairies, are omens to death, are the protectors of supernatural beings and creatures, which of that brought them here? Lost, rotten souls, or the soul of Eoin?"

"I don't know. And I've never seen *Slaugh*, or a practitioner kill a hound. There was something else here." I help shift her to her feet.

"Maybe the familiar?" She is leaning heavily on me as she limps to the stairs. "I guess the exorcism won't be needed now. The place has been bathed in Holy Water."

Gotta love her, and her push back.

"From what I've been told, the current practitioners are too weak to do the job anyway."

As I finally just pick her up, and carry her out the door, I'm thinking. As I ring Constance for a pickup, I'm fume-thinking; I'd like to ring a few Irish gods' necks. What is it in Mealla that the practitioners are so afraid of?

And the familiar, not anything I can think of that can take out a hellhound. In the newspaper picture is a pin-prick of a dark hole over Eoin's shoulder. You could think it was an ink spot.

Sure, Eoin fought the battle. He has the scars to prove that. It wasn't fought *for* him. *Slaugh* can divert a hellhound, but not kill it.

Constance honks as she pulls to the curb. "Hospital?" she asks through the rolled-down window.

"All superficial," says Mealla. "Maybe a sprained ankle."

"*Slaugh*. Eoin Hurley is dead. I have to go back and get a hellhound."

Back inside, I do an over-all survey. *Blood on the stairs. So hellhound. It bounds up the stairs, Eoin at the top. Why? Eoin is a Slaugh. Yeah, definitely not then, maybe now. Eoin is protecting Slaugh. Possible, but never heard of that before. Hound attack Eoin.*

You're joking. Never been done. Eoin attacks hound. Suicide. Also never been done.

As I take him in, he is a mess. The hellhound has done a right job on him. Jaysus. Water squeegees up through the carpet as I traverse the bedroom. No black cat... too big anyway. If he had a familiar, it's not here now. I stand in the middle of the bloody room, my feet wet and cold, puzzled. I don't know.

I have decided to bring the hellhound. Sounds fine like, but how do I go about picking it up? I poke at it. The eyes don't spring open. I wrap it in a bloody bed sheet, all the while watching for even a muscular spasm.

I dash outside, drop it into the boot, and slam the lid down. I'm sweating now.

I take the front passenger seat. "Know any familiars that can take out a hellhound?" I ask Constance.

"Niggets."

"Never heard of them."

"Nigget familiars are an infestation of small insects that are the power behind say a puny-armed practitioner's stroke with a bog-standard dagger, instead of an angel dagger. If that's what happened. As familiars, the bugs move as one in a topical layer of skin. They look as if a person's skin is loosely attached to its bones. Works on the arms, legs. An amazing source of magical energy."

"They're throwing everything they've got at this, including themselves."

"The prize is worth it to them."

NINE

Bríocht
Spell

Conversations about the weather in Ireland go like this: sure it's starting to stop raining; and ye wouldn't put a rumor out in that weather. And when the weather does turn...a drop of rain would do no harm. But mostly, it's to be expected that in the time Mealla and I limp to the door of the convent our jeans are soaked, hair dunked-wet, shoes sloshing like inflatable, children's swimming pools.

Constance did a drop-off, fly-off. It's a no-coddle directive here at St. Brigid's. We ring the bell at the very grand and imposing front door of the convent. Buttermilk opens it like she has been waiting there.

"Look what the cat dragged in," she says staring at the dead hellhound. "Bring it and yourselves."

Heartwarming. Sure, you're welcome. It was no bother to sort that shite out.

"Ye didn't leave in that shirt," she says as Mealla passes her.

"Puff off," I mutter as I wipe my wet feet on the mat like I'm trying to sandpaper off the soles. Mealla rolls her eyes at me and mimics Buttermilk's stern face.

"Come back here when you're dry, and we'll have some food for you," says Rose from the hallway.

"This one needs a bit of first aid, again," says Buttermilk.

If any of them are disappointed in us…bugger it. I'm in for a long shower and dry clothes and food, and a drink. Not in that order.

"What do we know?" Rose begins when we are seated in the dining room, slash, operation headquarters. The dog of hell has been wrapped in a fresh bed sheet a placed in a corner. Back in the spacious dining room, a plate of lamb and mash with mushy peas is put in front of me. I wash down the food with a bottle of lager. Highlight of the day.

"They have been all over our every move, Ladies. Their intel is deadly. This is deeper than it first appeared."

"Away with ye. Is it now?"

Buttermilk.

"Yes." Sister Rose sounds dead tired. "Eoin was meeting with the *Slaugh* you think?" Rose is not eating.

"You have any better ideas? How many bourgeois, flippin' gods are trying to capitalize on the magic money pot do you think?" That there may be others from the god spectrum in play does not startle Rose.

"One thing is, the practitioners don't know that I'm not working to what they think is my potential."

Buttermilk grunts. "Whatever that means, they'll pick up soon enough."

"The house on Westgate Road is on fire," says Rose.

"We left it fire-free, I swear," declares Mealla.

"Damn it, we just missed Eoin."

Mealla wipes her mouth and lays the napkin by the table. She's gone off her food. No appetite left.

"Bishop Crowley had Eoin under his protection. He and the

Franciscans brought him back here abruptly from missionary status. Times have changed since the old days when the church could do a blind eye. They went to the seminary together, the two, Saint Patrick's College, Maynooth.

"So the bishop knows something?"

"He's a good man. With him it was the good old boys. Vianney copped on to that house in Bishoptown. It's called a clergy rental, owned by the Church. That's where the Garda picked up one notorious Father Maxwell, about six months ago. Now there's a practitioner if there ever was one."

"So they were going to exorcize the place. Maxwell possessed they're advertising?"

"Looks like it. They wanted to sell it. The market is good in Bishopstown. Eoin, the hellhound, the *Slaugh* are complications they hadn't foreseen, and you two. Can't sell it now."

"Maybe that house was kipped-out to be special by Maxwell," Mealla adds. "Only we couldn't find anything. Maybe Eoin was there to decommission it."

I am silent. Rose is silent. Mealla goes silent. Even Buttermilk is silent. None of us has any answers. Our grasp of the situation is nonexistent. So far, we have only been putting out fires, or em, setting them, or missing fires by a whisker. Burning down Cork one place at a time.

It's not surprising that Ireland would be the chosen place of this the immortals hour. Setting perfect. It's an island where constant mists veil the places between reality, the past, and the unspoken. Entire villages disappear in the shroud to reappear only on clearing days. Faith was strong here once upon a time. The country's still pock-marked by stone circles, dolmans and perforated with holy wells, all conduits to the GrandOther. Soaked into the land is a long time of praying.

"John's Eve is coming up," I say into the void. A shite day of godly chaos. It's the night of the Wild Hunt when the dead souls fly, and the hounds chase them.

"Perfect night for an end-of-times magic grab." Mealla says

that like she gets it. We all get it. It's not just that a handful of bad men are up to no good. It's that the damn behind which magic is locked is breaking apart.

The practitioners are taking blows at it with insistent hammers. Shards flying, holes leaking. Releasing magic and attracting, like shiny bits of filigree, crows, The Crow. Who knows what else?

The room gets cold for all of us at the same time. Looking at my face, Sister Rose gets it that I get it and that I get it that Mealla has gotten it.

"One step at a time. We have to stop them from summoning what they are trying to summon. They are trying for something, and trying, relentlessly." Mealla says in a clear voice. She is the blood of two races of survivors.

"OK," I say straightening up and sitting more forward in my chair, "suggestions."

"We've always hypothesized... Sister Mary, bring a bottle of wine, would you? The practitioners are organizing through the setting up of a hellfire club."

"A hellfire club?"

"Secret societies meant to study magic. The secret wisdom of things inaccessible to human reason."

"A reaction to deregulation, in other words," injects Mealla.

"We are talking demons here," shoots back Sister Rose. "The hellfire clubs were associated with satanic rituals."

"And probably, lots of opium." That's me.

Rose begins pouring the wine all around. "The most depraved hellfire club here in Ireland was in Dublin. It's said that its creator, Colonel Jack Saint Leger still rides there, a ghost in a ghost coach with a headless driver. They supposedly drank hot *scaltheen*, a mixture of whiskey, butter, and brimstone. They toasted Satan. They had mock crucifixions. Once a cat chaired one of their meetings, then vanished in a puff of sulfur. Apparently, the cat was huge with red eyes. Their lodge there on Montpelier Hill was burned down. Their second meeting place,

Killakee Dower House has an invasion of ghosts. I'm not sure about the brimstone." She laughs a little. Nun's humor.

I shift in my chair. "Good history lesson. So what if they are? They're organizing. What does that change?"

"Yes." Gazing at her glass, she twirls the stem between her fingers she adds, "We're thinking it's more than that. It's not just Satan, demons, and magic, though saying that in one breath is enough. They're searching for immortality. Quite possibly the living dead. Not without precedence here in Ireland. It will make dealing with them much more complicated."

+++

It's anybody's bet when the nuns will let me drive the Fiat. Traffic in Cork City is mad. Mealla knows how but doesn't know the city, and its one-way systems, and she has to drive on what she refers to as the "wrong side." Still, the Fiat is small enough to fit on the footpaths should that be necessary, when there are footpaths. In the end, it's the nuns who decide the lot of us will walk to the District Criminal Court on Anglesea Street to watch Father Maxwell's arraignment. "He's intelligent, and evil, and worth watching even in gaol."

"Not intelligent enough to not get caught," I point out in that contrary way we Irish have. An Irishman says up, another within earshot will say down. That's why the phrase, "naff-off," is so popular here.

We walk from the River Lee, against traffic down Sharman Crawford. The nuns have the length of the street tied up in a day nursery, a national school and other modern red brick buildings. Turn left onto Proby's Quay, and we are walking along the original walls of the Brigid of the Isle Convent; a wall that I remember from the past. The road meets with the Lee again and we follow it through a few more Streets until a right on Anglesea.

This is the Cork City office area, the Cork City Council, City Hall, fire brigade, and a Garda Station. Not to mention a solicitor's office and a funeral director. Just a few more steps down the lane...Saints Joachim and Anne's Asylum, which has a four-bay window, Gothic-Tudor style, brick façade with mullioned windows. I see by the sign that elderly ladies live there now.

Old buildings have many lives. The courthouse used to be a red-brick school for four hundred and fifty students in the eighteen hundreds and then a maritime college. The courthouse has cream tile floors and blonde, wood-paneled walls.

"It's modern and restful," Mealla comments as we stroll down the center hallway. "That's good. All the people here are agitated."

The people waiting here and there on hard seats get free legal aid, a boon to solicitors. As does Sean Maxwell.

The courtroom where Sean Maxwell is being arraigned is packed. Within the crowd are supporters who have been spiritually-touched or helped by him. People of every background, religion, education, are saying, "I can't believe this." An older man near my seat in the public section wails, "I wanted him to do the eulogy at my funeral." Charismatic guy, Maxwell.

The crowd gasps as a frail-looking man in a maroon jumpsuit is brought in via wheelchair. He has the blotched skin of old age, and only tufts of white hair on his large head. Rimless, rectangular classes find a solid perch on his large nose.

"This is the man Sister Rose thinks needs watching?" Mealla whispers in my ear.

His blue eyes are fading but are clear, and his voice is potent. "I'm a good man," he begins. "Helpful. I believe in the theology of Gratitude. I believe that my legacy and reputation will be restored because all of this is not me. I ran into a wall and into evil things."

Cue in the exorcism.

His offences are read. This practitioner is one angry punter.

He's no slouch with higher degrees. He had written online that he thought he'd do something evil before he died.

Demon defense.

As the counts finish, the people in the room, who had collectively forgotten to breathe, who either loved or hated him, inhaled. As if a robotic part, his head rotates on his flaccid, hunched, ill body until it is in a direct visual line with Mealla. She gasps and grabs my arm. I lean in to break contact.

He huffs and turns his head back, but not before the evil in his eyes makes me want to yell, save yourselves.

"Merciless," mutters Mealla. She sinks into her seat. "He channels evil. He welcomes it. It's a relief to him." She looks at me with her almond, blue eyes that are darkened with a shaman's understanding of demons, of where they live, and who they are. She's winded, and it was just a glance.

"He's old. He's in a wheelchair, and he's in gaol," she intones.

"That's a setback for them then. Definitely, he is the man with the plan."

"He's been in here six months. I wonder if that's when all the face-melting started."

┼┼┼

"Who then?" Back at the convent I lean over my fish and chips towards Rose. "If The Club has had to cut Father Maxwell loose because this arrest has taken them by surprise, who would take over the lead? These are educated, ruthless men. Who could take over?"

"He's out, but not gone," says Rose.

"There could be many to choose from alive and dead," decides Mealla. "Say, they are trying to summon Pope Stephen the Sixth? He had the body of his predecessor dug up and put on trial for blasphemy. Didn't one pope sell the papacy? One, decreed that all humans on earth were subject to him." She looks down at her plate and spears a chunk of fish. "I'm just saying the selection of practitioners is large when it's alive or dead." Mealla glances up to the constipated, nun faces taking her in.

Nothing much to say after that. Anyway, a nun's head pops into the room from the kitchen like a wack-a-mole game. Wack-a-mole is a favorite pass time here. The messages are never that the sun has come out, and everything is coming up roses.

This sister says in a rush, which means she's serious and the house is about to blow, "There's a rotten body, just appeared in the kitchen, and it seems to be trying to retrieve its head from the refrigerator."

TEN

Creadair
Believer

A *geasa* is magic that creates a compulsion. In my case, after killing the Morrigan's son in a fight. Even after the son having all the advantages.

It's not that I don't feel guilty about killing that slabber. I didn't want to kill the Morrigan's son. I had no quarrel with the dose that was her son. Live on and prosper should be everyone's motto. I have no right to your life, nor do you mine.

Ogma must have understood the fouler of the Morrigan's temper tantrum because he gave me his hand as a *buada*, an act of good omen. The magic strength of that hand, and the magic of the Ogham written symbols are for events like this one with Luchar. Yeah, no, I don't need the *geasa*... let him not refuse combat to any...for Luchar. For this one, I personally give a shite.

Jaysus he looks bad. And that's looking at his arse end as his head is deep in the refrigerator.

The nuns keep a clean kitchen, but the large refrigerator is packed wall to wall with everything. I have to get to him before he finds it.

Luchar's face had once been Irish-god beautiful, even without glamour. His refrigerated version has alopecia. His eyes are sunken and perforated, and lacking in lids, his skin's in tatters. Luchar can't bare his black teeth without lips. No more lip-walking home from the pub for this guy. I wish the nuns had more mirrors.

I hit him square on his back. He back kicks me like a mule, effin sod, and takes out my knee. And I've lost the element of surprise. Now he's throwing ketchup and milk bottles and mayo jars at me like missiles. Sweeping out entire shelves with a stroke.

In the eureka-moment of his finding his head, he's blanked me for a split second. I swing at him as he raises it to shoulder height; holding it backwards mind you, so he can see me. He ducks. Effin' brilliant.

I'm pissed that he's managed to hold me off this long, what with having his head in his hands. I pull back to observe. I see, leaning next to the refrigerator, a shiny, rounded metal shield and a battle spear for both thrusting and for casting. Luchar's. You have to admire the design and finish of a Celtic battle-spear. The bronze head fixed on a wooden handle gleams. Celtic spears are broad and thick with the top rounded and very sharp. Very sharp.

His glaucomatous eyeballs are not lacking for visual perception. Shite. We both dive for the weapons he has brought and had to put down. How many hands does a dead, scut-god need to replace its head on its shoulders? Looks like it's going to be evens, so he decides to go for me, like an evil moth to a flame. He and the Morrigan's son were best friends. Scathach held him off me after the fight. The Gods do not forget or forgive… ever.

I have no idea how the thorns of my blackthorn club work

on the flesh of a dead *Tuatha*. He is all draped muscle, organs gone, including his heart (never had one.)

With one hand he throws me across the room. Pans clatter to the floor.

"Get back," I yell at the nuns gathering at the door of the kitchen as Luchar screws on his head. He grabs his spear takes his first thrust at my heart. The *geasa* magic has been inflating me like pressured air blown into my veins. That's the thing, at the beginning of any fight, I have to work through the pain. But now Ogma's hand glows and the veins in it pulse. I jump out of the line of the spear. The Ogma's hand swings the blackthorn club with such force it opens a crack in Luchar's shield.

I dance to the other side of a stainless-steel rolling counter. As Luchar lunges over and over with his spear, cooking ingredients like cut vegetables and cooling sauces fly, hitting walls and floors. The sharp sound of metal on metal reverberates around the room. This all from a dead man that looks like he's well beyond even being put on a spit and roasted with herbs. He is food-poisoning.

Using the hand's Ogma-strength, I push the counter-on-wheels into Luchar's midsection. From the force, he hits the wall behind him hard enough that he makes a body-shaped hole, and his head loosens. He has to whack it back on with two hands.

His shield dropped, I run at him, planning another hit with the blackthorn club. A thorn tears his various muscle groups down through to his groin. Now the muscles have a canal cut through them that's big enough for a cruise liner to sail port to port, but Luchar only pushes off the wall towards me using momentum to run me through. I hate battling the *Tuatha*. They are gods. They're that good.

He catches the blackthorn club in his free hand. The thorns pierce through his palm and fingers with the tip ends sticking out. It's the Celtic God Ogma's hand against the Celtic God Luchar's grip, arm, and shoulder strength.

Not to mention his other free hand. His two god-hands to my one. His free fist and attached shield connect with my head like a bat swinging on a ball. I stagger, shite, just trying to stay conscious. The blackthorn club flies from my hands and his, hitting a shelf of serving plates that scatter and drop to the floor. I'm just finding out that dead gods are worse to fight than live ones…being already deceased.

I'm on the floor. I want to puke under the overflow of poisonous *geasa* magic saturating my body. I'm just about standing, knife in hand, looking to take out an eye or something when a nun hits Luchar on the back of his head with a cast-iron skillet.

Luchar's loosely attached head hits me squarely in the stomach. Air is no longer in my lungs. It's like a vacuum there, and I can't inhale for the life of me.

The god plucks his head from the air on its rebound. With me wheezing, and he pounding his head into place, we square up. The thrusts of the spear are coming fast now. Some are inches from my head, shoulder, ribs. I'm effectively pinned down and tiring. I can't move for broken clutter on the floor.

I dive for the shield Luchar dropped when he caught his head. Reading him, I brace with the shield just before a spear point of contact.

The *geasa* will keep me fighting until death. Sure, I'm concussed, and there's Buttermilk's voice saying, he'll never stick it, and giving me odds twenty to one.

No more playtime for Luchar; a fierce jab towards my head and then another that skewers a chunk of prime arm muscle, mine, to the wall. *An donas ort*, you effin' god.

Mealla's voice. Luchar has heard it, knows it. It's good he is a stupid wanker. He yanks the spear back through me and turns. I pull my Ogma's Ogham knife from its sheath. I jump onto his retreating back. Clinging with my bad arm, I begin carving an Ogham letter into his shoulder. "*Luis,*" a straight down motion with two right side lines. "*Isteach sa tairseach,*"

This second letter of the Ogham alphabet functions as

apotropaic magic that wards against gods, and fairies, and opens portals. The blood from my shoulder is running down my arm into my hand. The Ogma's knife is slippery, as I carve the letter into Luchar's leathery muscle. I try to stay attached like a carbuncle on rock onto what's left of the flesh of his upper back.

Luchar wants to shake me. He rams backward against a wall. Time after time, the air is knocked from me. My head is bleeding. The knife nearly twists out of my blood-greased hand. I warrior-scream through the pain, the burn of a flare of *geasa* magic, the ache of the wound, the throbbing of my head.

I'm close to blacking out as I cut the last stroke of the Ogham letter. I yell *"Luis."* I feel the energy of the opening portal, only then do I let go. As I'm falling back, Luchar begins to shimmer and is gone. I hit the ground hard.

When a nun pulls on the damaged arm, some swear words eject from my lips like infectious pus oozing from the carbuncle I had been. *Geasa* magic is not painkilling.

"There's fire," she yells at me.

Of course there is.

$$\cancel{||||}$$

As they've just done up the place, the nuns, all fifteen of them like, with an average age of seventy, gather round ready to put out the fire. Good then that the sprinkler system in the ceiling comes on.

"Jaysus," I say while being rained on indoors. I know that I nearly ran out of road there.

I feel like I'm bleeding internally. Like my whole body is bruising as my tissues are saturated with blood. Or maybe it's just the magic leaving my system. My head aches and my neck.

My brain is on fire. My fingertips are sensitive like the nerve endings are inflamed. This is why I resist fighting. Actually this might be the actual dying part.

The ladies help me to a chair. "Do you think Luchar's body came through with the help?" Mealla asks, with the group standing around me.

"Maybe, or maybe through one or two of the three thousand holy wells that used to be connected to the GrandOther that Saint Patrick blocked. They could be unblocked," I say.

Vianney arrives with enough bandages to mummify me.

"Where's the nearest holy well?" I mewl because God I hurt. Vianney hands me a bottle of Jameson Whiskey. I tip back four fingers worth. "The cure."

+++

Down Washington Street to Saint Patrick's Street and then over the River Lee on Patrick's Bridge, another nun drives like it's a Sunday outing. Sure, it's easy to leave out that traffic is heavy and slow when all you want is to get to the only other not defunct holy well in Cork City and stop the deep and abiding pain.

Seems the Fran Well is closed, and anyway ghost-filled, and the Lady's Well is outside in a park. The other side of the river is a rust-belt of antiquated manufacturing, and of identical, lower-working-class row houses. The homeowners couldn't afford colored paint on this side of the river. The area looks like it might excel in bareknuckle boxing.

We drive up a steep Saint Patrick's Hill. Forced to stop in the middle of the road at an eighty-degree angle, I hear the nun zip up the parking brake, ready for a brake/clutch start that she pulls off, bang on it.

The nun eventually parks in the workers carpark across the street from what used to be Lady's Well Brewery and then Murphy's Brewery and now Heineken Brewery. The smell of hops as we emerge from the car would have been welcomed if someone handed me a full pint.

Most important to the brewery was the spring of water from the holy well up above. The water properties in this area rivaled the best European breweries of the day. Three hundred years of magical water making beer. Cork's been lucky that way.

My luck's run out as I stare up from the bottom of wide cement stairs, a hill-climb only goats would love. I swig from the half-empty Jamison Whiskey bottle, as I lift my foot up to stair one. The ancient cement retaining walls are coated with angst graffiti. I'm there. Gives me something to read and admire as I ascend, slow step by slow step. The tipsy, smoking, blue bunny is my favorite. And then at the top, as I'm absorbing the despair, disrespect, and disrepair of the unkempt greenspace around the well, I'm thinking blight. I'm thinking done I'm in. I'm thinking the well must be dry.

Which is reinforced when I see the well itself, and the empty beer cans there. I collapse on a low, stone retention wall that curves around the well. I drink more. I think I'm drunk, which is just fine with me.

"There's a grate over the well." Mealla calls back to me.

I swig more whiskey as I glance at the yellow duck with goggles painted on the alcove where the statue of the Virgin Mary used to reside. She has left the building.

I listen to the sound of traffic with falling hope.

"If there's water it could be gangrenous. Luchar for sure didn't come through here," she says.

I sit and drink and take in the nearly full moon.

Mealla climbs back up the steps from the well and sits next to me. "I think you can get a finger through the grating, but I'm not sure it will touch the water."

I take another slug of Ireland's cure all.

"Maybe I can find something to fit through." She walks up the slope across mowed grass. The thing about grass in Ireland is it's no problem. It grows and keeps growing, everywhere. Scrounging under the brush, I hear her call, "Eureka." She returns with an unopened condom packet and a green stick. "It says on the packet extra strong."

Ripping open the packet, she holes the condom at the top with my knife and threads the stick through. "How much water will you need? Should I find a storage something?"

"It all could be a fart in a pigs' sty," I slur a bit.

"Ah come on. This is, as you all say here, brilliant."

She pushes the stabbed condom through a one-inch square in the grate, and then pushes to the end of her stick. As it's hauled up, we notice that the condom is versatile; it widens for maximum water fill and then elongates to fit the shape of the grate.

She holds it up, the dripping, drooping, and bulging condom and says, "Success."

I try to shake away the doubt and the alcohol. As she ritual-walks circles around me with the stick of water, I mark myself in blood with an Ogham letter, down and across.

I pray the words of the well, and then say, *"Beith."* She pours the water from the condom. The cool of the water seems sinks into my skin. I'm dizzy within the healing relief. I get to my feet, with effort. I'm sore and feeling fragile and exhausted. I walk to the metal fence in front of the well. I gaze at the city of Cork. The Heineken Brewery tanks underneath the towering St Mary's Cathedral, and to the left the Shandon Bells Tower and Saint Anne's Church.

"Churches, churches, churches," Mealla says, joining me and leaning on the fence.

"Do you feel it?" I say.

"Yeah. Can you hear it?"

"And see it." The veil. It's so thin it's more like a mist than a covering. I see a shape sometimes like a dolphin surfacing in flat water. I smell the perfume of the GrandOther, flowers in a breeze.

There are about three thousand holy wells in Ireland, most of them forgotten in the middle of a farmer's field, or off some side road, or up a shale and rock path. Those three thousand remote places connect this world to the GrandOther. More if you count the stone circles, dolmens and the passage tombs. The island's a portal sieve to any amount of magical showers of shite.

ELEVEN

Dun Chur
Closing the entrance to a power site

People don't quit believing, they shift, to money as their new god that sort of thing. Except that lucky sod Bacchus, the god of wine and pleasure. He's always knee deep in faith. Your man, the devil isn't believed in much today. Currently 'evil' is just the opposite of 'good.'

"The hellfire clubs work off the idea of devilry, of flicking one's finger at everything, and welcoming necromancy," says Rose over her cup of cream-infused coffee. "Sorcery is the perfect medium for men who have expectations of power, and are not very Christian.

We have no clear idea if there's been a revival, when, or if so, how many branches it has. After an internet search, we discovered that a short-lived name of the group in the seventeen hundred's was, The Holy Fathers. You see, the germ of the idea."

Mealla is after licking cream off her spoon. She has inhaled the paté on brown bread starter, the broccoli soup, and the prime rib au jus with buttered carrots and parsnips. Spuds two ways, the meal to finish with a trifle and cream horns. She's lorrying it in.

It's good to feed your slaves.

"They have to be after a better source of magical energy than using their own blood. That can't last," says Mealla. "Which would be solstice of course. Or trying to trap a demon for a battery in the short term." She leans forward to tong lumps of sugar into her freshly poured coffee. If she were five, she'd be bouncing off walls.

"The point is are they uniting. United is worse as in more strength. But at the same time—"

"Bad because potentially we can find them and bust up their party," I say.

"The fires at all the summoning venues have destroyed any clues or magical tracing," finishes Rose.

The old and infirm nuns are excusing themselves from other tables around us. They're heading up for a midday nap. They smell of eucalyptus and camphor. The oldest smells like she's come to hate showers. Their voices are a pitch higher and weaker than when in their prime. Their walkers make a soft brushing noise as the tennis balls attached to the straight legs slide across the floor. They are not interested in our conversation. Peace and a good meal with a Bailey's Irish Cream top-off is all they want. They are too exhausted to face desperate times anymore.

These nuns of Ireland had a busy life running orphanages, schools, and laundries, and corralling young pregnant ladies. There's evidence that they didn't do it well. Bailey's Irish Cream it is now, and a good program on the telly. They are rich in property values and are enjoying their retirements. Even the chapel was refurbished with comfy chairs instead of hard-planked benches.

"We need to find someone of conscience to spill the beans," says Mealla when the hushed moving about is done.

I scoff. "Religion can be a hard life. They protect each other." I'm looking around and wondering where the old dears hide their Bailey's.

"Then a dead one. We could do a scrying spell."

I begin to sweat when Mealla decides to do magic. The results are, full stop, not worth the fun brush with death and the magical price to pay.

"What could go wrong?" When Mealla is digging deep into her books on magic, my heartburn flares.

"The mirror is two-way. Or, and no offence, let's stick with the living."

"Smart Ass."

"I hear that so often, it means half nothing."

"My idea is good. And here's why. I'm a descendent of Biddy Early. Her magical power was divination. All the articles I read about her talk about her Blue Bottle and how she could see the future, the past, and the present from it."

"'Seven odours, seven murmurs, seven woods I had not eyes like those enchanted eyes.'" With us all studying her, Rose says, "Yeats a poem about Biddy."

"Daft," I say.

"The components of her compounds were herbs, morning dew, and liquid from her magic well. Some articles say she was a descendent of the Irish goddess Danu. They both had red hair." Don't give me any cheek, Mealla's face says.

"She had the Blue Bottle to scry with. We don't have the Blue Bottle."

"Jesus Murphy!" Mealla pushes back from the trough and stands. "We can make do with a mirror eh…" She examines the room. "I know what I'm doing. It's safe."

A mirror in a convent takes some looking for. We end up in a corner of the girls' loo in the convent's school.

"Prophecy and revelation," she says as I watch. "It's an Original Native People thing. As well as a talent of Biddy's."

The sisters and I stare at the mirror as if it could do what people of the Middle Ages thought it could do, suck out your soul. Mealla settles herself in front of it, and I am beside her with my blackthorn club ready to bat it to shards if necessary. There are two nuns at the door with extinguishers. Biddy used the Blue Bottle for this, which makes me think why didn't the Morrigan bring it with her to give to Mealla, give her an edge. Yeah, no, not the Goddess of Death.

Mealla pops a couple of melatonin tablets to bathe her pineal gland, or third eye and increase its viability. She uses the activating time of the drug of twenty minutes to center.

Eventually she breathes condensation on the dark glass surface. With her index finger, she writes within it, *Eoin Hurley*. Mealla silences her mind to elevate her senses, to try to perceive the whisper. I feel magical energy quicken. The change of my pulse startles me, and I tighten my grip on the blackthorn club. Heat is increasing in the room. It's not that I don't believe Mealla can do the magic, any magic. It's almost like she does it too well, like a battering ram. Sweat roles into my eyes. I'm holding my breath, wishing we had the salamanders.

The nuns retreat to the other side of the loo door. I imagine them with their fire extinguishers, pins pulled and aiming at the shut door. With another gut twinge, I peer into the glossy surface of the mirror for an unknown face glaring out.

So flipping hot. Mealla becomes stiff and then her body shudders. Shite. I'm about to grab her, break the trance when she lifts her head.

"It's done."

My mind refuses to stand down. "What do you mean, it's done."

"I'm finished."

"What do you mean, you're finished?"

"Oh, for the love of God, put the club down. It's all over. I've done it."

"Done what?"

Mealla growls and walks to the door and opens it. There are two extinguishers aimed at her midsection. "I'm bloody done."

"Sure?" asks Rose. After a glance around, she signals the extinguishers down, the pins replaced. "Cup of tea I think."

Rose does look a bit chalky.

"Fine." Mealla exits the room. The rest of us take a necessary deep, collective breath.

So back to the nerve center of our operation, the dining room. It still smells a little of smoke, even with the plastic tarp that sets off the kitchen. "What about the hellhound do you think?" I ask Sister Rose as we walk.

"Nothing to do with the gods."

"You know for sure?"

"Yes."

"They were hunting souls. That's their job. The unforgiven dead were there. The hound was hunting. Eoin was protecting them."

"Mealla was attacked. Just Mealla."

"If the dog was sent by the *Tuatha* to protect her, then it failed."

+++

Mealla has filled the kettle and popped it on. She distributes creamy Belleek mugs. Plates of Jaffa Cakes, a combination of a chocolate Genoise sponge with orange jam, coated with more chocolate, arrive on a trolly. Vianney pours. The Irish add milk to tea later, as an after-thought.

"Thinking about it now, I don't know if it worked," Mealla begins.

There is a collective grumble. Some eyes close, some roll. These are all practiced schoolteachers and Rose says, "Tell us what you have."

"Well, fires and, and a large bird-human looking down at me." She glances at each face around the table hoping for a glimmer of understanding like when a psychic tosses out single words into a crowd and hopes someone will pick up the narrative.

There is no glimmer, just dull eyes, and a burned kitchen, and smoke-tinged air, so the fire part is spot on.

"Fires…bonfires!" Sister Vianney spits out most of her Jaffa Cake in the words pressing out of her mouth, and then she's embarrassed, because even if that's it, it's stuff we already know, Saint John's Eve. The busiest night of the year for fire brigades.

"Looking down at you, you say? Like from a hilltop?"

"Like a balcony."

"A high place, a building, to get less obstruction for the magic?" suggests a member of the coven as I'm thinking of them now.

Another coven member says, "What about the Elysian Apartment building? It's the tallest building in Cork. The practitioners seem to need an advantage."

"Is it too ironic a hellfire club in a building named after heaven?"

We are all just blinking stupidly at each other. And then the events of the two days coalesces my synapses. I have alarm-sweat from the clarity unfolding in my mind. "This, none of this is for stopping a simple demon summoning by an ambitious, incompetent practitioner or two. Club ladies club." I lean in. "This is the men preparing for a ritual. All those circles, all those failed summonings those were to bring in tools and demon energy. Because what they are doing is a long magical preparation for a higher-level spell. That's what it is, isn't it? Fatima. A replacement head of the new, improved, magic-controlling church they are forming. That's it. Jaysus."

Sister Rose is watching me closely like this is what she's been waiting for, me finally passing the exam.

"Invocation or evocation?" That's Mealla.

I speak to her like we are the only two in the room, because we are the slaves up to our necks in a situation, and not just a bit of craic with some wacko newbie practitioners. "What if even more than that? What if they are trying to orchestrate the six levels of transformation: filled with God, fed upon God, intoxicated with God, purified by the lustration of God, shedding earthy elements, matter replaced by spirit?" They want to become gods. It's the only way they can compete for the magic.

"Immortality. What the hell," says Mealla.

Rose opens her mouth. I raise my finger at her.

"High Roman Catholic Church magic."

"What?"

"Remember, I was a non-practicing priest for about a year, trying it out as protection from the *Tuatha*. Guess what, there are high secrets that come with ordination. Mostly do-not-dos-even-though-you-cans."

Mealla quotes, "'Turning and turning in the widening gyre, the falcon cannot hear the falconer; things fall apart; the centre cannot hold; mere anarchy is loosed upon the world, the blood-dimmed tide is loosed, and everywhere the ceremony of innocence is drowned; the best lack all conviction, while the worst are full of passionate intensity. Surely some revelation is at hand; surely the Second Coming is at hand.'"

Ok. Now we are all staring at Mealla.

"I like Yeats. I wonder now if that's because he was a great fan of Biddy Early."

I didn't think anyone could stun Sister Rose. She's a brick to the world. No ordeal by God is too much for her; a woman that has 'cut the crap' tattooed over her heart. And Mealla, she's a packet of biscuits and an Irish coffee by the fire in an evening when it won't stop flaming raining. Watching them reluctantly buzz off each other's Yeats, for god's sake. Two *fáidhbhean*, women of knowledge.

Impressive as that is, I break the moment. "Second coming or not doesn't change the objective. It just makes it all a more twisted shite-storm."

Rose spells it out. "What in God's name do you think I've been trying to say?"

With her nose back into the internet, Mealla reads from the screen, breaking the ice. "The Elysian. One, two, three, four-bedroom apartments…heart of the city…generous windows… tranquil Japanese gardens where nature looks her best. It has a dedicated onsite concierge. Takes care of package deliveries and maintains privacy, and it rents from three thousand four hundred, forty-seven euro a month. It is advertised as the highest building in Cork. It has potential."

"Vianney, take Mary with you, and talk to the concierge and check the roof."

TWELVE

Gealtachta
Incantation

Saint John's eve is in within days and magic is leaking. Come early morning, Mealla begins warding the convent. Making do with next to nothing. She has glass jam jars with lids lined in front of her for the four quarters. She's warding the place with witch bottles, a counter-magical item, and a protection against witchcraft. In them is urine, every-one's, pins, needles, sacramental wine, a sliced rowan berry and kaiju blood. She says the bottles generally are buried, but the convent is a sea of concrete.

It's a jumble sale of a bottle meant to capture evil. It goes as follows. Badness is impaled on the pins and needles, drowned by the wine, thumped by the Kaiju. The rowan berry is my contribution. Cut in half this berry has a pentagram inside. Protection against enchantment and preventing evil spirits from entering. All of it boiled up and bottled. Great stuff. Mealla will probably sell it on her web site.

Buttermilk trips down the stairs with two handfuls of Saint Brigid's crosses.

Brigid's crosses combine the protection of the Goddess Brigid, the Virgin Mary of the Gael. They are a true mix of pagan Catholicism. They keep away fire and are apotropaic, warding against evil. She's nailing them onto the all walls.

"Let's print out some *Sheela na gigs* on the printer," I hear Mealla say to Buttermilk. By lunch, all the exterior doors of the convent have pictures of medieval, stone-carved reliefs of ugly hags with pronounced vaginas duct taped above them. If nothing else, the Amazon delivery person will get a fright.

Women exposing their genitals drives away devils, evil spirits, and attacking troops. Female, body parts keep dangerous animals at bay, calm whirlwinds, and lightning and, ta-da, magical energy. What a woman's vagina can't do. The 'gig' in *Sheela na gig* means female bits. *Sheela* is a word for hag. The *Cailleach*, she who controls storms and winter. It's a throw down. The coven is after it.

+++

The *lunantisidhe*, the fairies who guard blackthorn trees, will let me cut branches on Esbats. A stroll to Bishop Lucey Park will give me some headspace. A pause from all the estrogen and vaginas. First though, speaking of fairies, I need to stop by the nearby Tesco shop for alcohol.

At the entrance to the park, I pass under the double freestanding stone arches, and around a piece of the original city wall. The park is a riot of rhododendron blooms. The grass is green. The park's a long narrow space with a red-brick church on one side, and the backs of three-story row houses on the other. The druids I knew would be shitting themselves at the loss of open spaces here now in Cork.

A Blackthorn tree is on the oppose side from me, off Grand Parade. It blossoms in May, but its purple berries are out closer to winter. They won't be ripe until after the first frost for making sloe gin. It's a soft day of little rain, the park is quiet. Perfect. I mean to cut stems and make a few blackthorn wands. But first the tree's *lunantisidhe*.

The blackthorn is a sinister tree. *Straif*, the Ogham letter of the blackthorn means sulphur, and where there's sulphur, there's fire. The blackthorn fruit, sloe means "slay," as in, you know, slay, slice, dismember. It's a crooked tree with septic thorns. The fruit is a metaphor for warriors and death, and for the Triple Goddesses, the Crone, and the Morrigan. It's short and fierce, and I'm about to cut off a branch.

First, I sit at the root. I settle in and wait.

"Padraic the Black," says a sultry, unpleasant voice that promises sex, dominatrix style. It's been half an hour. They like that, keeping me waiting. Her glamor is all glittery, with long pointed ears like the thorns of the tree. Her gown shimmers from dark green to black. Beautiful eyes, and deep blue lips like the berry of the tree, poisonous if ingested incorrectly, either of them. Blackthorn fairies are actually arthritic, gnarled-looking creatures, with thorny beaks of noses. This one's glamor is all in.

"Fer feck sake, tone it down," I say to her. "You'll give yourself a hernia. I have a present."

The change shortens her and curves her osteoporotic spine. Her nose suddenly has ample room for breathing. Maybe I should have left her the way she was. She makes a grab for the alcohol in my bag. Her thorny nails just miss my knuckles. In Ireland there are at least ten slang words for drunk. *Lunantisidhe*, mad keen for The Drink, fit all of them.

"The lager is for me. And I'm here to cut wands."

"As you please, mortal…as you please." She takes out her bottle of sloe gin and throws the two cans of lager at my head.

Good thing is sloe gin has a calming effect on the *lunantisidhe*. Feckin' nectar that can chloroform a bull.

"Take the weight off your legs. Settle in," she says as she knocks back the gin.

The *lunantisidhe* and I are adversaries with mutual dislike and toleration. This one is bored, the lone blackthorn tree in the park. As Ireland divided into fields, there is a decrease in the numbers of the low trees. The thorny plants still are used in hedgerows. Plenty enough fairies to make trouble together and sleep it off in the morning. Sloe gin stands at about thirty-seven percent proof. It's herbal medicine for kidney, lumbago, stomach, gallstones, gout. Very popular with the aging for their health. Keeps them youngish.

I open my own drink as I shelter under the tree. I wait for the results of the thirty-seven percent alcohol. These fairies have a high tolerance. It takes a while. I'm also here to try and cut out the middleman. I don't know how much Rose knows, but it's more than she's letting on.

The *lunantisidhe* lets out a long, loud burp. Getting there.

I reach into another bag for cheddar crisps. She settles in against the tree trunk and eats them like it's a holiday. Pieces get caught in her facial hair.

"Padraic O'Duibh. You're in great form tonight. What's your ugly arse after, besides the sticks?"

"GrandOther information. What the feck is going on here exactly?"

"It's uncanny the lack of thought ye have in ye're head."

The soft day is turning to rain in earnest with light patters on the leaves. I waggle a second bottle in her face. "It's a feckin' treat talking to you, too. I'll just take this with me then." I make to stand.

"Ye slack, mundane shite."

"What's the carry-on or this," I waggle the bottle, "remains mine."

"Keep the pressure on. Besides, they're making a mess."

"The clergy? What are they up to?"

"What are they up to! They're creating huge arsehole gaps. All sorts of things can get out."

"The gods, it's not about getting the magic back then?"

"Ignorant bollocks. Of course it is." She tosses the empty bottle aside. "We deserve it back. Weren't the Fomorians taxing us to our last coin? Didn't the Milesians trick us underground?"

I'm there. "Paragons."

"Bah." She reaches for the second bottle of sloe gin and another bag of crisps. "Cut ye're wands and away with ye." She laughs a happy, bubbly, drunken sound, takes up her second bottle and crisps, and merges into the tree.

I cut the wands, enough for each of the sisters and Mealla. The tree moves like a gale is blowing. A branch whips my face. *Tuatha*...fecking treats. I up and tear into a nearby shop for more sloe gin, the cause and the cure. I pour it into the bloody gash. The cut is going to leave a scar, minimum.

Blackthorn branches were used to burn witches, to cleanse the evil. The sloe berries are bittersweet. If you cut wood from the tree on Samhain or Beltane, the *lunantisidhe* whip the branches, like striking snakes. The trees are of the *Cailleach* and are known as the dark crones of the woods. All that is why my blackthorn club is wicked.

As I make my way back to the convent, infection could be spreading through my bloodstream, lowering my blood pressure, slowing my circulation, creating a drought of blood in my vital tissues and organs. Irish gods, biting the hand that feeds them.

┼┼┼

The sky gets darker, and the rain is pissing down now. I'm thinking of emigrating, somewhere hot and sunny. Not here where it's the wind that burns you. I drink at the gin. The Ali Baba Turkish Kebab takeout is a bright set of square windows in a red-painted storefront with a green, lit, sign above the open door. I am starving. I feel strangely calm as I eat the kabab and chips nestled in paper while watching the shower through the window. Big inhale and exhale. Always something.

My cheek smarts. One thing I know, never, ever show 'em you're capable. That was the problem in killing the Morrigan's son; I showed them I was capable.

As I walk across the concrete drive of the convent, I wipe the bits of my meal from the growth of red and brown beard stubble on my face. I approach the door mindful of the newly placed wards. I see the Sheela and her ultra-obvious vulva and think, yes please, but then I peruse her crone's face, er no. Shite, I'm just that side of drunk.

I try to feel the energy of the wards, but my mind is sodden and sloppy, as well as my clothes and hair. I can hear a whining vibrato in my head that says not to touch anything. Good on her. She did it.

Magic is a technical act of power. It takes self-confidence and practice. With Mealla, magic is something powered by unintentional nuclear fusion. I don't try the door.

Standing outside, water is dripping along my nose from my hair. I scoop up a handful of pea rocks, take them around the side and throw one at a lounge window. It comes back at me as an energized bullet. Shite, then I remember. I shove my wet, cold hand into my pocket to my brand-new, single-use mobile phone.

I ring Mealla. Almost like magic. It won't connect. "Exactly like magic," I mutter.

"Where were you?' A sign pops up in a window. Of course she'd start with that. As far as she is concerned, I was absent without leave.

"I was cutting witches' wands," I yell. I wave the Blackthorn sticks at her. "And talking to a *lunantisidhe*."

She points to her ears and shakes her head.

Another sign. 'The chapel is too holy. The wards refuse to stick there. Also, this building, the convent, is a place of power. The ambient energy is high. And there's something else adding to that. The wards are too electrified.'

"I know. I was almost killed by a pea rock."

She shakes her head.

"Maybe we should take the Sheelas down?" I point to my crotch and then shape my hands into an oval.

'The Sheelas are a construct of female empowerment.' Another sign. 'It was just all the sudden. We've tapped into something here that is producing orgasmic energy levels. We are like a high security prison, but also like a bomb.'

I'm thinking magical power sources out loud. "Chemical? Group belief? Blood? Potions? Portals? Emotions? Remains of demons? Angels?" I am definitely glancing into the corners around me. "Magical creatures—"

Shite. I know what it is.

I point to the door. "Get me inside."

'That's a problem.'

I point to the dining room and bark and pant. She should see the hellhound there thrumming like a substation. Which means it was not dead? A stunned torpor? She disappears. Next time I see her she's opening the front door.

"Where is it?"

"The chapel."

"The chapel? A hellhound?"

"We thought, they're on the side of good."

"How'd you not notice it?"

Mealla bristles. "It just started."

"How'd you get it in the chapel?"

She calms. "Pulled the sheet. We didn't touch it. They didn't kill it. The Wild Hunt is in two days' time. It's getting ready. Did you ask the *lunantisidhe* about the *Slaugh*?"

"What? Feck. Slipped my mind,"

It's her turn to roll her eyes. She does. "Too much sloe gin?"

"And ale. She ate all the crisps."

With The Wild Hunt days away, we drag the livelier hell-hound outside the chapel door and leave it in the courtyard. I feel protected having it around. My muscles relax like.

+++

In the dining room I'm whittling leaves and secondary branches from the wands and waiting for the nuns to return from the Elysian. "It may be the tallest building," says Vianney as she puts a coffee in front of me, "but we didn't see any activity."

"Cheers."

A backward nod in response.

She sinks into a chair with her own cuppa. "There is the UCC campus, which includes a mass grave of thirteen Irish Republican Army members who were executed by firing squads. There's the remains of a gaol there too. Between the two, magical energy there would be significant."

"Where is that?"

"Fifteen-minute walk from here. There's also Our Lady's Hospital. Now that has a long history. It was built under the Lunacy Act of eighteen forty-five. So you can imagine. But it has a chapel. I'm more thinking University College Cork. Maxwell is an alumni of UCC, a better place to set up a club.

THIRTEEN

Amhlaidh
So be it

T he discussion rages over whether Mealla should go with me to UCC or stay behind and stay protected for the final battle in a couple of days on Saint John's Eve. Mealla's saying that we should get them before the blow out. Nerves are thinning. The ladies are partially roaring at each other.

Mealla just says, "Not happening." She is staring at and turning the wand in her hands, as she continues, "This isn't a historical hellfire club, as in do whatever the hell you person-ally want, middle finger in your face adolescent men. Well, maybe partially. This is an in-training magical organization, and we have to continue scrambling them. Divide and conquer.

So, speaking of clubs, I researched UCC. I found the Godsills. They were a merchant family, into distributing mineral waters and chemicals in the eighteen hundreds. Part of the original site of the college belonged to them. They sold land to the college and were active in the college. It's their house on that land that's interesting. The son was obsessive about fire."

"Things went on fire then," points out Rose.

"What I mean is he built the entire house out of yellow fire-brick. The doors are all steel paneled, and there are five-thou-sand-gallon lead water tanks in the attic. Also, there was a slight explosion there six months ago, and it's not the chemistry building. The college has magical energy and a fireproof venue. If any of you leave without me, I will practice on you with this new wand."

In a maturity throw down, Mealla would kick my ass. I'm concerned about her though. Beginning in her is a shocking lack of fear of all of this. The awakened magical energy in her is pushing out, like adrenaline.

"How's the wand working for you?"

"I've used wands for rituals."

"That you've willed an outcome in."

"Well, I've been working on that. I carved a fire salamander onto it."

I inhale. "Right, so, let's go."

In her best, did-I-not-ban-this voice, Rose says, "Amazing discovery about the house, Mealla. You *will* establish backup. The Poor Clares Convent sits in the middle of the campus on College Road, practically next to the Godsill House. The Clares' level of devotion and prayer will keep them safer and you safer if you need a quick hideout nearby. Sister Vianney will take you there, I think. I'll ring them to expect you all."

†††

The Poor Clares aren't very poor. The convent is worth about ten million on the real estate market. We stroll under the wrought iron archway spelling out the name of the convent. The place is a plain, squat, single-level building with a simple, brown rectangular door. Next to that is a bell and a mail slot that has a written note above it. 'Prayer petitions here.'

Vianney presses the bell. It's an ugly sounding buzzer. Hard on the ear when I expected something more melodious of the angels. One of the six of the nuns living there opens the door. The rest are gathered behind a dove of peace art deco grille. This is a cloistered convent, a true sanctuary and inner sanctum. I hate to bring a sea of trouble here and say so.

The nun counters with, "We do what we can in prayer. This requires action."

The nuns' friendly twitter is as soft as their natures, "...so glad to be of help...will leave the door unlocked...if there's anything else we can do...going to pray for you," all served with tea and scones, strawberry jam and cream.

And then it's us off to fight the devil. "It's all of us using gods for our different end games," says Mealla as we walk down College Road.

We pass the Bon Secours Hospital and turn left onto Gaol Walk. Campuses in June are quiet places, so that's grand. There won't be screaming students in a demon attack. We want to get to the Old Gaol wall and Godsill House and back to the Clares' before the sun goes down.

"Did you go to college," I ask Mealla as we stroll deeper into campus.

"No, you? Oh, yeah, right."

The first change when magic in involved is temperature. As the air gets warmer, Mealla and I get quieter. Her fire salamander wand comes out of her pocket. I almost wish I hadn't given her the wand. Her and Buttermilk. Mealla's mind is buzzing with what's to be done. She is audaciously blunt, predictable, not reckless so much as not always forward thinking. I'm looking, as we head forward, for possible even closer than the Clares safe spaces. It could get desperate.

"I should touch the gaol wall. It could give us something."

"Don't touch the wall. Don't touch anything."

"It's the only way."

"Don't touch the wall."

"We need to know. We need information."

"Don't Touch The Wall."

Once within the footprint of the Old Gaol, the pressure and thrum in my ears makes me press forward, like there is a strong wind. My face is scrunched, and my breathing shallow.

"A lot of shit happened here." Mealla pushes out the words through her gritted teeth. The energy from the *unseeyn* is practically portal strength. As I close the distance, and within a few yards of the thing, I feel like a squeezed pimple.

"The magical energy is as thick as shite here. Enough to power the city. A ritual here would be possible, but out in the open?"

Mealla has tears in her eyes. "Outdoor mass?"

"Funny."

"Doubt it. Right here next to the Kane building in the middle of a parking lot?"

"It's possible the dead Irish Republicans won't easily subjugate to the practitioners' will." My ears start thumping. "Fall back." I turn, and Mealla too. We are both ready to get out. But Murphy's Law, she steps into a pothole, and is toppling. Her fingertips slide down the wall, as she reaches to break her fall.

A trance is a loss of personal identity. A shamanic aura glows around her. It's become all balls.

I grab for her. The heat in her arm startles me. I drag her off the wall. No change in her. And then I wonder if a sudden disruption of the trance will split her mind like. I don't know, she being a new shaman and all.

Her visions, through my hand on her arm, become our visions. The Morrigan once asked me why I fight my destiny so fiercely. Because my destiny is like being shite-faced daily from drinking Jäerbombs.

The spirits fixed to the area, their powerful anger, and want, and need loads into us. Her body jerks like being hit with multiple rounds of gunshot. Feck, she may be stroking.

In the vision, teeth, and roaring...feckin' treat-stuff all around. My heart is painfully foundering. It's along the lines of I have no idea what to do. Scáthach never taught me how to kick the shite out of a vision. Mealla is there, upright like a flaming sword. She's using her energy and mine, willing the souls away. A salamander arrives to save us.

Mealla opens her eyes. She turns her head and throws up. I help her sit. "Just like when I was ten."

I could drink the guts out of four bottles of lager.

"I used your energy and mine."

"To subdue them?"

"To stand my ground."

"What were they? I couldn't tell."

"I don't know, but it felt like madness."

I keep watch, as we retrace the length of Gaol Road. The pressure of magic eases with each step. Still, I have one arm around Mealla, and one hand on my club. I'm really hoping that's it for the night. "It's not my imagination. It's not me. It's you. It's always you."

"I know."

I stop short.

"What?" Mealla shifts her glance to where I'm looking. I feel her body tense, but she's getting used to ordeals by gods and their minions.

I toss us both down a side street, and up against a building. An energy wave, like a tidal tsunami, rolls down Gaol Road towards us. It is invisible, but for the explosions of streetlamps.

The two energies, one from the gaol, and the other from an energy-tsunami, slam into each other, creating wave interference. As the energies pass through each other, the amplitude is destructive. The gaol wall doesn't absorb the residual wave. Stones that have kept that wall upright for a hundred years, fly, making craters in the street. We crouch until the stone grit stops raining down, and then run, save yourself like. Lights go out as the college power plant, situated within the gaol footprint, explodes.

++++

"These practitioners are networked," says Mealla, her tone strong enough. Still, though, there's spillage of coffee, from the cup in her shaking hands, as we sit at the Mango Café and Shop, nearby on College Road. We watch the emergency vehicles go by. "What did you mean, stand your ground?"

"I don't know...Jesus Murphy...against a living force of dementia. "I don't think that it was souls, back there. Or a magical creature.

"A shapeshifting *Tuatha* possibly."

"But why?"

"When the *Tuatha*, want something, it is with a terrible clarity. They are pure emotion. Just to be clear, vacillation is for humans. The *Tuatha* are a compelling force, not just deities for summing. The Morrigan, the dark queen, giver of *geases*. Puck...the dreadful.

"You say shapeshifting? There might be something in that."

I wipe my hands on a serviette.

"Could it have been something worse?"

"I hope not. We'll never win."

"It was an accident, that I touched the wall." Mealla finally is beginning to look flamed-out.

"Was it though?"

"What was the thing doing?"

"Playing with you."

FOURTEEN

Díbirt

Exorcism

The Angelus bell rings from Saint Finbar's Cathedral each day at exactly twelve. A dirge sound foreshadowing change. A shift, when the portals, the dolmans, the wells, the passage tombs breach. "Patrick said, to let no one in and to let no one out. And then the Church loses the complete run of itself."

"Maybe we should try and summon Saint Patrick," suggests Mealla.

"How'd Luchar's body get through?"

"Lots of arse…holes. It means they are still summoning."

We are alone in the café. The rumble and roar of College Road outside is loud. The convent with Rose and the nuns sits feet from Sharman Crawford Street, but I never notice car noise there. The windows and walls are that thick. Stout against the elements. But when the convent is quiet, when I remember to listen for it, when the noise inside doesn't misdirect me, it would be there. It's always, barely there.

"Hey! Where are you?" Mealla taps by arm.

"What?"

"I was just saying, it must have taken a lot of collective magic, like all of them, the *Tuatha* working together, to bring you forward. That is if they're still as weak as you say they are. You know what I think. I think there's been enough of an uptick in faith to the old gods that they're feeling it. WICCA in North America is mostly based on the Irish Gods. My books are selling well."

"Stop it. You're taking away my will to live." I tick my head towards the windows. "It's dark clouds and greeny-grey light out there. Maybe a thunderstorm. Good for magic. They're around, the practitioners. Otherwise, where'd that wall of energy come from? Maybe we can catch them out."

"You want to go to the Godsill House?"

"Maybe we can surprise them. Maybe they think after all that carry-on, we're done for the day."

I glance down Gaol Road as we pass. The color of the magic that stains the sides of the buildings is red with purple tones.

"Can you see the coloration?" I ask Mealla. I didn't need to ask because she's pop-out-eye taking in the rainbow. She's still a newby.

"Purple means ambition and power. The crown chakra, the part of us that is connected to the Divine to the Universe.

Good to know if we didn't already. Here, at the rainbow, sounds from behind the veil are in and out with the noise of trucks hitting potholes.

"Can you hear it?" Mealla says. "This area is broken and is fluid. The veil is holding but by a thread. If I were a practitioner, I'd be crazy-out trying to take advantage."

"Where did Rose say Godsill House is?"

"The next road."

++++

Godsill Houses' yellow, London firebrick is like a flower bloom against the modern slate and stained-wood paneled buildings this section of campus.

The brick was specially imported, and inside there are steel paneled fire doors and a fifty-five-thousand-gallon lead water tank. Apparently, the tank has a slim lead lining that, with a fire underneath it, melts and then water pours over the house. The stairs are fireproof too.

Finally, a building that can't burn down. All perfect except for the crèche, for children, and an outdoor playground not thirty yards from its front door.

The house is classically Georgian in a soft glow of yellow-gold. It has a series of long, symmetrical windows on a flat front. Its three stories tower above us. There is an entrance portico with composite, white pillars.

There isn't a heightened buzz of magical energy.

"They didn't even ward," says I.

"They don't think of us a much of a threat," says she. "Old fashioned security cameras. They could be remotely watching us right now. Looks quiet. Maybe they've left the scene. I don't think there's anybody here in this minute." Acting on her intuition, she takes her lock-picking kit out of a backpack. "These are more reliable than magic, and less clean up."

"Two things. Just because there aren't exterior wards doesn't mean it's a zip though the inside. This stone is thick. We may not sense them. They could be watching, remotely.

Instead of, like leaving, she extracts her hawthorn wand.

"What can you do with it?"

"Channel a single blast of energy."

"If it comes to it, make it count."

She turns the knob and pushes the door open from the portico.

I want the door to creak as it opens. Seems appropriate for a hell-fire club. We step over the threshold like we are trying not to make contact with the floor. Off the floral–wallpapered, formal entrance hall are two opposing archways. I glance into a reception room, and then a dining room. Lots of comfy, leather upholstery, complicated crown molding, draping, red curtains, and a heavy mantle over the fireplaces in each room. The whole structure, inside and out, is every inch a gentleman's club, a place of privilege.

It was Pope John the twenty-second who went after priests who used the ritual magic indoctrinated to them for the invocation of demons. Whatever Laurent says about the mag-priests of his day, most of those accusations of magic were bogus, lies to create conspiracies and assassinations. There was mostly bounteous privilege to be protected.

The magical energy in the house is different from the Old Gaol wall. That energy comes from deprivation, a lack of justice, mourning, and is produced by the spirits locked there by their pasts. Full access there to the magical energy of the dead.

There's still a lingering smell of roast and potatoes, also the slight smell of ozone, like after the blow-out of birthday cake candles for a ninety-year-old great grandmother. Appears they had a lux afternoon meal and then sent a wall of energy at us as the entertainment. So close to the gaol they aren't concerned with paltry, weather-focused magical energy. Energy is available here in spades. Lots of energy. No skill. Melted faces.

Mealla follows me up the stairs. We look for circles, altars, any tools of magic.

"There's got to be something. There has to be," she says each time we meet in the hallways. "Did you notice any second set of stairs?"

"I want to know how we get onto the roof."

And there, on the roof, we have it. Mealla actually gasps at the invoking pentagram that has been burned into a plywood platform and is inside an etched circle. Stacked into corners are a cauldron, black candles, coal, and lighter fluid. She picks up dried herb jars and zip lighters. There is the faint residue of red and purple. It's all pure class.

They've gone home pulling themselves on their backs. They think we're dead.

Mealla wanders. Sniffs at the cauldron. Sifts through the herbs. Then she jumps three stairs at a time back down the ladder. I'm startled. I take in the place. I don't see anything alarming. "What?" I also hurry towards the ladder. I meet her at the bottom, coming back up with bed sheets in her arms.

She throws one at me. "We're clearing the place out. We can use this stuff. Tie it all inside."

Four white sheets filled and tied off later, we are like pregnant ladies with quadruplets just managing to get down flights of stairs and to an exit. We are stashing them in the garbage bins behind the Brookfield Therapy Clinic, when Mealla says she's going back in.

"Sure, what good would that do besides push on fate and luck? They're narky bollocks and we are not prepared. Remember the cameras."

"We have to rub out the circle. We need the cauldron."

"I'm sweating here from exertion. They can draw a new one with chalk."

"Not as powerful as that one. Come on."

"That's you outside watching, right?" I say to Mealla at the door. "The job at hand doesn't need two people." My last words before she disappears into the house and my blood pressure begins rising. Well, in case of fire, the house has her covered.

I watch the front of the house. In fifteen minutes, Mealla bolts out the porch door.

What in God's name? I glance behind her to see if she's being chased. My heart feckin' triple-thumps. I don't see anything behind her. Jaysus, I'm getting older before my time and that's saying a lot.

She drags me into the tree cover along the walking path.

"I saw someone returning, while I was up on the roof. Coming in fast, running actually."

"Of course he, jeepers-feck, was running."

"There!"

A man all in black approaches. We duck deeper into our greenery.

We hear him wheezing when he stops, death-breathing hard, before stepping onto the portico. As he looks around, his face towards us but not seeing. He quits searching the perimeter when, most likely from him pausing due to his hard breathing, it comes to his attention that the roof is on fire.

"I decided to burn the platform and the whole damn thing."

And the dark clouds start raining. Mealla swears. She wants the circle down to ashes. Not that the house needs the help of the rain. The lead lining must be heated through by now.

"The house is fireproof."

"Not the roof. It's not like the roof is going to be a big swimming pool. It will slow them anyway."

We take the long route to the sheet-cache and decide not to bring this shower of shite to the Clares'.

+++

With the smell of chocolate cake baking in the blackened kitchen, all the nuns of Saint Brigid pass around Mealla's mobile phone, and peer at the multiple pictures she took of the man at the house. She glances at me, a quick smile, delighted with herself. Fair dues to her. The camera, brilliant.

"Looks like James Buckley. He was just released."

"So what's this punter like?"

"He's a part of the set. His face is unfortunate and easy to recognize. He's unprincipled."

I stare at the man who looks like he'd battled with cystic acne during his teenage years and lost. That or his mother didn't care enough to find him some antibiotics. "And possessed. Look at his red-eye." I hand the mobile phone back to Mealla.

"I see it, and it's not the camera. 'And what rough beast, its hour come round at last, slouches towards Bethlehem to be born.'"

Rose nods.

Yeats again. He wasn't a cheerful bloke.

FIFTEEN

Ceocháin draíochta
Magic mists

Mealla hums as she itemizes her take. In a cellar room of the convent that smells like there might be buried bodies under the floor, I sit on a stool to watch her work as I lorry gooseberry crumble into my mouth. I'm just giving my head and stomach some peace. The nuns have put her here thinking the room is insular. I'm thinking she could weaken the foundation of the convent.

Mealla is tall for a woman at my height exactly, but I'm not particularly tall for a man. She is muscular, not gym muscular but from lift and toil...so work built. It's not a body that attracts men usually, square, robust...but busty, some points there. Her face is something to look at, though. High cheek bones. Blue eyes pop from her darker skin. And the mouth, never better.

"What are you staring at?"

"Can't a body enjoy ten minutes of peace?"

"In a three-minute situation...no."

"Where'd you get so awful…resilient?" I was going to add "positive" but to me it's not a thing, or a real word.

"Habit. There's some great stuff here. In this little jar is the-impossible-to-find herb, *Angelica archangelica*. This stuff," she shakes the jar a bit, and I cringe, "is legend. In sixteen sixty-five, the Archangel Michael came to a monk in a dream to tell him that this could help against the plague. It didn't work."

"I would say so, no."

"Too bad. Well, now it's used to make conjure-bags. The practitioners are trying everything. The smoke from it induces visions and luck. Mixed with cumin and salt, it drives away unwanted people and evil spirits."

"But would it work against Buttermilk?" I toss the words over my shoulder.

She weird-smiley-faces me. "She'd take a bullet for you."

"Sure," I grunt.

These, just simple walnuts, were the portrait of the human brain to the Romans. The outer green husk, the scalp. The hard outer shell, the skull, the paper-like skin between the two halves, the membrane. In compounds, this jewel helps us to think faster. Oh look, they have garlic."

"Garlic, imagine. The kitchen has garlic. Come to think of it, they're all witches."

"You're on fire here. It's a protection repellant. Wards off hexes, curses, and the common cold. Look, and, drum roll here, butternut root bark. It expels worms. Keeps you regular."

"The shites."

"God, even myrrh, for exorcisms. And even Irish moss."

She shows me a fan-shaped frond brownish-red seaweed. "Carrageenan," I correct her.

Buttermilk walks in as Mealla is turning it over observing its shining surface. "A famine food," the nun says and then, "Rose wants ye." And she leaves. Not without sticking out her tongue at me, because the elderly get to be brats, again.

"You go," Mealla says as she throws the seaweed into

boiling water in a pot on a camping stove. She says words to Brigid and her spirit animal the Salamander. The greenish liquid soon smells like the sea.

Be it compounds or words or actions, magic is about confidence. It's visible to the trained senses, but the rational mind is another thing altogether. Mealla is there now confidence wise.

I climb wooden stairs. The main floor still has the background residue of smoke smell that is impossible to air after a fire. I reach the sitting room. Rose is staring out a window. There are stars out, shocking for Ireland, and a sixth day waxing gibbous, humpbacked, moon.

"Maybe we have set them back?" she says to me.

"They can't draw a new circle? Probably on it now."

"You're ever chipper. Maybe so, but they may be scrambling. At least we know the spot. They can't change that so easily for what they are doing. We need to find the Blue Bottle. It will get us a step ahead. It's where Mealla's Irish magic comes from. It's used to see the future."

"Where is it?"

"The bottom of a lake. Possibly. Biddy Early died in April, eighteen seventy-four, buried in an unmarked grave in Feakle. Unmarked, so people couldn't try to contact her spirit for magic or dig her up. It *was* a priest who said she wanted it thrown in the lake near her cottage."

"So you want Mealla and I to go to Feakle and try to like call it?"

+++

The mind-blast of information after the time bend didn't prepare me for the visual change in the countryside in Ireland.

The N20 Toll Road took forever to get out of Cork City. Blarney is more like a suburb.

All the ancient oak forests are gone, replaced by the green fields, which are crisscrossed by dry, stone walls. Farther up the Mallow Road the carriage way becomes two lane with curves, so the lorries are setting the pace until the by-pass around Limerick. In just under two hours, Feakle comes into view.

On the lane in, loads of derelict, Famine cottages have been a part of the landscape. Feakle is starved-looking village of fifteen buildings in the interior rolling hills of Ireland. The low buildings are attached, end to end, but with different facades of bare stone, pebble finish or smooth plaster. All variations of the color brown except for J. Moloney's Pub. The lower half of the building is painted light yellow with bright green stripes, boxing in the front large window and door. There is no wind, so the Irish flag above the signage plate lies twisted and limp. The pub has traditional Irish music.

Feakle was one of the most superstitious areas in Ireland. Biddy did it all. Busted through *pishogues,* curses. She boiled potions, cures, and veterinary poultices, all while gazing into the future and mediating with the fairies. Priests didn't like her, accused her of witchcraft. She gave them no notice.

Constance parks in front of the Gallery Café, sign, plumb in color. "Give them a bit of trade," she says.

The front window is large and arched with brick-a-brack, giving it flair. Mealla hoots at the rusted bicycle screwed onto the face of the building, with the dummy of a woman riding it. Orange scarf on her head, purple wellington boots on her feet, gloves and a teal long raincoat.

Mealla leans in. "Think that's supposed to be Biddy?"

"The White Witch, the Wise Woman of Clare in purple Wellington, mud boots? I'd say yes."

Inside, the walls are covered with paintings of all sizes and content, no frames, and pottery on makeshift shelves. Constance insists on tea and scones.

"I can spread our trade to the pub across the street." The glare tells me tea it is.

"Is Biddy Early bringing in tourists?" Mealla asks an end-of-age woman as she lays a jar of strawberry jam on the wooden tabletop. The woman doesn't look like she's expecting customers. She hasn't as much as taken a brush to her hair.

"If you're looking for the house, it's about a mile down the road. Good luck finding it though. There's only a bit of a rope across a track."

"The blue bottle?" I hazard to ask.

She scoffs like I'm a one-electric-bar fire. "Thrown in a bog. So they say."

"Which bog?"

"Kilbarron Lake was close to her cottage. Only I've heard you can buy it on EBay."

+++

Biddy as a child used to talk to herself, but some said it was with the *Tuatha*, at the *rath*, a circular earthwork, in Jack Brian's field, beside his farm at Coolreagh. There could be a line of wagons from the village to her cottage, and down the lane to Kilbarron Lake. Desperate people looking for help. Still, there were twenty-seven priests at her funeral.

Constance drives us up and down the lane as Mealla and I, our noses to the car windows, try to spy a broken cottage or a path with a rope across it. The lane is like a roller-coaster. With no luck, the nun parks on a slim lay-by. I take one side of the lane with Mealla and Constance the other. We walk.

I go off-road looking in thickets of trees for any low stones lying one on the other in the shape of a cottage. I sink to my shoe tops in the bog. "I found the effing lake. What's effing left of it."

Shite. I squish bog water and mud between my toes in my socks inside my trainers. If it's here, the blue bottle has gone underground.

"Any house?"

"In the effing bog?"

"It must be this side then," Mealla says with her cheery tone wrecking my head.

Feckin' must be.

"You're kind of picky, ya know, considering the dirty'ish time you came from," she says when I join her.

"Maybe a path here," yells Constance.

I perk up. "Where?"

"Here. A break in the trees with a bit of rope."

We all see, now, the nearly invisible rope that touches the ground, and is stretched between two ancient posts.

We collectively hoot.

Nettles, and a canopy of sorrel hide the path in. The house at the end is being held up by the grout of ivy, brambles and creepers. Next to the derelict cottage is a grove of blackthorn. The house gazes at me with two small, square, pane-free window shapes on either side of a door-shaped opening.

Yeah, seriously gazing at me.

There's no roof but the sky and the over-hanging trees. The inside still has one whitewashed wall from a refurbishment in the seventies. The trunks of vines grow up it like brown varicose veins. There's scatterings of bottles, some blue, around the indentation for the fire and on the windowsills. There's a sleeping bag that didn't go home with the owner.

I am looking in from the outside, hesitant to go in. The café proprietor said the man who bought and refurbished the cottage to restore as a tourist attraction, seems his wife died soon after and then his son.

Magic buzzes around the house like it's a beehive. I wonder

if it is a good idea to be here. I'm moving to Mealla's side. Biddy is known as the *Spéirbhean*, a wise woman. She probably warded the house in some way.

Mealla is aware, so it's hard to believe that she strides into the house anyway. I hear the sound of a door shutting behind her. The GrandOther is having an effing laugh.

CHAPTER

SIXTEEN

Feath
Miracle

Magic works in three's. The perfect number, three. Harmony, wisdom, and understanding; past, present, future; beginning, middle, end. The optimum number in fairy tales. It is elemental, healing, and psychic. Also, foreboding, vanished, and shite.

I'm taking in Biddy's ruined cottage, rooted from surprise. I'm there staring, groping for what to do as I see nothing but the inside of a skeleton of a cottage.

There is that gut reaction to call the lost person's name. Like that would help. I rush in. It's only the inside of a skeleton of a cottage that meets me. The portal was waiting for her, and only her. She answered its want. We stepped right into the shite like the total tools that we are.

Sister Constance is stunned, mouth open. It's hard to take the nuns by surprise. Then she gets over it. I see her, through a window with no glass, point at the house. She eyes me with a hard glare that says get cracking.

"Do you see the well there? Keep an eye on it," I call at her, as I leg it to a lone ash tree. The house won't work for me, but I have my own method of shifting.

This is an extreme action that I do only under the threat of death or dismemberment, and sometimes either of those is preferable. I cut the Ogham letter *Nion* for the sacred ash tree into its trunk with the Ogma's knife. It's a surface scratch really, but I man up for the carry on from the fairy associated with this particular ash. The keening is a bit much. The mark is a little less that a bite from a year-old baby that's still nursing.

"Sorry," I say. "I'll make it up to you. Whaduhyousay, some fertilizer?" It's a sad looking ash tree. I'm just saying.

It's not necessary to use the ash generally. Just sitting under a Hawthorn would get me where I want to go, if I have alcohol, and I do not.

The letter *Nion* is sacred to the *Tuatha* as an entry Ogham letter to the GrandOther. It's a portal I discovered by accident and couldn't get the feck out of the place for twenty-four hours afterward. I evade, dodge, or duck the GrandOther as if sanity depends on it. Which it does.

I thank the fae who is just sniffling now. "You are part of the *Yggdrdasill*, the world tree thing, roots to the underworld, and to the homes of the Gods. Get over it. *Nion!*" I'm gone before she can cream my horn.

A mighty wind pushes me. I'm assuming that Biddy, befriended by the fairies at a young age, given bottles and all sorts, must be there. I'm hoping that's the only reason Mealla was sucked in. Mostly I'm fuming. Just another ordeal by gods when they are supposed to be on our side.

The *Aes Sídhe*, the People of the Mounds, the *Tuatha*, the Irish Gods live in a parallel universe, a self-contained place of existence. They've made the best of things with eternal youth, beauty, bounty, good health. They got to keep remnants of their magic.

As I said, I've been here before, once. It's similar to having a near death experience. After the darkness of transport, you see a landscape of running streams, and ever-blossoming trees, and more varieties of birds than you can take in.

There's a glare straight into my eyes from jeweled mountains with castles on top. Should have brought shades. It never rains here. Even the *Tuatha* are sick of rain. The scent of perpetual spring, youth, and glamour makes me sneeze. I'm allergic to magic like.

To me the changeless blossoms have always seemed colorized, fragile even, like days-old cut flowers. The air smells cloy like the gods have discovered glade plugins. That's just me. Really, the place seems perked up a bit. A sense that something immemorial is coming, and they're getting ready for the remodel.

Nobody here is going to lash on the kettle for me. I admit it, I can be irritating. And then, large as life, my bitter enemy.

"Padraic O'Duibh."

Feckin treat. And always coming up on my back, the dose. Turning to face the Morrigan herself, I say, and give me credit, "You wouldn't know where I can find Mealla? You do know each other."

I ask the Morrigan like she is the *Tir na Og*, or as I call it, the GrandOther tour guide and information center. The Morrrigan is war and fate personified. She foretells doom and death. Standing within her aura is like the day you qualify for hospice. Just from her perfume, I'm ready to drink myself into oblivion, and then throw myself under a bus. She's had like four husbands who, even though the sex was fantastic, probably did just that, throw themselves under busses. Drank themselves silly.

Then there is the rising fear that makes my heart thump so hard she can hear it. She loves that. This is the Goddess that washes the bloodstained clothes of men she has prophesized to die. The only thing keeping me together is trying to guess her opening line, something like, you're an ignorant bollocks.

"You are useless."

Close.

"The effort it took to send you to the future. For this very easy number, shut down a few priests. Wasted."

"Practitioners."

The Morrigan's dark, sensual beauty is beguiling to anyone but me. All I see are the talons and beak of the crow, as a shapeshifting overlay of that divine face.

"Why will-o-wisp Mealla away to fairyland." She hates me to call it fairyland. I should give over to her; I'm powerless here, but it's not in me. Never has been. Orphans have nothing to lose.

She just smiles a double-dealing, evasive grin. My fists ball. I'm about to lose the complete run of myself.

"So predictable. Going to take me down, are you?"

"Worried are you?"

"We are always worried about Catholic priests. That's who you are supposed to take care of," she snaps.

"Practitioners."

She flips her hand like she's swatting a fly. "Find out what they are doing, and stop it," she roars.

I'm discombobulating the Morrigan. She is not really discombobable. Which is telling and would be more fun if she wasn't so scary. "You're looking a bit poorly. Nerves?"

She opens her mouth but there's a full stop on the words. She sniffs the air. I can't help but to do the same.

It goes to show how a situation can turn.

Paracelsus thought that faeries are in the four elemental categories of water, air, earth, and fire. He thought there were salamander fairies, the fairies of heat, of energy, of anger, and of passion, courage and boldness. He's the guy who named their breath, 'bellows breath,' but it wasn't her breath I smelled.

"Mealla! Shite."

As I speak, the very woman is running hell bent out of the increasing smoke, and screaming, "Shittttt!"

It's a knee-jerk reaction that the Morrigan goes for my throat. Like Mealla, running hell-bent for sanctuary from beings halfway between flesh and spirit, is somehow my fault.

She is one angry Morrigan with blood in her veined eyes, but I'm a factional stick fighter, a *bataireacht,* and I've been ready to fight since she surprised me from behind. She is counting on home court advantage of her goddess-ness and super strength.

I am counting on being one step ahead.

I bring my club around and thrust forward with the hard root-knob end. Air wheezes out of her. Weakness slumps her. She doesn't know that I bored out the center of the root knob and added iron to the core of the stick. She grabs for my black-thorn club, and I leave it there, let her close in on the spines pointing up. I pull back on it hard. She screams. As I run towards Mealla, I hear the Morrigan calling for the god of healing. Her next breath is a long shrill whistle.

Calling her shite dogs.

Fire explodes in the near distance. There's an aura of flame blowing from Mealla's back, a shape writhes within that orange glow, her fire salamander. The woman has set fire to the Grand-Other, no less.

I join her. "Keep running," I say. Er, like she is going to stop.

A pack of the Morrigan's Barghest dogs are like a silent fart. They can be invisible with only the sound of rattling collar chains, and then your Achilles tendon is ripped by canine teeth that can put an elephant's tusks to shame. The silent death-howlers. If the teeth are not enough, they have claws.

There is the story of a man who tried to summon and confront a Barghest. His dead body was discovered soon after with death-marks on his chest. The dogs can take the forms of headless men, women, white cats, and rabbits.

Mealla glances back, and then at me.

"I hear they can't cross rivers."

"See any...rivers?"

The first one makes a long jump towards her, fire and all. It's invisible but for a shadow outlined by the bright flames. My blackthorn club is quick, and hard-hitting, and the dog flies.

The grassy meadow is thick with the damn dogs. I know that only because the yellow flowers growing there are being trampled. The green turns to mud. I take a hit to the side. The supernatural part of the animal makes them stronger. My head snaps. I struggle to keep my feet under me. They are trying to flank us.

"Go to the ash tree," I yell. My Ogma hand and knife slashes air, and sometimes fir and muscle. I'm already calling on the Ogham letter for power. The tree seems miles away.

A Barghest bites at her thigh, I swing. She dodges. It's a one-two that protects her side from deep, bone-crunching harm, but not enough to protect her completely. She cries out. I kick at the thing with all the tight anger inside me. Good thing is, as we zip along with the both of us leaking blood, I've made a dent. I hear less jingling.

I glance back. The dogs are visible in death. I see the septic bodies, ugly on the pristine landscape. "*Nion,*" I keep saying until it feels like an echo in my head. We touch the tree at the same time, Mealla is still flaming. The GrandOther fades.

⌗

"Right," says Constance. When she sees us.

"I have it," pants Mealla. "I have the bottle."

Constance sucks in air between her teeth. She is that surprised, again, then she sees the blood. "Into the car." She helps Mealla struggle to lie across the back seat. I hardly see the landscape as we fly down narrow lanes. She set her dogs after us. The Morrigan doesn't think we are worth saving. That is a problem.

The nuns are in chapel when Constance, Mealla and I tumble into the rarified air of the convent. The organ is blaring, and then all sound dies. From their individual carrels along the soft, golden-colored length the chapel, black-scarved heads turn.

Rose waves us away, until Constance points out Mealla. Constance is apologizing. "No need, no need. It's just we need Our Lord in this too." Rose takes in that my shoes are caked with dried mud, and Mealla is…just wild looking like, as if she's been caught in a tornado, and thrown a few hundred feet. Go bathe and—"

"More than that," explains Constance. Rose notices the saturated blood at Mealla hip.

"Keep praying," Rose says to the others as she motions us into the convent.

I sit on a dining chair. I am folded over, my elbows on my knees seemingly studying my dank shoes and socks. I'm thinking about the Morrigan's face. Under the haughtiness and the glamour, it was there, panic. They had sent a champion… two champions. They expended great energy that could have been used elsewhere, and we are effing it up. They are afraid.

The Irish Gods have a knee-jerk fear of priests. But they have adjusted over the hundreds of years. Irish religion has always been a blend of Catholicism and Paganism. It's more than that in the Morrigan's face. It's something that has the nuns and the goddesses working together, sort of. One hand doesn't know what the other is doing.

+++

. . .

The blue bottle. Large as life but not taller than five inches. A deep, sea blue, the color of the Atlantic as it crashes on the rocks at the base of the cliffs along the Wild Atlantic Way. Mealla has brought it down, and placed it there, as the center-piece on a table in the dining room. I'm feeling for an energy spike in case the bottle decides to self-destruct in a convent.

Biddy was accused of witchcraft, the bad kind with the devil and all. She was released on lack of evidence. No one would testify against her.

The liquid inside the bottle swirls. Activated like. It was what called Mealla to the GrandOther. Mealla, with her magical awakening, has been be changing on a fundamental level. The bottle senses her.

"It's a stored arcane energy," says Rose when she drops a Guinness in front of me. "Can't you feel it, the power of the original energy fields of the universe?"

"Think Mealla can direct that?"

"The house recognized her. The bottle called her." We stare at the bottle as if it might bite. "Biddy managed to direct it." Silence. "The bottle was enchanted when it was made. It's the bottle." Rose makes clear.

"It could take out the city."

"She just has to work out how to use it."

"The *Tuatha*, they don't want it here," I point out. "After she set the castle ablaze, she was running with it. She stole it." Sure, that fact should have had the nuns cursing the Irish gods for their lack of support. It doesn't.

It isn't the first time I am wondering about the nuns and the GrandOther crowd. Arcane magical energy is exactly what we need here. We had to steal it to get it.

And then I know. Our Arcane-magical-energy-tool gain is the *Tuatha's* loss. Right now, they need it themselves, more than ever, for something.

SEVENTEEN

Gorm

Blue- protection and magic

Sleepless myself at the witching hour, I see a light under Mealla's door. Inside her room, I find her trying to bond with the bottle. I feel it. She glances up as I enter, and then gets up to move a chair from a corner in closer. At the surprise in my face that her limp is improved, she says, "Just Tylenol. It's not as good as your holy wells."

"Do you see anything? There in the bottle."

"You look. Do *you* see anything because I don't? There's nothing," she says. I notice her goggled, stress-filled eyes... don't take gifts from a fairy. She picks it up and shakes it like a snow globe. "Why would it call, and then not work?" Her voice is fed-up and at a breaking point, like *it's* a glass bottle.

I take it from her, gently like. "Maybe a goddess has blocked it. It was not given willingly. Maybe it has to be given? It's theirs after all."

Good I have it. She looks like she'd throw it against the wall.

Feeling hard done by for her, I lay the bottle down like placing an egg in an egg carton. Mealla cares, fights, teaches, nurses, bears up, laughs, and then when all that is exhausted, when she is exhausted, she comes pegging out like a...smoldering-fire-salamander-flare-up.

"I need to control this." Her voice is calmer. She is trying to stuff her frustration back into the box where it lives. "Anxiety is a magic killer," she adds as she rubs her neck.

"That's Irish magic," I say, indicating with my head to the blue bottle. "Arsehole magic."

She laughs. Meditatively, she closes her eyes and inhales, then exhales. Rubbing her temples she says, "There is a legend within Native Americans that the monster, as big as the valley, was eating all the animals. To stop him, the brave coyote allowed the monster to swallow him. He had on him stone knives, and he cut apart the monster from the inside out."

"Sounds like a brave and complete tit. Your point?"

"I don't know." Her eyes look overheated. "Break the bottle? From the inside out?"

"Full of Arcane energy."

"Yes."

"Demented."

Now she's just looking bat-shit crazy. "What? No. We've enchanted our own bottle. Bottle within a bottle. So was can access the energy inside the bottle."

Feck, she's gone mental. "Oh, please do that. I want to watch the fireworks before *my* face melts. You are tired. We can't enchant a bottle to hold arcane energy and remember, the magic is the bottle."

"Oh, for hell's sake." She'd just now take a swing at me if she'd let herself. That's the way with mopping up after gods and their wannabes. "It's the enchanted bottle that's being controlled," she insists. She does that fed-up, you-figure-it-out arm toss.

This is a lot for me. It's an awful lot for her. Most of the time

I'm alone, dealing, and I don't have to shift to nice and kind. But she is the nice and kind I didn't think was still out there. So I try harder. "Just to be clear, before I leave you to get some sleep, you don't know how to... ah...sort of bottle in a bottle... arcane energy." I leave out, and don't say you're going to google it. See, I'm there.

"Maybe it's like transferring a mad hornet from one jar to another, jar to jar, pull out the cardboard between them." Only she's pulling my leg. Though my eyes feel like they're bulging from my scull. Cardboard! Jaysus I'd murder for a pint right now.

"I'm joking. The look on your face. I'm joking. So, figure out the enchantment," she says in an off-hand voice that sounds like she'd miss the bells, whistles, and face-melting. She flops back on her minimalist bed and rubs her temples. She's going to wear out the skin there. Running up against magical problems is migrainey. I know after twenty minutes here that I want to lie down.

"How did your parents come together?" I ask.

"Horse racing. My father is a betting man. He breeds horses and sometimes races them. My mother also likes betting on horses, a lot. I was a girl, so the birth didn't matter to my father."

"Vindication for you then, all this?"

"I yelled at my father that I wouldn't be a shaman if hell froze over anyway."

"So you became a fake one."

"We needed money."

The glass is so clear in the windows in this epoch that the full moon is easy to see. Something flies in front of the moon, then drops down, out of the frame of the window.

Another flying dark shape and another, then multiples. I spring to the window, peering down. The black shapes are landing in the courtyard, amassing there.

"Shite." Right off, I'm thinking revenge of the Morrigan. It doesn't make sense the god attacking the nuns' home territory. Usually when she cools off, she's more rational.

"What?" asks Mealla.

"Come look."

There were so many now that the courtyard shifts and moves like a black, undulating ocean under the bright moon. The door opens. "Padraic."

"We see them. Do you know what they are?"

"Is the hound still outside?"

"I haven't checked lately." I feel like it's my hellhound which is mental, and I'm worried about it. I pound down the stairs, which have never been pounded down before, and really never to save a hound from hell. I join Rose at a larger, street-level window.

"*Sluagh*."

"Large as life."

Human-beast creatures are landing, growing, and forming muscular bodies with long arms, the size of tree trunks, and with branch-like fingers. Thighs like the hind end of a deer, springy and bent at the knee, and acres of sharp toenails that would blind a mani-pedi tech.

This type of *Sluagh* have hair like a mane of dried blood. In the face are mouths of overlapping sharp, yellow teeth and lit, vacant eyes. I hate vacant eyes. It means there's naff-all there, just manic, mindless, twisted extermination. They are landing, swelling, and filling the courtyard, probably, if I could see, all the way around the building.

Hellhounds have been herding *Sluagh* for forever. Now *my* one is lying there for them sweet and docile. I am scared of both the *Sluagh* and the hellhound. But still, it's going to have to be open, grab, and drag. I actually count in my head for motivation. One, two, three. It's all in, in these situations. Only one go. With my heart pounding out an Irish step dance, I grab the door handle, which is freezing, or is it that my hand is hot from all that extra blood flowing to it? If I'm not careful, I'll invoke the *geasa*.

Still, fear-energy pulses into Ogma's hand. I pull open the door with my mortal hand, reserving the true strength for shifting the dog.

"I'm behind you," calls Mealla because it's also her magical creature.

"No, you're not," I yell back.

But she is in battle stance with her hawthorn wand out and pointed towards the door.

I call out, *"Luis,"* to the rowan tree for a shot in the arm of apotropaic, aversion magic. I pull open the door and take one step over the threshold.

And step back just as rapidly, slamming the door closed in front of me.

"What the hell?" asks Mealla.

"The hellhound is up and is being joined by his friends. Good news. Brilliant news."

"Do they need help?"

"The hellhounds?" I think my heart is settling. "It's their job."

"Maybe they're outnumbered."

"They're hellhounds."

"The *Slaugh* are more of a deluge than a hunt."

"All good. All normal. It's got help." I'm talking to the air, because Mealla is gone, and then back again just as my word, "help" floats to ground. This is where it gets mental...she has the blue bottle.

"When I googled Biddy and her bottle—"

"You were shaking it just a second ago."

My whole being is screaming. My face must be a portrait of anguish and fear because she says, "Before, and I know what you're thinking, but that was trying to see into the future. This is different. I read that when Biddy's first husband died, and she couldn't pay the rent, she got an eviction notice."

I now hear the dogs and the *Sluagh* tearing into each other, growls from both sides, the second death screams of the already mostly dead. The hounds crying out. And next, what's not wrong with this, Mealla, without finishing her story, with a glance that says stand back, opens the door and steps out.

It's as if I'm being tortured by an advanced case of shingles. That's the reaction of my body.

In her fear, the flames of the salamander trace down her back. I can see the blue bottle trembling in her hands as she holds it out away from her body.

I with my club and Ogma's knife, I rip through the first *Sluagh* that gets close enough to rip out her throat, and the second. After that I quit counting, and just fight beside the hounds.

A *Sluagh* crashes into me. I'm on my back, skidding away from Mealla with the beast on top of me. With Ogma's hand, I tear into its back with the knife. *Sluagh* can't be septic.

In my peripheral vision, I try to see what's happening at the door, at the same time as trying to beat a *Slaugh* silly. I can't kill them. Only the hounds can do that. I can only dissuade them from coming closer.

In going for my neck, a *Sluagh* clamps into my golden torc. It screams as if burned, which it was. I smash in its face. It's a sea of *Sluagh* between me and Mealla. I have to let the *geasa* take me, swinging at anything that moves like the madman I become. The hounds, now in front of her, are like kill machines. More are *Sluagh* are coming.

"Get inside," I yell and gesture, as I try to close in on her, but then there is the next *Sluagh* and the next.

She's staring into the blue bottle like she been doing all night. I've never felt so much overwhelming dread.

Gripping the blue bottle so tightly that I think she's trying to break it...a real thought in the space of a second in my mind. Standing there she's beginning to look every bit the most powerful, insane sorcerous on the planet.

"Stay where you are," she yells.

She chants.

The dogs stand. They are breathing hard but sense a change in fortune. Like all the *Slaugh*, at the sound of Mealla's voice, sticking to the pavers, like she coated them with glue.

Mealla and I dive for the door. I shut and lock it behind me. I immediately pull into myself to control the will to do battle. I press on my chest like I'm having a heart attack. It's all been too precious, too precarious. Every moment strident. I breathe.

Mealla reaches out.

"Don't touch me," I yell. I curve into a ball on the floor. With a strength of will I've had to develop over time since I was a young teen, I mentally force my body to filter the *geasa* poisoning from my blood. I never let myself go like that. It's all I can do wrapped in on myself to soothe and repair. I force my mind into unconsciousness. When I come to, the nuns are all around me, waiting and praying.

I'm shaking as they help me up. "I will get better quickly from now."

"I'm sorry," Mealla says.

"Couldn't you have done it from behind the door?"

"I'm sorry. I don't think so. Don't you ever do that again. Whatever that was."

I hear the dogs taking care of things. The sound trying to put the wind up me again, the wail of so many nearly dead being shredded by the dagger-teeth of the Hounds of Hell. I've spent most of my life working not to fight. I'm the meaning of the word "placatory." I assess right off whether I'm likely to win a fight and then act appropriately. I go the long way around people. Now they all have seen why.

What's changed here that I let it all go? The women praying around me...mostly though, Mealla.

"Let's move to a quieter place," says Rose. I nod my head and follow Rose. Away from the pitched sounds that could burst eardrums and rouse *geasas*. The dogs know their jobs. They are not made for mercy.

But there is no quiet place. Buttermilk arrives with wax ear plugs for me.

"How did you know to bind them?"

"I read that Biddy used the bottle to bind the men who were going to evict her. Instructions included in the story. The hell hounds. You need to trust me more."

"You need to communicate."

"The hell hounds."

"Yeah, Jaysus." I slump into my chair.

I tell Mealla to unbind the *Slaugh*. "They're damaged enough that the hounds can finish their job herding them to hell.

"Right," says Buttermilk. "Hadn't our Lord said that they would be cast into the furnace of hell and gnashing and wailing and so on?"

She could jockey on a horse with fright.

┼┼┼

"The practitioners are that desperate now. It means they will do things they might not normally have done. They've decided to try and contain us here."

Rose coughs. The sound is loud in the silence at the end of the *Sluagh* massacre. "It appears you are both warming to the job. Stars all round for intelligence and fast-thinking. Those are unteachable gifts."

She's scrutinizing me as she talks, like I'm an effin photo of insanity. I agree with her. They might feel threatened by me now. I would. Sister Rose catches my eye and holds it. "We were told that you are the epitome of the Irish personality." She leans towards me. "Which is ego, temper, charm, warmth, and caustic wit. We've been waiting for the last one, buoyancy." She smiles at my face, my thoughts, my being. A genuine sort of a thumbs up.

"I'd add devious and artful..." I tap my finger on my nose, "...basically, a cunning little shite."

We smile at each other. Her smile says she agrees without doubt. Mine says I am what I am. "We are very glad you both are here."

Maybe, but still the cats are herding us.

CHAPTER

EIGHTEEN

Fiorainn
True name

I'm in the shower getting *Sluagh* guts out of my hair. I press the guts through the drain slots and into the pipe. I hope I'm well gone before they may have to call a plumber. Souls of the dead smell. It's like a sewer in here.

I take the time to look in the mirror. Beard-less, my face is still not familiar. I take a razor to the stubble and notice the red strands from my mother's hair in the brown. The blue of my eyes is rimmed in red from the soap. There's a bruise on my cheek. I don't check out the rest of my body, which is a bruise.

Taking in the effect, I bark-howl, a sound from the past when I ran with my *bataireacht*, stick fighting, gang in medieval times, through the countryside. We were the *fianna*, Irish warriors of our time. Landless, orphaned teenagers out for trouble. A few of the gang, like me, had been released from training, from Alba and the home of Scáthach, *Dun Scáith*, the Fortress of Shadows. All after I killed the Morrigan's son, the man with three serpents in his heart, the Mighty Shite.

I bark-howl again, remembering those days. A thought comes from it, clear as the cold water from the tap. The sense of it takes me inside myself, thinking the idea forward. I run from the room, and then have to return to change out of the towel around my waist. I hop around the room while throwing on my pants. Shoe-less, hair wet and flying, I take the stairs two at a time and burst into the kitchen, where all hands are on deck for a late-night after-Slaugh charcuterie board.

"Everyone, listen."

They stop what they're doing. The state of them. The exhaustion in their bearing dampens my enthusiasm in the moment. "Now what?" one of them actually says.

"Don't eat my head off. This is good. Would the name *Laignech Fáelad*, bring some air into the room?" A flutter of puzzled looks flies about the room.

Riding rings around them.

Stupidly delighted with myself, I say, "He's a medieval legendary warrior—"

"Thinking of a summoning?" Asks Mealla. The nuns' body language is suddenly trial-by–a thousand-knives like.

We have gotten to that point. But this, ladies, you will be buzzing about this.

"And a werewolf."

I wait for the spiritual lift. Nothing.

"It's not a summoning. *Not* a summoning. As a supernatural being, he still will be alive." Ok, some of them are stirring. "He's from a tribe of werewolves who are related to the kings of Ossory. He ran with my gang of stick fighters. We'd all go "a-wolfing" together, I fully kipped-out in wolf-skins."

I watch Rose trying to catch up to me. When she does, her eyes widen. My head nods up and down, encouraging her thoughts.

"The Book of Ballymote?" she asks

"Yeah, sure, probably." Never heard of it but knowing her she's on it.

Rose explains. "It's a medieval book that references 'descendants of the wolf,' who have the power to change. It was written that they ate people."

"Move past that."

"They were said to leave their bodies behind. Their bodies had to be protected for the lupine to come back to. The bodies couldn't be moved. If the lupine was stabbed, so would the body be stabbed."

"Some old things are pure mythology. The car have petrol in it?"

"We're too close in now. There's no time to go driving about the countryside, and we just can't risk it."

"If he's alive, why don't you just call him?" Mealla takes out her cell. "What is his name again?" she asks as she is typing away. "Laignech Fáelad" did produce a number of hits, only all of it medieval information, like a site titled, 'Werewolves of Ossory.' While palming the mobile, she shows me the bright screen.

I read the headlines out loud, "'Kings of Osraige—Wikipedia, The Kings of Ossory—Irish Pedigrees—Library Ireland, Ireland's History in Maps—Ancient Ossory, Osraige, Osraighe—'"

"That's the County of Kilkenny now," says Rose.

I push up on the glass of the phone. I read the next selection: "'Kings of Ossory Brewery and Pub.'" Instinct tells me that this is the place we will find *Laignech*. I touch the headline, and then read, "'Liam Fahey, Master Brewer. Liam has studied the art of brewing as a passion. Finding a new hop, a new flavor, is his true passion. He's the best brewer in Ireland.' That's him, and never short on praise for himself."

The man in the picture wears a creaseless, black t-shirt. His dark, browed eyes look directly at me. Hair crests the crew neck of his shirt. He sports an urban-male, black beard with a full mustache. Black hair rolls thickly around his head. He hasn't aged since I ran with him. Whatever the dangers of going out to meet him personally, it has to be done. I have to explain this face to face. There's no, I'm your old mate from the thirteen hundreds, come forward to fight practitioners, sort of thing over a mobile phone.

The nuns realize the potential but are risk adverse.

"I'm going," I say without inviting anyone. "Mealla stays here and practices. You have to keep each other and Mealla safe until I get back."

There's never a clean or dignified exit with Buttermilk in house. She asks, "Which way do you go, after ye've walked out the door?"

"It's ten pm. We could get there by eleven," says Sister Constance.

✝✝✝

I don't know that anything is following us. If they are, they are sucking diesel as Constance is flooring it on the motorway, and the engine is screaming as it powers through a top speed of ninety kilometers an hour. We don't see *gardaí* until outskirts of Kilkenny, where they are prowling outside the pubs for drunk drivers. We should have done the distance in an hour and a half. She did it in one. She's a nun. Unstoppable. When this is over, if I survive, I'm going to ask her for driving lessons.

The Kings of Ossory Brewery has a red-painted front with four vertical long windows and the name on the signboard in scripted gold. Classy.

"Would you ever look at that?" I'm pointing to the midnight blue painted pub next door. "It's called The Biddy Early."

"Sure, isn't that an omen? Just the thing," encourages Constance.

"Only it's in the wrong county." I open the car door.

I let a punter pass me out before walking into a room so dark that, if it had been bright daylight outside, I would have been blinded. The décor is carved mahogany chairs and brown, leather, button-tucked upholstery. Pure money spent. From the stained herringbone floor rises along one side a shining mahogany bar. Advertising-mirrors on the back wall reflect the lager on tap: Werewolf of Ossory IPA, Wolf Picker Experimental IPA, Dirtwolf Double IPA Pilsnes, Kilkenny Werewolf Red Ale. I'm getting used to choice.

This is the place. I rub my hands together and clap once. A bit of joy can't hurt. It's a weekday and the room is empty of any more punters except for the one and a man wiping down tables. A turf fire is burning down. The air is malt scented. I inhale deeply. Clearly, a pint is required.

"What'll you have?" asks the man as pint glasses clink together, dangling by their lips in his large hands. He strolls to the ornately carved bar.

"*Laignech Fáelad*?"

He leaves the glasses on the bar and turns. A suspicious face brightens. "It's been a good many years, but I'd know that face in me sleep. *Padraic O'Duibh*. Shouldn't ye be dead by now?"

We hug and beat each other's backs. He goes behind the bar. "It's Liam Fahey in today's money. Jaysus, would ye sit down there? *Padraic O'Duibh*. I'll get us a pint. It's a long story, no doubt."

"I've got a nun with me."

Laigneach laughs. "I don't remember the religious appealing to you much."

"I'm still there, believe me. After the drive here, I'm pretty sure she'll have a whiskey."

His eyebrows raise. He shakes his head and laughs. "Always large as life you." He isn't saying, I can't believe you're here like. He's supernatural himself. He gets it. We all settle with strong alcohol at a table. I take a long drink of his Red Ale.

The brew master in him has to ask even in these circumstances, "How is it?"

"Excellent."

"Should be overtones of rye, toasted malt, and burnt caramel."

"Wow," slips out of me as I sip for flavor. "That is interesting." I look around me. I study *Laigneach*. "Looks like you're fitting in here."

"Yeah, thanks to a witch named Alice De Kyteler. The pack helped her leave Ireland in the sixteen hundreds. She and another were the only witches ever tried for witchcraft in Ireland. Such was their luck. The other was her assistant Petronella De Meath. I'm afraid we couldn't help Petronella in time. Alice left us with a potion that's works...like shifting control—we change when we want, and only when we want."

"So do you...ever change?" I'm afraid to ask. So much depends on his answer.

"Not so much. The country is small, the forests are gone, along with animals to hunt and the natural wolves to blend in with. And business is ripping."

It's like my hole was kicked. He must see the craic in me deflate, because he says, "What's this about?" He leans against the back of his seat. As he listens, strokes his black beard. "We've been feeling a number of warming, magical surges. Was one of them you?"

"Probably. In an impossible united front, the Tuatha combined their magic and bent time sending me forward."

"Wow. Fair dues to them." Liam blows out his lips. "I wouldn't have half-thought they could do it." He takes me in head to toe. "No worse for wear, seemingly. So there has been an environmental uptick in magic. Reassuring really. I thought I was going a bit mad with age or something."

"Magic's leaking, and mag-ex-priests are desperately trying to control the leak for themselves, by desperately summoning an ordeal by supernatural being. The wankers. I guess I'm here to stop it."

Laigneach can't miss the fierceness of the situation with the wankers, or what it is I want from him. "Slack, poxy shites," is all he says. I'm asking him to upset the life he has built. I watch as he takes in his pub. He downs his drink.

"The long and the short...magic is becoming unbound," I say before taking an equally long drink. The ale is that good that I nod my head in tribute. Liam nods back. He's losing joy, though. I'm sorry to keep explaining. Sorry to involve him. Sorry about Mealla. The nuns can take care of themselves.

I speak to him in the old *Gaelinn*. *"The Catholic Church is weak and losing control. They've kept magic out of Ireland since Patrick, out of the entire world. Here we are at a reckoning, and subsequent power grab."* Another long drink and another. I feel it warming up the cold spaces. "These practitioners have been using low magic in their rites for centuries. It's that a little power has always created an appetite for more. You know that."

"Big egos."

"In fairness, the Church did try. They designed the rites as an action of and from God Himself and left the practitioners with only incidental ministering significance. It was never going to stick."

I couldn't tell if I was convincing him to shift. I kept going. "The *Tuatha* are in play. They want back what Patrick took from them. Human faith. Ordinary human consciousness hasn't anything within it to perform magic. The gods are hemi-parasitic. So it's symbiotic. Ordinary humans get power from gods and gods get power from human faith, with magic at the center."

"I stay away from all things religious." Liam laughs. "Always did."

"My motto has always been "god-awful.""

We sit quietly with the largeness of it all and drink. I get that he is not *Laignech* any longer; the man who used to go wolfing, the brother of *Feradach Mac Duach*, the king of Ossory; the man who opposed Saint Patrick more stubbornly than any other. "Remember the stories you'd tell about Saint Patrick?" I say out of the blue.

Laignech blows out another laugh-grunt.

"What's coming is evil. Ordinary humans will be fodder, like your witch Petronella De Meath."

"I don't know. Feck it. Maybe we need to start shapeshifting again. Use it or lose it, eh? The others are pretty comfortable though."

"There's a cabal, sort of hellfire club of them trying to shift the magic from the whole of the church to themselves."

"It's what's the Club always been for.

"We don't know what's coming, but the practitioners are melting their faces to get there. We have the where and the when. Saint John's Eve. We need numbers."

"It's just you and the nun so far?"

"Nuns and a sorcerous of sorts. She's a genetic melding of American indigenous tribes and the Irish through Biddy Early ancestry. A druidic-shaman. She just discovered her talents two days ago." That last definitely didn't help sell it. "Just one man brought down the Gods and Goddesses of Ireland and all the druids. You didn't like him."

Liam is staring at me, and then through me, then around me.

These wolves have been lazy for too long. "As I said, they've been melting their faces off. Remember Father Timothy Laurent of the Franciscans?"

"He's in with them? That skint blackguard."

"He is, but thanks be to god, he's tethered to the Franciscan Brewery."

"Should have gone worse for him."

We tap our glasses and try to drink to that, but we both need a refill.

"So, ye came forward with it?" Liam eyes me again.

"Intact, with of it, the hand of Ogma, the Ogham magic, the knife of Ogma, the blackthorn club and my high intelligence."

The werewolf flicks his head back and grins. "God, you're still at it. Didn't you run with a knight of Scottish heritage for a while?"

"I did so, a grand reprieve. His death and now this."

"You want the pack to strengthen your position?"

"Is there a pack?"

"Of course there's a pack." Liam stands with both pint glasses in his hands.

"I think it's inevitable."

He leans in. "And her?" he indicates with his head to the nun.

"They're on the forefront with the *Tuatha*. She's a Sisters of Saint Brigid."

"Women were never fools." We both glance at the nun. She tips her head and pops her eyebrows. These nuns are as bad as the Tuatha for giving away nothing. "If I'm hearing you right," Liam begins, "ye're looking at a takeover of the Catholic Church and the magic contained there by its laicized priests."

"Practitioners."

"All the men who have had their day in court."

"Pope dead. Something, something, something. Prophesy of Fatima takeover."

"Jaysus."

Of all the things we've been talking about, this is what shocks Liam?

"Once a priest, always a priest, isn't that right?" asks Liam.

"The mark from the Sacrament of Holy Orders, the ceremony that transforms them, is permanent and immovable upon their souls."

"These practitioners, they're something special then."

"Something like that," I concur.

"Exactly like that."

Laignech strolls to his bar, in his establishment. He pours out two fingers of Jameson Irish Whiskey for himself, and drinks it in one, burning toss down his throat. Wiping his mouth with the back of his sleeve, he takes in all that is his, and probably the peace and prosperity he has been enjoying for a good many years. "See that mahogany grandfather clock there with the swan neck pediment? Bought that at auction. Pride of place in the hellfire club of Mount Pelier. Provenance linked straight to the Connolly family."

"Were you part of The Club, then?"

"Feck no," he spits out. "I was there when the area had a passage grave. Stones were taken from it to build the lodge. The lodge's roof blew off right after it was finished. Lots of paranormal stories are told from up there. Shite. You're wreaking my head, so you are, but you're in luck," he says as he pours more whiskey. "For a while there, we used to run with The Hunt on the Eve of Saint John. Clears our systems of the potion once a year for good health. The timing of the potion's effects is still there. Free of it by tomorrow. Mind, I can't guarantee everyone."

"How many left?"

"Fifty-six. Some will come for the *craig*. They've been missing it. Some will because they just hate priests. I'll ring me brother, Connor."

"Conner. Same old shite?"

"Dotes on his daughter. You wouldn't know him. He has the Kings of Ossory butcher's shop in the next lane. He'll get out the word. Where is the meeting place?"

"Her place," I nod towards the nun. "Cork City."

A slosh more of Jameson, and Liam drains his glass. "We've been smelling burnt magic for weeks now."

"My first few minutes here, coming out of Saint Peter's Church in Cork, I was met by a Kaiju. A hell hound was stunned. The nunnery is warded to the hilt. *Sluagh* attacked just hours ago."

Liam's eyes pop out. "You're taking the piss."

"Not a bit."

"Feck."

I eat a bag of sour cream and onion chips that I love. The spice powder from them stays on my tongue, and I get to ask for more lager to go with it. Liam pours a pint of the Wulver and then begins ringing various numbers, and then the nun, the werewolf, and I pile into the Fiat. Sounds like the setup to a cheap joke, and I am laughing. Necessary because, at this point, the *geasa* inside me won't completely still. My human body is struggling under the onslaught of continual magic.

"We've got the werewolves," the nun is saying into her mobile as she drives one-handed through Kilkenny.

But then about that laugh. Never ever be positive. There's always a shite out there that will consider the challenge.

NINETEEN

Foirteagal
Words of power

"The hellfire clubs were after your time," Liam says, while grabbing the back of my car seat to steady himself as the Fiat takes a corner. "It all began, once upon a time ago with a French priest named Rabelais, a Benedictine. He decided, rightly so, that the ideal monastic community should have both men and women living in it 'doing what they will.'" Liam laughs. "In theory, for the church, sin has always been a by-word for anything fun. Rabelais opened the door to anti-morality, and eventually the hellfire clubs. Stupidly, women weren't admitted to the hellfires, but at times they *were* left in, if they were beautiful, well built and sweet natured."

Constance hits the brakes hard. My seat belt squeezes my heart, stomach and liver. My head flings forward. At first, I'm thinking she's responding to Liam's story, but as the car skids to a halt, she yells, "snakes." She pushes open her door and flings her body to the tarmac.

According to a Welsh monk, the multitasking Saint Patrick drew all the snakes, and any other magical crawly animals with venom, to the holy mountain *Cruach Phádraig*, where he'd been fasting and collecting magical energy. From the mountain, all the snakes and any other venomous creatures were forced to the seaside where they were given the choice to sink, not swim. So when the nun calls out snake, Liam and I immediately think end of days. When we see the snake, a *Gnaddr*, we are sure about end of days. This snake is a descendant of the one in Eden. They are associated with demons."

We shouldn't have left the car unguarded.

The snake drops onto the road…and it multiplies, exploding like a confetti cannon.

Constance glances around. "We're on a bridge. I can't swim."

It's a short bridge. But it is water on either side of the rails, and vipers at both ends.

Meanwhile, chicken feet pop from the chests of the snakes, and then heads at both ends. They move by slithering; or for speed, by clamping their mouths together and rolling like a tire, the legs pressing on the earth for acceleration, jumping, and stopping. Double fanged with poison dripping from both mouths, the creatures move backwards as fast as they move forwards. Eyes that glow like a steady, red on-button follow our every move.

I ready my knife and blackthorn club. I slice through the first one that flings itself at me. The halves fall to the ground to rejoin again.

"Well, shite."

I'm worried about Constance, but also Liam. He hasn't changed for centuries. His cells, maybe, have been human for too long. He's a day off the end of the anti-change juice in his system.

"I can't swim," Constance reiterates as another snake jumps at her.

I bat it into the Glashaboy River and hope it can't either. Like a switch has been thrown they all attack at once. The blackthorns on the blackthorn club are not piercing the skins of these snake-chickens. Like the Kaiju, the scales on the sides of these vermin are like metal armor. The snakes are shying away from the iron in the club, which tells me something.

"Come to me!" I yell to her, as I take swing after swing at anything in the air. It's like every snake banished from Ireland has found its way back. Sister Constance's having none of it and is using the tire iron. Not a fear, except water. God bless her. And damn it, why can't anyone take orders?

It's hard to avoid a viper attack at close range. These, magically enhanced, will really catch up to her and overwhelm her, overwhelm all of us, just by numbers.

The werewolf has no defense against snakes but thick skin. But this werewolf hasn't changed in three hundred or so years. I used to wonder what snakes had ever done to Saint Patrick to deserve mass extinction. Now I know. With these two-headed snakes, even a small bite will bring death.

I see Liam's change isn't happening fast enough. "Here." I throw him my blackthorn club, which he neatly catches from long range.

"Are you mental? What are you going to use?"

"Just keep swinging at them, into the water."

Liam changes as he's batting. Some vipers explode on being hit. All fly like comets across the sky with Liam at bat. Impressive control. Don't know why I thought any less of him.

I take out of my leather bag stone arrowheads, *gae sí*, fairy darts. The darts have holes in them with fairy toxin. Hurling the darts is a particular expertise of mine. The toxin, upon contact, paralyzes the arms and legs of any animal, including humans. It's called a *poc sídhe,* a fairy stroke. Other symptoms, sore eyes, red, raw skin, unable to see or hear. I am a master thrower because fairy darts, by their nature, can't miss. So I'm cheating.

They will not penetrate the skin of the snake, but there are three soft places...two eyes and a mouth, doubled. Using, but controlling the *geasa*, I'm hitting my targets with rapid fire. Still I'm just keeping the enemy at bay. Constance is tiring. I'm surprised she's still upright. I'm running out of darts. Toxin-paralyzed snakes are everywhere, and new snakes are just crawling through them. The road is slick with their spit.

"Where's the magic coming from?" I call to Liam.

"Maybe Blackrock Castle across the river. Radio telescope there...magical signals with pinpoint precision."

"Lota's Children's Home down river," Constance says one expelled word at a time. "Ugg," I hear her expel air. She glances up at me with stricken eyes.

"Are you bit?" I call to her.

Liam bats his way to her, and lifts her onto his shoulder, mid-fall. He's supporting her weight and swinging at the, once again, swarming vipers. I remember the conjure bag Mealla made for me. It's in my pocket. *Angelica archangelica*. Can't hurt.

As I wedge the packet out of my pocket, I slip and fall hard. I roll and toss the whole package at an in-my-face viper, its mouth open and fangs dripping. So satisfying as the snake catches it, and better yet, feckin' bursts into flame, which I did not expect, except that I should, because Mealla concocted it. Then, in a brilliant, feckin' treat, it seems that all the vermin are connected, a sort of fuse line. It's pop, pop, pop, and then flame out.

"Fecking hell," says Liam, as he lowers the Constance to the pavement.

I'm there. I remember the other compound in my posses-sion. I have her drink the plastic bottle dry. Just in case, I slice off the crispy head of one of the snakes, if the hospital needs a venom match like.

Liam can't drive. His partial change-back will take time. Or

Sister Constance, obviously. I'm there. I'm at the wheel and starting the engine. "Better let me, Mate," says Liam. "You're looking a bit wired."

"Better that you're half wolf?" I ask, and then his legs change to normal. "It's easier to go wolf to human."

At the emergency room entrance, a nurse is taking charge. Holding out the snake head, I approach him.

"Viper bite."

He is not looking at me. "Yeah, right, Mate."

I can't blame him. This is Ireland. "Things are changing, Mate," I reply and move the snakehead into his line of vision.

He jumps. "What the hell? Are you mental bringing in that?"

"You're going to need this." I can tell from his tight-lipped expression, that he's not inclined to take it. He hands me the bag he's just opened that had medical tubes in it. I drop the head in. As he's looking for puncture wounds on her arm. I say, "It's not drugs. It's snakes. Down around her ankles where snakes roam."

He scowls.

I don't care, Mate. There may not be any snakes in Ireland, but I'm sure that you've heard of them.

"We don't carry anti-venom. I doubt there's a hospital in Ireland that has any. Venom has hundreds of bioactive elements."

"Call somebody."

"You want Captopril," Liam says to them in a voice that says find it.

The nun's ashen color is bad.

This is too much for the compound.

They wheel her through double doors; one man with an intravenous bag under his arm, another cradling his mobile phone between his shoulder and his ear, as he's yelling into it. "Find some Captopril. Captopril, C-A-P, yeah, yeah, for snake bites. You heard me. Just do it."

The double doors close in our faces.

"I've got to ring Rose."

"Let's find a place to do that, and then we can talk."

I tap the screen of the mobile to disengage from Rose.

"How'd that go?"

"She all but, I-told-you-so'ed me. She's sending someone."

"I got us tea." Liam hands me a disposable cup with something smelling like tea. Its heat brings down the moment, as my muscles loosen and my fingers warm.

Liam stretches his legs out in front of him. His pants are torn. His shoes are bare. He drains his cup.

A doctor walks into the waiting area. Not for us, though. Medical smells are mostly the same over time. Combinations of herbs, chemicals and alcohol. We hear stat calls as background noise. Doors opening and closing. Murmuring voices. Shite.

"Sure, back in the day popes wrote the Grimoires," Liam says.

"Remember Luchar? Headless, he found a way through, all by himself. You know what that means?"

"There's no control anymore. So it's Saint John's Eve, then," says Liam. "You're the *Tuatha's* champion. What do they want?"

"Pft," I blow out. "The priests dead and buried upside down and under rocks. I think they want the prophecy of the Lady of Fatima to be fulfilled. They want to be able to slide back in gracefully, without blowback. The practitioners are melting their faces off. Is that because they're slack shites, or because whatever *it* is, is so big, that they can't wrap their heads around it?"

A doc in a white coat with trim brown hair and a young dark-skinned face comes up to us. "It was a near thing, and she's still not one hundred percent, but she began to rally a few minutes ago. We gave her steroids. We think it might have been an allergic reaction to something.

Sure, let's go with that.

TWENTY

Nealla fola
Blood invocation

S aint Brigid of the Isle Convent dining area is now like a
Gardai procedural room, and it doesn't come weirder
than that. With the help of the convent school's Canon
large-format Inkjet printer with sub-ink tank system, we have
photocopied a map of the City of Cork with landmarks and ley
lines. It's taped up on the wall. It's the morning of the day
before Saint John's Eve.

Twenty of the Werewolves of Ossary, the nuns, Mealla and
myself appear ordinary enough, like we might be planning a
fund drive. Only Liam is the head of a pack of ancient warriors
of old Ireland, wolves as warriors. They fight with savage
unpredictability, a spectacular martial prowess.

Or fought.

Currently they're looking round-bellied which, considering
the metabolism of werewolves, speaks for far too much of the
beer and meat they sell or the witch's potion is potent.

Then the nuns. I still don't know which side or both they are playing for. It's a desperate individual who would cross these nuns. Kind of historically nuns have been good and ruthless... good or ruthless, might be better.

And Mealla...trying...getting better.

Myself and my *geasa*, Ogma's hand, Ogma's knife, Ogham magic, my club. Seems enough on the face of it, but the face of it is like the top half of a tooth. The nerve endings are invisible.

I feel a flare of anticipation in my geasa. I need to catch myself on. Maybe I'm over thinking. Yeah, no. Can't convince myself of that.

As the day before Saint John's Eve, the sisters are getting ready for it early. In the courtyard, sisters chatter as they build a bonfire pile of peat and bones. Then there's the weedy smell of yarrow that will be thrown onto the fire for health and protection against evil. The nuns are running in both camps.

"How to precede, then?" Rose redirects our attention like a master teacher who has a classroom of mostly boys.

Liam snorts, and the front legs of his chair hit the floor. He grabs a chocolate digestive from the plate on the table. Nothing happens in Ireland without beer, whiskey, tea, and or cake and biscuits. He hands me one. Chocolate. Sugar straight to the brain.

It's perfect to have Liam here.

Like he's reading my mind, he says, *"N'an sgrioslaich mhor a sios agusa suas air uachdar an domhain mar na truidean.* This reminds me of the quote, 'down and up on the face of the earth like lightning and thunder.' Remember who used to say that?"

"The lovely Siobhan."

"She was never one to have a good word to say. But she didn't need to. Hips like the broad beam of a ship, mouth like the sea that welcomes it."

"And many a ship did," I say.

Rose clears her throat.

"The *Sluagh*," says Liam towards her with a wink. "How to defeat the tossers."

"*Sloo-ah, shee*," Mealla mimics. "Makes me feel drunk. *Sloo-ah, shee* me another cup of tea, Bartender."

"Got it in one," he says. "You make a decent drunk. You *can* just call them sons of bitches, but then that's back to the perfect Siobhan.

Liam and I toast with teacups.

"I actually don't know what *Slaugh* are exactly," says Mealla. "They're aren't magical creatures."

"That's been a question since I can remember. Pre-Christian they were considered fairies gone amuck. Fairies without any degree of mercy or restraint." Not a far fall I think. "Post-Patrick they became packs of unforgiven souls, dead and unrepentant. One or the other or both, they steal souls of the living. They travel together and look like a vast flock of dark, brooding ravens."

"You can call them." Liam glances around him and whispers, "Just by saying their name." He laughs. "Hopelessness in the heart calls them too. Once you've got their attention you have to sacrifice another in your stead to get rid of them. Then there's the boils, skin lesions, abrasions after an airborne attack. Blood stains on rocks and stones of a dawn—"

"Thank you, Liam," Rose injects.

"It's not like bats though. They won't get stuck in your hair." He winks at Mealla. "Usually, they reserve their kills to cats, dogs, and sheep. If cats and dogs are the end point tomorrow, sure, we could all go home." He finishes with another wink at Rose. If you can't laugh in the face of danger, you're bullock'd.

"They seem to have gotten more aggressive," I add. They used to just carry the odd person away. They're being been influenced." What to do about these crowds of souls who roam without the constraints of mortal life, and outside the boundaries of the GrandOther.

Liam is studying the map of University College Cork. "Why here? Why not the ruins of the hellfire club on Montpelier Hill in Dublin? That place is brimming with energy from evil. Richard Parsons started the thing there in the seventeen hundreds. He was a black magic practitioner...satanist, devil worship the lot. A real hole-of-a-bugger. *Scaltheen* was his booze of choice."

"What *is scaltheen?*" asks Mealla.

"Considered putting in on my menu as a tourist attraction. I was playing with the ingredients. It's salted butter, brown sugar, ground pepper, water and Tullamore whiskey. My motto, a drop of *scaltheen* clears ye're head.

I knew him, Parsons. Never sat a drink with him, the 'King of Hell.' He was one scary boyo even for me. At their club meetings he used to wear horns, wings, hooves... the lot. He drank his *scaltheen* boiling hot. He'd get pished and talk a lot of shite."

"If you didn't associate, how do you know all that?" asks Mealla. Her face opens. "Ahhhh, you drank with someone else in the club."

One of the other wolves says, "There's was a hellfire in Askeaton off the N69 on an island in the River Deel."

"I know the one," another wolf says. "One Reverend Matthew Pilkington was a member, an absolute shite. Ladies-man, jailed, divorced. His ex, flat out broke had to become a prostitute. When she died, he married his mistress. He was loved by the then Archbishop of Dublin."

"All contenders. But there's real evidence for University College Cork," I say. "The *Tuatha* brought me *here*. Practitioners are melting their faces *here*. We found a hell of a magic circle in a hellfire meeting place on the campus *here*. If the place is not *here*, then the whole universe is having us on."

A battery-operated kitchen clock ticks off a few more precious minutes. I rub my whiskers and finish my cup of cold tea in one gulp. There are no prophetic leaves in the bottom of the cup, just five teabags in the pot. Our third pot. I'm wired.

"Raining soup and all we have are forks," says Buttermilk.

Fair enough.

"We still don't know what's coming. Any of you tried to battle a host of demons, on top of the *Slaugh,* like?" I take in their stricken faces. "Me either. It's got to be a nightmare."

"Nightmare fits. Think," Liam says. "Religion needs the faithful. It's symbiotic relationship. How to get those faithful back in a church...scare the shite out of them. It's worked over the ages. Sure, if we're about to confront demons of Hell with only our wankers in our hands, they better be pretty pointy."

"If I may," interrupts Rose in a give-me-strength tone of voice. "If we stop the practitioners, as we are going to, as is our job here, there won't *be* any demons. Let's not run away with ourselves."

"She's right," says Liam. "My apologies."

"Something else. To control magic, you either are a god, or you work for one, or you are aligned with something with eternal energy," says Mealla. "How about this. These practitioners are pretty old. This power-play won't last them very long. What, men are lucky to last to eighty? Most of these are in their sixties and seventies already. They aren't doing this for those who come after. Why do this at all without longevity, power over death? *That's* an immortal prerogative."

"Like tiny gods. Hey, shouldn't that be some short guy's porn handle?" Liam says. "Oh jaysus, sorry sisters."

Gotta give it to him. He's knocked it on the head. I start laughing uproariously. "Tiny God, the movie."

"Boys, boys, boys," chimes Rose, though she is smirking. To be honest with you, just now, I like her a bit better.

Mealla, carrying on, says, "Maybe it's that they're trying to resurrect...something, or someone. Not just summon them. That's would be face-melting job. Though that's a god-only job, and they're not there yet. Also how does that help them?"

I think of myself, "or time bend."

I can think of a lot of dead punters, and deceased, gifted practitioners, who fit into an end-of-world scenario. We all can, and that's why the table has gone quiet again. Desperate. Liam's probably rethinking his pack's involvement. This is something big, and we haven't gotten past tiny-god jokes.

That's how we've all gotten through life, though. We're all traumatized here. I've been under a *geasa* for half my life. The werewolves have seen the arsehole of life. Mealla… something's there. The nuns historically have created the arsehole of life. Point being. We can think on our feet.

"I *have* been working on the Blue Bottle." All eyeballs on Mealla. "It's a direct but murky conduit to the *Tuatha*. The thing about prophesies from most deities is that they're mostly inspirational, or a revelation of truth or knowledge. The barrier between worlds has to maintain an opaqueness. The children of Fatima would agree with me on that. Also, prophesies are available only at enough distance from their future so there's sufficient time for change. So there's that. The Tuatha didn't intend me to have the bottle; I took it. So they aren't going to be very helpful."

"So squat all," says Buttermilk.

"Maybe not. I'm working on getting a message from any one of them. There are lots of Irish gods, hundreds. I only need one, a D-list celebrity eavesdropper with a grudge. My chances could be decent."

"All we need to do is disrupt?" Liam asks. "Then let's put some people around the other areas as insurance."

"The Godsill's is uber prepared for something important. The old gaol a thin mile from the house. The *Slaugh* hit after we raided the house."

"Disrupting," Rose brings back Liam's thought, "is correct. Mealla, I'm not sure you've had time to realize all your gifts." Rose says.

The girl has hardly had time to shower, like.

"We are a small—"

There is a buzzer from the front door. The warded front door. The warded buzzer.

"Liam?" I ask.

"I'm not expecting anyone else," Liam replies. "I wouldn't think evil would press the buzzer though. Stupid way of going on if you're the bad yoke."

There is no scream of pain.

The buzzer sounds again, this time longer, like the yoke is leaning on it.

This is somebody. The thing about wards, there are naturally occurring loopholes. Mundane, benign bodies of the universe like the everyday postman get a pass. They can't get in, but ringing the bell will not produce instant cremation. In a word, semi-impermeable. A ward-hackers dream that.

Our barrier is anchored to the apotropaic magic of the Shelana-gigs. I also cut, with the tip of my Ogma's knife, the Ogham *Luis* into the doors. It's not complicated with a vertical line drawn downwards and a horizontal line drawn from the middle of that line out to the right. Symbolic of the rowan tree, *Luis* is strong apotropaic magic that protects against enchantment. It averts gods, and fairies, and black magic. It is the Ogham letter of Brigid. Our buzzer ringing is none of those then.

We use a simple, non-magical solution to the buzzer-ringer, the camera on the door. Liam, Rose, Mealla, and I walk to the front of the convent to check the computer. There is one spindly, old man, with sporadic grey whiskers, not more than five feet six inches if he was wearing heels. Of course size means nothing. As a practitioner, he could lift his arm to try and fireball through our defenses. Instead, he is pressing our warded bell, again. Then, looking into the camera, he mouths, "You don't have all the time in the world. I'm here to help."

Brillant and unbelievable. Sure, we can't move for people offering to help.

"He's not leaving," says Mealla. "It's weird, but then my weird barometer has run dry. Anyone?"

As an answer, the guys are turning into wolves behind me. Hundreds of years out of practice, the swearing, cracking of bones, and moaning is not encouraging. A pack of old men getting out of recliners. I glance over my shoulder to the were-wolves behind me—looking like they have alopecia. Good thing the buzzer is giving them a trial run.

I have to actually laugh when Mealla leans in and says, "Aren't they supposed to look fuller?" Then there's a concerned scrunch to her face. "Jesus Murphy, I hope I didn't hurt their feelings." God love her.

I turn back to the screen. I'm watching as our ten-foot, solid oak door, double thick, and warded is opening.

TWENTY-ONE

Millteoracht
Destruction

I get to the front door just as I hear a stranger say, "Liam. Looks like I found the right place."

"Bob the Knob," Liam returns. "Stand down everyone." As Bob steps inside, he pats my shoulder. "Jaysus, that's one powerful ward thee has."

Upon closer inspection, the fella looks real old with a smile revealing teeth so perfect and clean that he must take them out to eat to save on the wear and tear. In contrast, his clothes look like he never takes them off, and were picked up, years ago, from a free-stuff dustbin in front of a Depaul Homeless Charities Store.

He is relaxed, smoking. His elflocks a tangled, ropy red in color, and down to his shoulders. He senses my magical aggression because he brings up his smoke free hand.

I let Liam clear up the why-are-you-here bit. "What are you doing here?"

There you go.

"We've been watching since we felt thee," he says, glancing at me, a long look that is all about appraising what has been sent. "The electromagnetic shock of thee's arrival from the past. And then Moira, me sister, wasn't she in the church, and saw Saint Brigid turn her head, and a bright light exploding."

"How'd you figure out where we are?" I ask.

"Sean there, of Liam's pack, donates meat to travelers of the Saint Catherine's halting site in Kilkenny. We have a convoy of twenty-five families in white caravans setting up camp at the Curragh of Kildare currently. A bit of horse racing, as we're want. Just in the field above McDonagh Pitch and Putt Club. Sean dropped by saying he was leaving for Cork and a convent there. I didn't need to know which one. The magic around this one is a lighthouse in a bog.

When she's in Kilkenny my sister goes in of a morning to Saint Brigid's Church in the village. It's spare, just her and the cross, and she likes it. She returns the next day thinking she'd maybe do a double take, and what she sees then, over the front door of the carved timber, is the statue of Saint Brigid moving. This is Ireland. We get a particular buzz off moving statues. Like they are all step dancing to music only they can hear. Anyway, we figured that we should find thee."

"Bob here is a *Pavee* Magician. The *Pavee* means "'walking people in the Shelta language. They are commonly known as Travelers here in Ireland,'" says Liam.

"A Gypsy?" asks Mealla as she closes the big wooden door and checks the wards.

"He wouldn't be delighted if you called him that. The Irish *Pavee* and the Romani Gypsies aren't genetically similar, just their lifestyle. The Pavee could be pre-Celtic. They've been distinct genetically from today's mainstream Irish person for one thousand years."

"So you're here to help? How many?" I'm hoping for the feckin' United Front of *Pavee*.

"I have me brother Rory bringing a crowd. We are good at bare-knuckle boxing."

I can see from his dancing, blue eyes that he's taking the piss. That the help is most likely Bob and Moira. I glance at Liam. If I'm honest I can only think, he's a nutcase.

Buttermilk arrives and tosses out, "Spellthrower."

Now I'm interested.

+++

The kettle is put on the boil. Bob has his tea and is in a chair at the round table. The act of saving Ireland begins again. The prophecy of Fatima, the end of times. In fairness, every battle through the ages must have felt like the end of times to somebody.

If you had told Celts, back in time, that witches and Satan walked hand in hand, they would have thought you mad. The Irish only put to death one witch, Liam's friend. So what about witches. Join the group. The druids, the Tuatha, Saint Patrick, various saints, holy wells, all had powers.

Today, few Irish people consider themselves religious. Religioned out. But it's still there...the magic of spirituality, a hum of energy in the mists, valleys, passage tombs, dolmans, wells, and in the remains of stone circles.

"Thanks for coming, Bob," I say. He has the most neutral face I've ever seen. "Let me introduce you to Mealla. She's a descendant of Biddy Early." That brings a glance of interest to her direction from him. "And shamanic from her American side."

Bob stands and bows. *Pavee* are no nonsense. They call it as it lies. They are tribal, and deeply religious. The *Pavee* and Mealla's strain both love horses.

"You know Liam." I don't bother introducing myself. He knows. "When the goddesses put together this time bend, you'd think they'd had more of a plan going forward. They made a holy show disaster of the whole thing. I was attacked before I could cross the street. Not to mention what we've got here, great-lumps-of-stupid practitioners dissolving barriers so they can source magical energy."

Rose takes over. "We think they are using the concept of hellfire clubs, to organize themselves. We were wondering how to check on the two other club locations in Ireland, their involvement. Maybe now we can have the *Pavee* watch them on Saint John's Eve."

Bob scratches the scruff of beard. His face is fine-boned. His white skin appears nearly translucent. The man is outside all his life, but this is Ireland. His hands are not as fine as his face. They look used. His nose has been broken more than once, and leans. "Saint John's, is it? I'd think so. A brilliant day for magical energy." He reaches out to pat Mealla's hand. "Attacked straight out the gate? The shitehawks. Normally, the Eve is a fun time. There's dancing and music, and the pipes around the fire. Lots of drink. The fires are kept burning to dawn."

"Right then," Rose injects. "Bob, will you ask some *Pavees*, to light fires tomorrow night near the Dublin hellfire and the Limerick one, and to be ready for whatever? What does everyone think? We'll concentrate on the diabolical within the University College Cork campus, and its hellfire club. We are after disruption and containment. With any luck, the modern Irish will link what they may see to what they have been drinking."

"What about the *Garda*?" asks Bob. *Pavee* and the *Garda* don't mix too well.

"They'll be busy with partiers. We need a plan for when the *Slaugh* come back."

"Back?" Asks Bob.

"We took care of it," says Rose. "The other side would prefer not to let us get as far as tomorrow." From the kitchen, the sound of a pot hitting the bottom of a sink through greasy fingers startles us.

Bob is studying the walls, the ceiling, and the windows of the room. "Sure, this is a big building to defend. Good wards, but I can make them a bit better for thee."

"May I?" He wraps his hand around the open air in front of him and says Latin words under his breath. I feel energy rush towards him, like a table-top cyclone. The wind moves our hair, and cups fall from the table to the floor. Chocolate digestives slide off their plates, and then the plates slide off the table. Sister Rose grabs the floral teapot. With an easy javelin-like toss from Bob's hand, the invisible spell moves through walls and doors. We can hear it take hold, as timbers moan, and bricks clink. Savage skills. An asset worth having.

Here's one of my takeaways on all this: the statue of Saint Brigid of Kildare is moving. Which means Brigid of the Tuatha is active. "I've got to meet someone." No one asks why; it's gone beyond that. "I'm going to take Liam. I want to talk to a goddess. We'll be back before sundown." I say. Like I can guarantee that.

CHAPTER
TWENTY-TWO

Nasc
Binding

The gods draw their power from humans through prayer and faith. The humans get their magic from the gods through prayer and faith. Magic manipulates the energy of the world. To use it, humans need intermediaries, demons, angels, and even things like blessed amulets. Every religion sells holy trinkets. Who said magic comes at a price first...the Roman Church.

Numinomantic magic draws its power directly from supernatural beings. These beings are unpredictable, vainglorious, and outright bastards. They require a lot of tender loving care and groveling.

Not my style. But there's nothing for it today, I tell myself as I head for the blackthorn tree. Time to get some things straight, because the lot of us can't show up at the party without a gift. If the schizophrenic personality of the combined saint and the goddess Brigit is in the game, I get to ask her questions. She might even answer.

I return to Bishop Lucey Park. The *lunantisidhe* is going to be as accommodating as usual. The night is busy with traffic, but the park is dark. It's too far from the pubs, kababs, and the evening late-night-curry-and-chips crowd. It's not raining... hard, but that could change with a good wind.

A car screams by me and Liam. A percussion of air pushes against my side. The pace of life is modern. Mundane humans fill every minute of every day with trivia. It's not hard to understand why religion is losing ground. Only telling yourself there are no gods or things that go bump in the night, doesn't make it so. There's a shock is store.

The *Tuatha* will try. They'll sell themselves as the new-old. Or just take it all by storm, or fear. Gut-wrenching fear. It's worked before. It will work again. Humans are vulnerable and sometimes not very bright.

I'm mentally preparing myself for what I'm about to do, by telling myself that it has to be done. It's all been a bit fast. Mealla was a few days ago selling shamanic and Wicca claptrap on the internet. Well-informed, but unbelieving. Now she's being asked to trigger spells, under intense pressure, using a gift she's only known about for days, using the knowledge she had no faith in, using only her innate senses. Her willpower and mental dominance have never been tried or tested.

And then the werewolves that haven't changed or fought for centuries, soft as lambs, but they make damn good ale.

And then the *Pavees* and the nuns, both devoted to the power church as it was in the sixties and to druidic beliefs.

Not to mention the *Tuatha* of the GrandOther, a realm superimposed over the mundane world waiting and playing coy until they can lean in a bit closer.

Forest for the trees. What I need is something against the *Slaugh*. Dead things don't die twice, but they can be extinguished to Hell. The only way to get a magical item is to ask for it. They only way to ask for it is to go to the source.

With Liam at watch, I stand before the blackthorn tree. Its magic twisted and dark. Its goddesses and powers, the crones, the *Cailleach*, the waning of life, and the Morrigan—goddess of war and death. Guarded by *lunantisidhe*, mean troll-like fairies with manes of hair growing from their heads and their faces, and with teeth as sharp as the thorns of the tree and with pronounced noses that alert them to trespassers. *Straif*, the Ogham name of the blackthorn tree means 'sulphur.' It is a symbol of the vision of death and of sacrifice.

There's an old saying, 'Better the bramble than the black-thorn, better the blackthorn than the devil." And I'm not talking shite.

A man falls asleep under a blackthorn bush. He dreams that the fairies have stolen his corn. He learns how to get the corn back, but the fairies have enchanted the corn to kill the cows and pigs who eat it. That's the fairy way, and I've come knocking on their door. *Pog mo thóin*. Kiss my....

Using my Ogma knife, I scratch the Ogham, "Straith into the dirt against the roots of the tree." Three tipped horizontal lines cut by a vertical line and call out its sound.

"Ye're back." Her teeth click as she speaks.

"I'm reques—demanding an audience with Brigit."

The fairy laughs like she or I am mental, or both. How the *lunantisidhe* got the moniker, 'fairy lover,' is one of the great mysteries of this and the GrandOther. More like 'luna-tic-sidhe.'

The only cure for insanity is drink. I know the blackthorn fairies well and have brought lager. Not just any lager, Were-wolf lager. Not just one can, a twenty-four-pack. When she has drunk it all, I step over her, and feel the suction of The GrandOther.

"If it's drowning ye're after, it's the deep water ye're looking for," I hear the *lunantisidhe* call as an echo of the portal, and then a long belch.

"Feck off," I call back to her. I hear her laugh. Exercising her stomach muscles makes her fart.

Fairy Lover my arse.

It's true though about the deep water. I barely got out with my balls intact last time.

The place is singed looking. In all fairness, even as I'm stealth itself through the trees along the path, they aren't expecting to turf me out twice in twenty-four hours. I know where Brigit lives and am using the walking-time to remind myself that it's always a person's mouth that breaks his nose. So this is what I say to Brigit when I find her sleeping beside a pool of turquoise glacier water, "You all must be delighted with yourselves."

Because on the walk here I realize, Morrigan or not, they have to let me back out, and in one piece, or fight this war themselves. They haven't a notion. The Morrigan probably got a reprimand for the dogs the last time.

The *Tuatha* have a love for hiddenness and invisibility. The females change shape to hide their secrets. Some are phantasmal and appear to sight and sense but are not really there. Some are clairvoyant, while others need messengers.

To get to the pool out back, I walked through a doorway twenty paces wide to get inside the *Crédé,* or royal house. Inside are racks for weapons. Interesting. There are vats, warring platforms, a dais, and eventually gardens with cows and trees and water.

The Irish gods are perfection in artistic and professional skill. Skill without heredity is not sufficient in the GrandOther, or in my case partial heredity without skill. Hey, I'm not bitter.

Brigit is in good form. Eating from the feast of Goibniu that gives her immortality. Servants skitter around her.

Me too. Ick.

The daughter of the great Dagda is multitalented in magic.

"We need to talk."

"Do we, Padraic O'Duibh?"

I didn't come for this, but it's just so stuck to the side of my brain. "When is my *geasa*, unfairly hexed onto me by the Morrigan, going to end?"

"Stop standing over me boy and sit down. Ye've always been difficult."

Can you say shut your face to the Goddess of Poetry and Wisdom from whom you want a weapon of mass destruction?

I don't sit, and she sighs the mothers' sigh when they are tired and want to put up their feet with a strong alcoholic beverage, over ice, in their hand, and with a bath of hot water running in a scented bathroom with candles.

"Twasn't wasn't the Morrigan who loaned you out."

That explains the dogs.

"'Twas your father, Ogma."

"What?" Anger flashes red though my pricked skin.

"She waves a dismissive hand at me.

"Why, for feck's sake?"

"Why you? Well, this I *can* say. 'Tis not your way with words...legendary. Or your ways with women...hopeless. In fact, we were afraid you'd antagonize Mealla, and she'd get on the next airplane. Which almost happened but for the Kaiju. Was it Scathach who pointed out your impatience, impiety, and prideful, rebellious nature? Her best and her worst student ever. Then there's the aimlessness, the hubris—"

"Stop, you're making me blush."

"Oh, sit down, Padraic. Ogma did it because he believes in ye. He made quite the strong case. He had to. Ye came for a conversation; we're having one. Let's finish before someone discovers ye're here again. You've made enemies, and your contributing to my headache."

"Too much of the feast of Goibniu?"

Her face scrunches in pain, real and maybe psychological. I

work hard at being a pain in the arse because they deserve it. Maybe not the wise Brigit, though. But it's become a habit.

"You're right there," says Brigit, reading my thoughts. "You're not a young man anymore, and adolescent truculence is unbecoming in adulthood." She fixes an eye on me, which you do not want from the Goddess Brigit. "It has become a habit." She deep-inhales the rose-scented air as a calming gesture. "Ogma suggested you as a way to snap the tether on the *geasa* and also to prove yourself. You're coming of age, a bit late, but I'll have you know, he is ever mindful of you."

"No warning, no information."

"You don't attach to people. You hide behind humor and a clownish face. You are highly intelligent, but deeply hurt, and dismissive, and cynical. How else was it to be done? You do see though the pain of others. It's that strength, and the element of surprise, that we have been counting on. I think it is working. Here you are looking for weapons," she finishes.

"What do the *Tuatha* get out of this?"

"We've simply been asked."

"By the nuns? What's their angle?"

"Pursuing evil is their...angle."

I study her. That can't be all. Her current glamour has been chosen to hide secrets, and to act on my nature. Motherly. Of course, the moment I stepped onto the GrandOther, she sensed I was here. Of course, there is more to this than pursuing evil. Maybe not for the nuns, but for the *Tuatha*. The nuns are enabling them.

I note a halo of light around her. Probably from her being syncretized by the monks in my old time with the holy Saint Brigid of Kildare. Two became one.

"What do you have back in there to fight *Sluagh*?"

"Nothing there will work for the mundane on the earthly plane. The Ogma's knife, and the Ogham letters are in your bloodline. We sent with ye and to you all that will be useful. You have the, *gae sí*, fairy darts and the blackthorn."

"The souls of the *Slaugh* don't swell or get sepsis," I say.

"What of your priestly knowledge? Their black arts? Their plans are invisible to us. You, being a priest of the Catholic Church still, we hoped that would be of some benefit to you. When ye proselytized yourself to the church for protection from the Morrigan and from your *geasa*, it was a permanent act, was it not?"

"Yes because of the sacramental character of ordination I maintain the power of orders. But I have been signed off from the priesthood through laicization and dispensation. I'm not involved anymore. I'm not privy to their conversations."

She studies me. "Is there any magic in that, which ye can use against the *Sluagh*?"

"Would I be here if there was?" Tiredness strikes my heart like a bolt, dead on target. I drop into the previously offered chair. I'd been fighting who I am for too long. I'd never really liked making my way alone, of being mixed in with, but not part of these antediluvian aboriginals, who have been taking the piss off me since I was left to them at my mother's death. Yes, I'd become a priest to get some upper hand. After all Patrick had defeated them. But then I found as much devilry there.

The *geasa* sucked what was left dry.

Brigit is taking in my hang-dog face because she says, "The *geasa* will end. The Morrigan has pledged it." Brigit means it, with kindness.

"I only have to defeat practitioners, the Prophecy of Fatima, and the Wild Hunt of soul-sucking *Sluagh* to get there," I mumble.

"You just have to stop them from whatever their shenanigans are. The rest will follow."

I glance up at the goddess. Her eyes are on the next strawberry she is selecting from a crystal bowl, not on me. Secrets. She is full of them. "What is it you really want? What are you afraid of?"

"What ridiculous nonsense."

Effin' Gods.

I clap my hands and then rub them together. "That's it then. I see it's proceed as normal, half-assed, and practically naked. You lot are a lot of fun. Never a boring second. The *geasa* will be finished anyway when this body is dead and buried."

"I'm not surprised the priest are using the *Slaugh*," muses Brigit. "They've been praying for the dead for so long in their rituals, that all that attention is paying off."

"We figured that out."

"Then there you are. Go away with ye now and do your job," says Brigit, like the great nit she can be."

Posers

"I was lucky coming in. It could be a bit of a bother getting out. You might raise up off the sofa for a moment, and sort that out, seeing as I'm the Champion."

She walks me out herself, and with me giving every god that dislikes me the finger on the way. Now this is service.

"People are depending on you," the clairvoyant Goddess says as she gives me a "little" push into the portal.

"Ok then. Definitely happening," I say to Liam as we walk away from Bishop Lucey Park. "I will fight every fight, but not as the Tuatha's champion, but as me, as a human with choice."

"They give you anything besides a pep talk?"

"Not a thing. Seems I'm too mundane to use such fancy things here."

Liam elbows me. I'm thinking he's commiserating with me like. Yeah, no. Werewoves have sharp eyes, and he motions with his head out the park gate and into the shadows of a building. He peels from my side, a flanking motion.

As I leave the park, I see the man loitering just out of the light of a lamp. I glance around the dark spaces for hidden beings…searching for hidden pictures like in the foliage and in the patterns of rock walls. I sniff for demon scent or the floral musk of gods of The GrandOther. There is an aura from the man, the light from the sacramental character of ordination. Good guy or bad, he is waiting for me. As I walk forward, it comes to me why the nuns are involved. Nuns have always known what these chancers are capable of.

He helps me close the space by sauntering towards me; his hands in front of him. A lit smoke in his right hand, he stops within earshot, takes a long drag, and drops it to the cement. Embers bounce. He squashes it. No wonder Cork is a tip. I am open-sensed and aware of anything thing that moves. Basically, I'm jumpy with weapons ready.

"Just returned from Mag Mell?"

Bad guy. "You mean Gag Mell or Hag Mell? Sometimes I'm partial to Shag Mell, but then there's always Nag Mell. Just dropping in to see my old friend Brigit."

The practitioner smiles one of those depreciating smiles that the powerful are so good at. "So you're Padraic O'Duibh. It's a sad state of affairs the old gods had to reach so far into the past for help. They just aren't current to the world. Scathach hasn't trained a warrior in centuries. They are only large in their own minds, the Tuatha."

"It took a time bend."

"So it did." He fake-gasps and then chuckles.

"Yup, I'm all they've got."

"And that Métis woman."

This twice-over depreciation tells me the practitioners are underestimating Mealla and me, even more than I underestimate Mealla and me. To them we are bargain-basement, half off, of half off. So I don't know why they are trying so hard to kill us.

He's all in black, like…a stereotype, with his white collar. His belly bespeaks good food and plenty of libations. A man who chose his employment for the vacation time, job security, the handouts, and the power over other people's lives.

"I'm here to offer you a place on the winning side. From what I hear, you aren't fond of the old guard, or them of you."

"Now how'd you get that idea? The gods and I have been shagging each other over right, left, and center." I'm upping my bad-ass ratio if he's been sent to negotiate loyalties.

"Lot of money in magic," he offers.

"I've been on both sides, and I don't like either of them."

"From what I hear you've never been on either side."

"I'm really not a 'sides' sort. I'm more like a, 'are-you-a-wanker' deciding sort. I'm thinking that you are. When's your day in court?" Probably digging my grave with my mouth, again.

Right full of himself, the practitioner laughs. His lungs have that wheeziness that comes from smoking too much. I could take him in a fight, unless he pulls a gun, which he does. Why complicate things with magic.

"Suit yourself. Thought we'd try."

"So original. What are you all the mafia now?" I blather on asking how many people has he shot? Is there dispensation for maybe two, like?

"Surprise," says a creature with claws, teeth, and fur that lands squarely on the wanker's head. The shot goes wide as Liam tears out the practitioner's throat.

Liam changes to human form seamlessly.

"Getting good at that."

"All in the wrist. What should we do with him?"

"Leave him. Let the garda figure him out. I say we leg it."

We walk. "They sent one...one fat bloke with a gun to take me out."

"You should be insulted."

His soul left to join the Wild Hunt. We'll see him tomorrow. He'll probably be more effective dead.

CHAPTER

TWENTY-THREE

Taibhse
Ghost

T he *Tuatha* rules of war are first win by trickery, then bring some magical weapons with you, carry sharp swords, and have some powerful druids for mists and storms.

Also, bring a ringer.

After my one-sided gunfight in the streets of Cork, I realize that weapon-wise humans have choices that we are underutilizing. I don't have to just bring a magical club to a gunfight. We can use weapons that are less up close and personal, something with a striking distance.

Still, we're fighting magic. So a gun with a kick.

"Guns easy to come by?" I ask Liam.

"There aren't a lot in Ireland, so it depends on where you're looking."

"The *Pavees*?"

"Of course."

To any observer, we are two lads chatting and walking, in the evening dark, through fog and rain. Normal. Cork is a dense city of row shops and terraced houses, with preserved medieval lanes that can lead to nowhere. Plenty of concealment in narrow dark corners. As mist and haze was a favored tactical magic of the druids, we are marking obscure movement and shapes, on the road back to the convent.

We pass the defunct, Beamish Ale building with a mock-Tudor façade. "I cut my teeth there," comments Liam. Beamish Draught Irish Stout. Bought out by Heineken. Mild roasted and bittersweet. Excellent on nitro."

I'm reminded that he is a werewolf that has become accustomed to the good life. I won't ask him if he's gone good. He just killed a human. He's been a werewolf for a longer time than he's been a peaceful brewer. He didn't kill men as a werewolf. He was bang on that practitioner though.

Alongside the brewery is a wee lane I remember from my old days, Lamley's Lane, a narrow cut-through, off the main road to the River Lee and to the convent. At the end of it, we are standing with the toes of our shoes just on the edge of the concrete wall that confines the river. The stone walls of buildings on both sides, and the river mean dead end lane. The close-by bridge, inaccessible.

"This wall couldn't be closer to the river if it was in it."

The water is dark and funereal, as it runs past us to the sea. Shite dark. I move away from the edge of blackness flowing past. Originally, taking us down Lanley Lane, I thought concealment and cut-through, but now we are blocked, a deadly position. "Shite," and to Liam, "I'm sorry." On the other side of the Lee, I see an edge of the red brick of the convent, in between two river-front, four-story apartment blocks.

Not one hundred feet away is the small bridge I'd thought to cross. It drops us on the lap of the courtyard of the convent. If we can get there. On our left, the old Beamish and Crawford warehouse was built on the edge of the cement wall of the river. Same on the right.

"Let's double back."

Liam points out a fire escape off the side of the left-hand building.

The feeling that luck is not a bitch, and that all mistakes are forgiven is always brief. If we cross the roof, it's a skip and a jump to the bridge. Fifty more feet to another lane, and into the green courtyard of the convent. I'm just saying, what could go wrong in say one hundred and fifty feet?

A screeching that the Banshee would be jealous of, like?

Liam's sensitive ears must have exploded. Ashrays, or river ghosts of those souls drowned in water, grab for our ankles. More controlled the souls of the dead. Proof that evil never gets to rest.

Slaughs, and ashrays, and ghosts. The practitioners *are* good at commanding the souls of the dead. It's brilliant. A Requiem is the liturgy for the dead. It's offered for the repose of souls, a shortcut out of Purgatory. Priests have been praying souls out of Purgatory and Hell for thousands of years. That's a lot of grateful, captive souls with nowhere to go.

The movement of the translucent souls causes the river to foam. Their lashes of seaweed cut through our clothes and our flesh, even with us turning to leg it.

One well aimed lash snakes around my leg, and an Ashray yanks me onto my arse. Ashrays drown anything that seeks air to live. They are nocturnal, when exposed to sun, they melt into puddles of water. Not happening at midnight. I grab the seaweed and pull back, but six more whips wrap my arms.

I glance at the werewolf. Liam has shifted. Torn clothing remains on his hairy, built musculature. With huge teeth, he is tearing through the green bindings that constrain him. A single chomp severs rope after rope.

I press my heels against the lip of the river wall to keep on land.

At the same time, I strain against the pull on my arm I'm working to unsheathe the Ogma's knife. The muscles in my Ogma's hand strain against the force. I'm too bound, but I manage to free and grasp the knife just as I'm yanked midair over the River Lee.

Irish water is artic in temperature. It's a freezing baptism that knocks my lungs airless. I concentrate on one thing…don't drop the effin' knife.

The river has been so encased that the sides have no purchase. It's a tributary, so smaller than the main river, and shallower, but tidal, and the tide is in. They will find my body by the seaside. With my legs wrapped in sea rope, it's down to mermaid kicks towards air. Squirming really. I don't know how to swim. Even though it's an island nation, and even though it was a country of fishermen, the Irish didn't learn to swim. The water's frigid; there's no lasting. I'm moving by instinct. Dog-like. When even just hovering over water a dog starts moving its legs.

Hopeless though. I'm sinking, like you would if you can't swim, and have two legs bound like a mummy.

My slammed lungs burn. I slash with the knife and free my arms, but I'm still bound below. What ropes I cut are back return on steroids. The dead are relentless.

I hear the percussion of another something large hitting the water. Shite, must be Liam.

You're a priest. Brigit's words come to me. *There's some magic in that.*

It's high tide. Salt mixed with the river water. The simple ritual flows through my mind. I begin with the consecration of the salt. This river is tidal and mixes with the sea. The prayer itself is long, but I'm panic-reciting. Next, I exorcise the water. I stir the salt and the water with my bound legs and make a kind of sign of the cross with my fingertips, and then let even more prayer words flow through my mind.

If this works…jaysus.

I bless the water. By now, my entire torso is wrapped, a bun around sausage, like

"Amen," I call out.

The river rolls like it's boiling hot. I hope that means vaporizing invisible Ashrays. The green falls from my body. I hit bottom. My last effort is to push off and up with my legs. My head breaks the water line. I take a breath and go under again. I'm kicking like maniacal scissors. How can so much motion produce so little thrust? My arms thrash as my head again reaches air. I don't know if Liam is already drowned.

I grab at the lichen and fern growth out of cracks in the concrete. It tears off in my hand. The practitioners didn't need the Ashrays to drown me. They just needed to push me in.

I sink again. I push off the bottom, I breathe. Repeat. When my head breaks the surface a fourth time, I'm grabbed and hauled to shore. Liam pulls me up and onto the concrete surface. I turn over and cough and sputter and breathe for a few minutes.

"Jaysus, that was close," says the wet werewolf as he slides down next to me.

"So you aren't dead yet." I'm rocket-snotting river-water from my nose.

"Nearest thing I've been in a long, long time."

I cough, trying to wring out my lungs. "Holy water."

"Feckin'-A. You had some?"

"I made some." I glance at the slow-moving water. "A river full."

He pats me on the back. "If you drown in consecrated water, do you go to heaven?" he jokes.

"I must ask a knowledgeable priest when I find one. Let's get across that bridge before all this holy water runs into the ocean."

Our feet pound across the bridge and down the lane between apartment buildings. We don't stop until the grass in the convent courtyard. I'm dripping in Lee water. Liam is naked. It's pissing down buckets, and we are laughing as you have to when you have stared at death, and not flinched, and survived.

"Feckin'-A," Liam huffs out. "It's been a long time."

+++

I hear a beer tab pop as Liam walks into the dining room from the kitchen. We are all back at this feckin' table. "The practitioners have been historically a strong adversary. They owned the world at one time. They dominated from those massive churches on the hill."

"It's a hard sell, if they want that power back." Mealla's turn. "Human faith is low. They'd have to bring in the power of hell."

"That's always been their go to. "The punters wouldn't blink an eye." I tuck into cold ham and bread and salami. "It's taking us too long to remember how many types of dead souls there are. It's going to be all head and quick thinking."

Rose drops into the chair she has brought with her. She is still put together, her hair tight in a bun, her clothes immaculate and pressed within an inch of life, but she sits as though her legs won't stand any longer. Exhaustion pours from her like sweat. Talk about faith. Hers is fading in general or in us, hard to tell.

"You brought up guns, if only we could shoot holy water, long range, like a tsunami," says Mealla who is creativity gone wild in personality. "Like fire hydrants with hoses."

"Hard to holy-up one of those."

One of the younger *Pavee* lads speaks up. "SplatRBall." He glances at our faces that probably look blank, but desperate. He shakes his head at us oldies. "You've never heard of that? Semi to full auto action. Shoots eight rounds per second; four hundred round magazine of water beads."

Mealla looks delighted with herself.

Liam puts his fork down and rubs his hands on his pants before picking up his phone. We are silent enough to hear the mobile phone assist ask if she can help him. "Call Michael. Hey, yeah, we need SpatRBalls, couple dozen." He folds the mobile closed. "The water guns use water beads that are made of water and an absorbing polymer. When immerse in water, they fill up like a sponge….and splat! Got two in the boot."

—///—

I'm stirring a rainbow of beads, with my hand in the holy water, watching them engorge. So satisfying. "We should test the theory on some dead soul."

Sister Rose's lips are pressed like she's trying to keep words in.

"Have some faith," I insist to a nun.

She clicks her tongue. She doesn't need words to say, that's a stupid way of going-on. Taking a half–cracked risk and exposing ourselves to danger, as we have ben doing. But if the guns works a very big problem will be sorted. And shooting holy water pellets into *Slaugh*, how can that not be the best craic ever?

I know the dead man I want to try the beads on; the one haunting the Franciscan Well Brewery.

"It's over two bridges to get there, and then you're along the river." Rose's silence breaks.

I huff. "Options? See if it works as the *Sluagh* are soul-sucking us? The water beads should work on the Ashrays too. We're not walking over the river."

Silence.

"Rose, it's a test for all of us. Jaysus, if we can't handle the one dead fella in a pub, we might as well stay home on the night." That's Liam.

"It's a very easy number," I say.

"How do we get the yoke to materialize?" asks a werewolf.

The room is quiet because there is always someone who comes up with the point that there is always one more thing.

"He'll know Sean and Liam are werewolves when you walk in," says Mealla.

"He'll show. He's that vain. He'll want the entertainment. It's his home turf."

"If the pellets don't work?" asks Rose.

I pull a largish bottle of water out of my jacket. "Just in case the water beads don't have enough water in them." I thumb-indicate to bottles on the table. "Each of you has one."

Liam lets the front legs of his chair drop to the floor. Seems his thing. "Aren't you the lad?"

"Yeah, but…" a werewolf begins.

Everyone sighs as hope is once again hole-punched.

"…how are we going to get in?"

I look at lock-pick nun, "No problem."

Buttermilk is there. "You ever shot a gun of any kind? Bow and arrow?" She is watching my face. "No, I didn't think so. It's harder to hit something than you think, especially when it's moving about."

Completely believable that she knows that.

TWENTY-FOUR

Toghairm
Summoning

We are flying down Main Street, in the Mini, Sean, Liam and I. Constance, wasn't going to be left behind. The Garda don't give nuns tickets she has explained. Still, it's great not to worry about tickets, or other cars in the light traffic of what's now early morning. The worry is all about the mythological dead. Why can't dead mean dead?

Loads of parking in front of the arched tunnel of the old Franciscan Friary.

"Why'd we leave Mealla? Wasn't she sent for this too?" asks Liam as he is standing beside me.

"Last time we were here, Laurent went for her, like she was the woman who killed his mother."

"He didn't have a mother."

"He's afraid of her shaman'ness."

"That he is," Liam agrees.

I explain that the magic Laurent uses to make himself corporal enough to do damage to us will take a lot of energy. "The magic comes from the essence of the priory that was here, and the graveyard. He can't leave. So any problems, just make for the door."

The nun picks the lock, and once again I pass through the copper-plated door surround. This time I'm more wary, and with two werewolves.

"Ah smell that." Liam inhales the smell of hops as he follows. As I walk to the back, and out into the Plexiglas-roofed outdoor area, he samples a few taps behind the bar and then begins to change. The Pompeii Pizza hutch has the low glow of left-on lighting. I smell the coming rain and pepperoni.

There's no sitting with my back to the wall for protection. Laurent's hands can come through it and choke the life out of me. I hop over the front counter of the pizza place, and glance around for anything the corporal dead can pick up and throw. I feel easier when all I see are rotary pizza cutters. We gather, Liam, Sean and I in the middle of the outdoor patio area on the monk's graves, so our backs are to each other.

I hear each of the werewolves breathing hard, waiting.

The walls have eyes, and the taps have ears. Though Laurent knows what Liam is...evil narcissists, they always think they're better.

I feel the coarse hair of Liam and Sean's wolf through my shirt.

So still. Maybe I overestimated Laurent's ego.

"I hear your bitty, human heart thrumming like it's an expert on a *bodhran* drum," says Liam.

"I'm fine," I say back.

That is, until a milky mist, much like a druid-conjured fog, rises from the floor. Freezing as a Finnish grave, the spreading mist numbs my toes. It can, if cold enough, freeze your lungs if you inhale it. I raise my weapons and stamp my feet. There is no substance to the enemy. The mist swirls as Liam tries to punch through it.

My freezing feet feel clumsy as we move away. I fall over a stool. The mist reaches for me. Liam hauls me up. I tried to hold my breath on the way down, but I'm coughing from the ice crystals embedded in my throat.

The mist is up to our chests now. Their fur and metabolism keep them warm, but even werewolves have to breathe. The crystals will freeze over wolf eyes. Laurent will be able to pick us off at his leisure.

We are hustling into the rain that has begun to fall through the open spaces in the Plexiglas roof. The precipitation is beating down the mist. Warm drops wash my face. It's the first time an Irishman has ever been thankful for pelting rain.

I'm feeling movement return. The floor is like an early spring thaw. Warmer air melts the crystals in our lungs.

Recovering, I head to the pizza counter. I stumble and rise and then fall, then claw my way over the top of the counter. I switch on the ventilating system. "Feckin' yeah," I say at its powerful suction. I watch the mist straight-line up and out.

Laurent is, in the moment, a creepy, invisible laugh. He's not done. We haven't seen as much as a ghostly eyeball.

At least two dozen *bagairts*, ghosts, are becoming as corporal as any army unit.

"Give them time to become substantial," I remind the wolves.

From Liam, "Let's sort this shite out."

I love that guy. I always have.

"Let's see if these arseholes are corporal enough to die twice."

The dead have resurrected with pieces of coffin wood as shields. Their weapons I recognize, *bolines*. The curved, double blade of Damascus steel with a bone and wood grip was a trademark of the Franciscan order. Each *boline* was matched to its monk-owner and eventually buried with him. We are surrounded. I don't have enough rounds, but I have were-wolves. The werewolves descend on the bogles and open their backs, tearing off arms, legs, and heads. All three werewolves are a frenzy of teeth and claws.

The bogles fight back, slashing at the werewolves' thick pelts. The bogles don't bleed, but the wolves do.

One ghost-monk, his face a decayed pulp of an eye, and a lipless grin, slashes towards my chest. I dodge, and swing for his head, and miss. I shoot him. The water burns him. He falls back but doesn't die. Shite. There's two more on either side going for me, *bolines* raised to slice through my neck.

These bogles have been brought back from the dead to be used as weapons. Death magic, wielded by Laurent, who is dead. Impressive. He was educated and knew exorcism and demonology. Laurent was the life and soul of necromancy, a sort of madness in him. Not unbelieved the rumor that he ritualized his death.

One thing about reanimating the dead, the brain tissue is the first to decay and the last to arrive. I slip between them, and let the *bogles* carve into each other, long cuts that catch their eye sockets, mouths, and necks. Primordial goop is everywhere.

Blood is mixing with water and goop. The floor is slick. The shower-of-shite *bogles* are thinning, but not fast enough. The werewolves are looking like their pelts are being stripped off in lengths to make coats. We are not winning.

I shoot holy-water pellets at a *bogle* as a machine gun round. He evaporates like. Finally. The shite. I'm not sure if he's gone. He was dead before. Feckin' treat, these resurrecting dogs.

Liam falls against me. I slam hard on the ground. My head hits the cement floor. The hit reverberates into my neck and arms. The bead gun flies from my viscose hand.

Laurent's laugh has been background music the whole time.

I grab the *bogle*-feet next to me and pull. *It's gotta stop.* The animated bones hit the ground. I dose them in a slug of holy water. The werewolves are still upright; only Liam has two hanging off him.

Magic has a price; it eats up energy like a race car eats up petrol. Laurent is pouring copious amounts of his energy into his dead army. These punters will flag soon. Before or after we're dead is debatable.

I rake the thorns of my blackthorn up through the pelvis and ribs of the nearest monk. Not for sepsis. I call, *"Luis."* The zombie portals somewhere. Hasta Luego.

Next, I smash in the leering face of another punter. I duck at as a spinning blade fire-flies at me.

Give over, you stupid bollocks.

I'm slammed from behind and am back down in the muck. My blackthorn is kicked away. Liam sees it. God, he looks like offal from a meat factory covered in black fur.

Still, Liam bares his teeth at the corporal specter in his face. He pounds on it until its spiritual fluids are ejecting from its mouth. He's not holding back on these sonofabitches either.

The blackthorn is kicked around in a brawl of entities pounding each other in a small space. Wooden stools and chairs lay broken on the floor, skeleton like. The werewolves are using wooden parts, and skeletal parts as bats. It's become an Irish *bataireacht*, a stick fight, after all.

Sean slides across the top of the outdoor bar. There are small explosions of breaking glass. The magic is heating the area like a fever.

There has to be an end. Laurent has to run out of energy. This is a hell of a lot of magic here. He's always had endurance.

Show yourself, you wanker.

I don't have to try and stand, because my throat compresses, and I'm lifted from my feet. It's not long to black out. I scratch at my neck with my free hand. Laurent. His arms are corporal. That's got to be enough to get at him. I grasp Ogma's knife. Carve onto an arm the Ogham for the Rowan Tree, the portal tree, with the pentagram inside the seeds.

"*Luis,*" I croak.

The hands shimmer into nothing. The army of monks melt into the floor.

"That's for you, you slack, medieval shite."

Sean, Liam and I do what you do after a challenging fight, stand in place, take it in, and breathe—or try to breathe with the sear of over-worked magic still strong in the air. The inside of the place is in bits. Smoke and grain dust make the air opaque. Within the brewing part of the brewery, an explosion sends glass shards flying. Us too.

Constance is there. Moving us through the smoke and flames, piling the lot of us into the Mini one by one.

"The authorities will put it down to a grain dust explosion," she says with her foot on the gas. "They'll have to because there is no other explanation in their minds."

The two werewolves are in the back. Their heads lean back on the seat. "What the hell just happened back there?" moans Liam.

I cough up grain and smoke.

"How'd you end it?"

"Portal'ed him to hell. I think. I hope. It might not stick."

"These guys mean business."

"I'll agree with that for nothing."

╫

Mealla finds me slumped in a reception room chair avoiding the nuns and letting the werewolves heal. The room is cold and lonely; the chairs rarely sat in, the carpet as if new. It's a room that exudes the feeling that people are meant to be here by invitation only. She sits next to me. The firm sofa cushion doesn't dent under her weight. The thing was bought to last.

"The wolves did a hell of a job," I say to her in a tone that says shit hit the fan, and there was nothing to be done for it.

"Don't worry. I think they enjoyed it."

I back-nod as in agreeing. "The holy water beads only burned them unless you used up the lot. We'll run out of ammo quickly."

"It's a deterrent. That's something. I should have been there. You can't keep leaving me with the nuns."

"You," my hand pops a pointed finger at her, "are the ringer." Ok, I was getting a little pissed as in drunk. She pours herself a whiskey with a glass she brought with her. I am drinking from the bottle.

"Did you know that shamanic beliefs are the primal religion of mankind?"

"Yeah? Well only old people attend services here anymore. But, Liam told me, people still baptize their babies, have first communion and confirmation, because the church runs ninety percent of the hospitals and schools."

She sips some of the elixir of life. "One foot in the door. One foot out."

"The collection basket is heavy...with coins."

"Slowly going broke."

"Did I tell you that the shower-of-shite gods didn't tell me that I couldn't work magical weapons on the mundane plane? I'm not magical enough."

"I think you're pretty magical." She clinks glasses with me. "This isn't going to be waltz in, disrupt the proceedings, and waltz out, is it?"

"I wouldn't say so."

"At least this time you burned the place down without me."

We clink glass to bottle and each pour two fiery fingers of whiskey down our throats.

TWENTY-FIVE

Tuar
Omen, prophesy

The day of Saint John's Eve and all of us, I, Mealla, the werewolves, and the *Pavee* hadn't slept. Nobody could sleep. No one wanted to sleep. We didn't think we had cracked what was ahead of us.

Four o'clock in the morning, we hear the nuns' hymns of praise. Women are made of sterner stuff.

The nuns need the praying of the Liturgy of the Hours, which praise God, and sanctify the day. There's magical energy there for them that we're all going to need.

A few nuns cook breakfast while the rest of us gather what we have prepared, amulets, blessed charms for luck and healing, crosses. Like a multi-denominational, religious boot camp.

We bolt down a full Irish, white and black pudding sausages, fried eggs, tinned beans, brown soda bread, rashers. Pots of strong tea. The dining room smells glorious. Can't help but think, last supper…uh breakfast.

I sit with the *Pavee.* I need some assurances.

"What's your source of power?" I ask Bob without preamble. He's slender, but wiry with old ropy muscles. I put his age at fifty. Closer in though, seeing the thick, blue veins and arthritis bumps on his hands, I put that out farther.

"I see what thee is thinking. Is it possible to do it alone without the women?" He pats my shoulder. "The concern is good."

I wasn't thinking that. These women can and will always speak for themselves.

"They said ye'd never stick it. I said ye would."

"Who's 'they.'"

He laughs as he moves away. He talks to all the tables as he meanders to the kitchen.

I move over to a seat next to Liam. "What/who is Bob?"

"He's sort of everything, I guess."

"I'm half torn about him."

"He's an arsehole that you need, to clear out the shite."

"So you don't like him."

"Nah, I like lots of arseholes, even you."

There's the sound of dishes and cutlery being cleaned, and soft conversation. I watch Bob chat up a nun to get another egg. She wasn't going to give him one, like? I don't know, maybe she wasn't. It's a convent.

Liam sees me studying Bob.

"He's an enchanter from a long line of magicians. He can put a spell on an ant to run backwards. He's *Pavee.* Their moral compass is not mainstream. Not bad, but they look at the world differently. They're very religious. He's *the* man in The Sodality of Our Lady. You wouldn't have heard of it. Started by a Belgian Jesuit in fifteen sixty-three. It was started then for young boys in college. It got bigger, mainstream. It was the beginning of the church serving the poor. A dusty conservative, he's a pain in the asset that way. He's also a bit druidy. He's a blending of the old religion and the new. Almost its own church."

"Would you trust him with your life?"

"I'm just saying, if he's in for a cause, he's in."

+++

"Let's make a start, shall we?" Rose begins like she's organizing a charity walkathon. "The objective is to keep the practitioners from being successful at whatever they are attempting to do at the Godsill house on the UCC campus. We have a where. We have seen the circle there. It was the Lamborghini of circles. We did destroy it, but it can be rebuilt. Anything to add to any of that?"

"Do we kill the practitioners, like?" asks one of the two young *Pavees* in the room.

A murmur animates the dining room.

"Let's see if they don't take care of that themselves." She compresses her mouth and shakes her head. "No. Whatever you can do, do. That means take care of anything you see that you can influence. Don't wait for orders. Be watchful, watch everything. Watch out for each other."

"So you say. But how do we stay out of fooking trouble with the guards?" Fair dues, the *Pavee* lad is rightly concerned.

Bob pipes up, bright, like. He's not bothered, "I'll take you all in hand. We'll all take care of the outcome."

"And thanks for coming out to help," pipes up Mealla. I get the feeling she's very glad that in end, it's not just the nuns, me and her.

"The werewolves are escorting all the civilian sisters to the Poor Clares. Some members of the *Pavee* traveling community are watching over the Limerick hellfire club. They know what they're up against. Same in Dublin for the hellfire club there."

Rose is there, dressed in black pants, shirt and weatherproof jacket. Same with her nuns. And not a fear of it.

I'm feeling something like shite, and the fan, and all that bollocks.

I notice that we all hear it at the same time; heads raise, motion stops. A sound noticed in a split second of silence, like millions of ants walking and shifting grains of sand, or like entire walls of termites eating. The windows darken as if covered, and then pinpoints of light flashes in them in a chaotic but slow rhythm.

"What do you think?" I put out there for anyone to grab.

"Magical lightening bugs," says Bob. "Blanketing the wards."

"What? Shite, never heard of it."

"The flash is simultaneous bioluminescence. They are injecting oxidized luciferin into the ward. Millions of pin-prick injections."

Under the pressure of these millions of minute, fiery explosions like, the wards will fall.

Then, there's a cacophony of sound as something is smashing against the walls, breaking, cracking, pushing through.

I'm thinking chapel. Knee-jerk to the days between me and the *Tuatha*. That's when an exterior wall collapses. A wind blast gut-punches me. We're all blown against interior walls and ground into them.

The wind is like a stampede in my ears. Debris pummels my spleen, ribs, and head like professional punches only there is no one to fight against. Glass pieces cut my arms and face.

A *Pavee* is sucked into the vortex, flying to the apex of the ceiling. Pinned there like a kite. Even the superior strength of the werewolves is no match.

I can hardly breathe. It's like drowning again, but in air

pressure. Incrementally, I try to move my arm down to my hips. Any global movement in any direction will snap your bones.

I can't get to my knife. Using the fingernail of my index finger from Ogma's hand, I try to carve, "*Beith,*" into the plaster of the wall. The Ogham letter is release, rebirth. I recite the magic of the Ogham word against pressure of the wind on my lips and my lungs. I can't speak it.

Something crashes through the brick wall and flies at me hitting my left arm. The gale picks up the Fiat in the driveway and hurls it through the open wall, just missing Mealla. I watch it miss her by inches and explode into the wall holing it. Shite.

I carve the letter again as deeply as I can. Trying for more depth than before into the wall behind me. Maybe the first time it wasn't the Ogham letter at all but just disconnected lines. A single vertical line with a single horizontal line branching out from the middle. In desperation, I force out the word that is the catalyst, expelling the last gasp of breath-pressure from my lungs.

The release is sudden. I fall to the floor. The poor lad on the ceiling screams his way down. With Bob now able to stand, he positions his body to mimic a crane standing in the water. One eye closed, standing on one leg, his arm outstretched, he evokes *Corra-Griothach,* Crane Knowledge, a higher level of magic known only to ancient priests such as Saint Columba of Iona. Now I get who he is. He couldn't have told me sooner, using words.

An upward force cushions the lads fall.

And then shite, the airborne articles follow him down, pots, pans, and a stone statue of Saint Brigit.

Bob the Enchanter, with hot words pouring from him, stops it all mid fall like. The debris hovers. Only the *Pavee* magician is pouring energy into the room. His eyes are bloodshot. Mealla is extending a circle, making it a hard mass over our heads. At her signal, Bob lets his leg down. We all duck anyway as the contents of the room fall. Mealla notes our reactions and insult-huffs.

"It's all down," I call to Mealla.

We look like war refugees. All of us grey-tinged with ancient building dust. Coughing up black sputum. All of us moving slowly and shaking off building bits like dogs. Dust motes have created a fog.

There's Rose saying something to me. I can't hear a thing over the ringing in my head, but I read her lips. My arm. I look. It's not hanging well. That's the stuff.

The deadly destruction of the building is neatly contained to the south side, but everything inside the rooms adjoining is a crushed, snapped, splintered version of its former self. There's no safe place.

The chapel. I climb and trip over the broken everything to get out of the dining room and into the church.

There are invisible recurring patterns of forces and light in the form of a spire in the front of the intact room. Not many can see the light patterns. I can. Probably the nuns here as well.

Whoa. High magic.

Low magic. That's the energy available to magicians, witches, sorcerers. It's all about the operator and connections. It works off the needs of the particular practitioner, and the power sources of the practitioner.

This is higher up the food chain. Within the spire's illumination I feel calmer, grand like. Rose comes in next. She gasps and then kneels. The light fades.

Rose and I, looking desperate, white-powdered, bruised, and broken, are refreshed. Not one of us is dead; we didn't burn the place down. The chapel is still a safe place. That looks like a good day for us.

Refreshed, but knowing. That all was, once again, precious close.

CHAPTER

TWENTY-SIX

Ceo dhraíochta
Irish mist

"They'll, whoever, just come in here to finish the job."

"I don't think they can afford to expend any more energy," says Mealla.

Bob sniffs the air. "Residual magic, but nothing active. Not to say there's nobody around in the minute."

"We can deal with humans," says Liam.

"Donal, take Padriac and get that arm improved," says Bob to a *Pavee* lad.

"And then what?" asks Mealla. She's looking the most banjaxed since we ran into each other. "We can't do this without some confidence." Like her's is waning.

I feel the room mentally leaving the cause, feeling beaten. Sure, if I'm honest I'm a bit there myself. They've had us from the get-go. It's all been us foundering hit by hit. I give the faces a once over. They're looking like they want the kettle lashed on and a duvet pulled up over their heads.

Rose is having none of it. She's still got a glow on. And she's raging inside. I can see it in the set of her heavy jaw. "They are expecting us before the ceremony. What if we wait until they're busy, doing the ceremony?"

I want to say, won't that make it too close to call? But I fear she'd eat me.

"All we'd need is a grenade." That's a *Pavee* lad thinking on his feet.

"We should split up as we leave. You stay with Bob, Mealla. The wolves with the nuns. I'm with the lads." We are going to have to be heroes, but heroes mostly die and are given metals, posthumously.

"Meet at the Springfield Halting Site," says Bob.

++++

To mend my arm, three young *Pavee* are driving an old banger, white Renault up the N20. I've been up here before. My arm hurts something awful; I smell the Heineken hops. I'm afraid going forward the aroma will be associated with pain in my mind.

Donal sprays gravel as he turns off the road and into a *boreen*. The lane climbs. At a high point, the car comes to a hard stop. One hand turning the steering wheel, Donal parallel parks into a space that if the car exhales, we wouldn't fit.

The lads pop the boot and grab an oxygen/acetylene torch. A short stroll down a grassy hill this time. Back to Lady's Well, the stair-free route. Up here, at the top of the hill, is *Pavee* territory.

I duck as three black birds fly over our heads. I watch them, my club ready. They alight onto the branches of scrub trees on the edge of the patch of lawn.

"They's just crows, so," says the *Pavee* lad.

"Sure," I retort, though I'm not sure. There's never sure.

The lads make two cuts, about a foot apart, to the middle section of the iron grate over the well. Then all round to make a cut-out big enough for my arm. Some final tugs, and the metal releases. This holy well is now open for business.

One of the lads sticks his hand down the hole. "Jaysus, the water's low." He sinks down to his shoulder, still reaching, pressing his body into the grate. Both of the lads glance at me, and then they break into laughter.

I say the words every Irishman says in this situation, "Feck off." Which makes every Irishman laugh more. But I have the last word. "I've been here, yesterday."

"Just kicking your hole."

"Yeah, not in the mood."

The bone is through the skin. It's painful to put my arm in the water. It's a holy well, not a clean well, and I'm thinking gangrene. Same routine. The relief is immediate. I'm grateful the wells are nearby. I slump against the grating, not from the pain relief, more like from something has gone right. It's a bit of hope when everywhere else it seems you're just running out of road.

+++

We've agreed to meet at the Spring Hill Halting Site that is up from Lady's Well. It's a bit over a mile further up the N20 and down the North Ring Road. If you ask anyone in Cork where the travelers have a massive halting site, they'd say, those slack shites, they're up the hill in Blackrock.

For one or two generations, the *Pavee* haven't been traveling much. Without having gotten into land, or house buying, ever, they own nothing but their car-pulled caravans.

Their traditions as seasonal labor have been shredded. They used to craft tin. Not anymore with mechanization, and industrialization.

The halting site is a collection of identical, battered metal homes on wheels with khaki stripes on their broad sides and with front picture windows. They were once an overall purer white. The picture framed within the picture windows is piles of junk.

There are traditional tow-behind caravans tucked into here-and-there corners. These haven't moved for a good many years. The area resembles stagnation, with the odd laundry line stretched across brimming potholes.

The halting site is on tarmac at the bottom of a quarry and is not far removed in looks from a tip yard. Two cars with flat tires mark the entrance road. I watch a car stop at the lip of the quarry and tip a load of rubbish down its rocky side. Lovely altogether.

Children run around, yelling at each other. A pony grazes in the only patch of grass. Dogs with dirty fur bark at me, as I follow the lads to a home only they can distinguish from the others in camp.

The tension of the magical energy of the place buzzes in my ears. The *Pavee*, each one, holds the power-magic of the old soul. The buzz is also the magical energy of belief. There's a spectrum of color that bounces off the occasional ray of sunlight.

The *Pavee* were one of the first people in Ireland. They know the *Tuatha* well. When Catholicism arrived, they embraced that too, and mixed the whole mess together. Not well liked as a group, there's the joke that traveler babies be used as shark bait or for testing new vaccines. So yeah, they stick together. They're faithful people. High magic from that faith shelters the place.

Used to be they traveled. Gathered here, in large numbers, and for so long, the magic is at saturation point. This is the place from which to fight a war of magic, I think.

And then a baby cries.

Inside, Bob takes hold of my arm, turning it, examining it. "Good job." After he gives my arm back to me, he ushers the lads and me to a red Formica table. I note a cupboard-sized room with a child's bed in it...with two pillows. Wall boards and the electrical wires behind them have been chewed. Probably by rats. Rain begins. The roof leaks.

Hanging from a hook in a corner is the Irish god, Manannan's Crane Bag.

The crane is imperturbable; patient to the point of dying from boredom and is associated with the *Cailleach*. It's a magical bird.

Pretty gagging that the skin of this bag came from Aoife, Manannan's son's mistress who got changed into a crane at some point. Pretty standard. The reason was jealousy. Really all the reasons for any action among the *Tuatha* are jealousy.

So given to Bob maybe, like my Ogma's knife? In it should be Manannan's knife, and smith's hook of Goibniu, the shears of the King of Alba, the helmet of the King of Lochlann, and the bones of Assal's pig. The bones connect back to Luchar.

Crane Magic is magic that kills.

I'm watching Bob in new light. Magic is what we're up against, and controlled magic is what we need. Not to be a Mealla-doubter, but magic is like herding cats and experience is a plus.

If we have a guy with a Crane Bag already here, and Mealla, already here; why squander precious energy on me?

Unlike Mealla and me, Bob invited himself to the dance. "What are you up to, Bob?"

"Same as you. Saving the world."

"Sure. With that crane bag, you're powerful. The only

reason I can think of that *I'm* here is that you didn't want the job.

"Here's what *I* want to know." He leans in. "You have the hand, the Ogma's knife, the Ogham's power. Who are you then, Padraic the Black? You'd have more power within yourself if you knew who that is."

When I'm feeling very hard done by, which has been most days of my life, it shows on my face, so people tell me. Bob starts laughing. I want to punch him. The feeling is so strong; I have to disengage, or I'll lose the complete run of myself.

"Here's who I am. I'm the Morrigan's tool."

Bob passes a packet of chocolate biscuits across the table. I smell the tea brewing. I concentrate on that, and not on kicking Bob's hole. He's sidestepped my questions, as the *Pavee* do. Is he with us? Shite. I don't know. But then who better in this world to side with?

"Are you on our side, Bob?"

"You need help with the *Slaugh*. There will be so many more than you battled before, and it's Saint John's Eve with the thin spaces even thinner. They will be at their most powerful. This fight, any fight, must be fair."

"To be honest, I'm not all that fond of fair."

"Padraic, you are like my old car out there. Reliable. I put it in drive, and it goes forward. I put it in reverse it goes backwards. When I don't oil it, it whines. You have a part in this. We all have a part in this."

"'So we go blindly and headlong to our tasks, the head helping the heart, and we deserve to win even if we lose.'"

The quote startles Bob, which I like. Maybe rejiggering his opinion of me.

Mealla walks in. She sits next to me and pokes my arm. She goes, "All better. We can take on the world." I glance at her, a little stunned. She has already regained her force of buoyancy. I look into her Biddy-blue eyes, take in her face. It hits me that she's too everything to be sacrificed. And if I can't keep her alive; if she can't keep herself alive, it will hurt me. She puts her arm around me and pats my shoulder as women do.

"We can do this."

"What are you on?"

She laughs.

I know what she's on, though. Herself. That practical-order, completion, internalization, strong and resilient in the face of tragedy part of her. That caring, fighting, nursing, bearing-up part that makes the world a better place, or dies trying.

"We're going to Crunch Fitness the dead bastards," I say in my let's-get-on-with-it voice. "The re-killing of a few million fairy *Sluagh* sounds about right. I have no notion of letting any of them resurrect."

"'Let us not grow weary of doing good,'" Mealla says into my ear.

"Galatians six-nine."

"So you were a priest."

The werewolves and two nuns walk into the mobile home. Sure, a brilliant set up to a joke that I will have to work on later. Let me add that I nearly fall off my seat at seeing Rose and the *Cruaidín Catutchenn* strapped to her side. The sword that can cut a man in half, without either half knowing. The mobile home is crowded with magical talent. We may be desperate, but we are there, and with our senses of humor. Let's wake the house.

Food is shared around as the lads carry in vats of holy water. We've scrapped the water bead guns and are going for super-soakers. Simple mechanism, but Bob enchants them from being bound anyway. We wet our clothes in the holy water. Freezing. The lads, all ten of them, look like they've robbed the Royal Irish Academy that houses medieval Irish weapons.

The *Pavee* scare me a little. And I want to run my hand over the weapons, feel their weight. Not just because they're so shiny, like.

We all have our wands. "I've heavily enchanted the *Luis*

Ogham into all our wands. It's a portal enchantment as well as protects against enchantment."

It is Saint John's Eve.

TWENTY-SEVEN

Nára bheire an mhaidin ort
That you may not see the morning

In Medieval times, on Saint John's Eve, Saint John's fire dotted every hilltop. The bonfires were a combination of wood and bone that repelled witches and evil spirits. There is a special power from the saint on this night, against the evil forces at work. Only Saint John may be upset with the current lack of rituals in his honor. He'll be a no-show.

The faithful in Ireland were a riotous blend of pagan-christianity. On this eve, we used to burn yarrow against evil. We'd walk, with torches lit from the bonfires, through fields to aid crop growth. In the morning, we walked animals through bonfire ashes to keep the livestock healthy.

On the night there were steaming pots of Goody on the fire, which was shop bread soaked in hot milk with sugar and spices. Bring your own spoon. Blessed Saint John's wort was spread, a plant used for depression. Pretty usual herb for a country constantly rained on.

But not tonight, any of it.

As we drive closer to University College Cork, I can't see a single fire this night in the hills around the city. The churches are shut due to a lack of personnel. No scent of burning yarrow.

"It's a very easy number for evil these days," I mumble from the back of the car. The evening is in good form so far, with an early moon showing. Pissing rain has let up with the clouds getting lighter and shifting north at an alarming rate, like they want to get the hell out.

We have to put in at the Poor Clare's car park. The gates to all roads in UCC are closed. Conversation is minimal as we walk the short distance down College Road. We are looking to be in position before sunset. The house will be warded, guaranteed. The air is redolent of a thinning veil, a whiff of sulphur, with a perfume of flowers. The *Slaugh* won't be here before midnight. So there's that, hopefully.

The house is dark. The campus quiet. For Mealla and Bob, finding the ambient magical energy will be easy tonight. Only the reaching-out-for-energy is itself a trigger, a marker of where we are.

In Ireland, the weather can go, all in one day, from Jack Frost on the car's windscreen, to the sun splitting the stones, to a wind cutting you in two, to a soft day, to a pissing-down, dirty, old day. Not surprising that the easiest spells to perform in Ireland are about weather or wind. An apprentice druid could do it.

With these more talented practitioners, we could be facing a straight-line windstorm with force winds, heavy rain and severe thunder. Our wee group has that strained-look about their shoulders and faces...waiting for what the shower-of-shites bring.

I'm squatting on the tarmac of a walking path sheltering behind a hedge and watching Mealla. Herself has copped on to magic, feeling it more intensely. There is a fire lit on the roof of the hellfire club. They're there.

We are hidden in the tall hedgerow, along a walking path through campus. At our backs is a steel ten-foot fence with spikes on top, which runs the length of the walkway to the river Lee, where presumably there are Ashrays. The access to the house from here is up broad cement stairs onto a paved, open courtyard area. Retreat will be sticky in all directions. The entrance from College Road is gated, but the lock has been picked.

The werewolves shift. "Start the Crane Magic," I call to Bob. He rises to one leg his arms out. Words form on his lips. He's absorbing magic and pushing it out, protecting us. The air glitters. I'm first, heading for the stairs.

Only Bob's magic triggers hell.

Clouds close in. Mist rises. We can't see each other. Bob chants louder.

The clap of thunder is so loud it vibrates against our bodies. Next the wind. Stereotypic shite. I'm off my feet. I glance back. The lads' faces are stretched, like they're on the descent after jumping out a plane and waiting to release the chute.

And all that is from Bob. "Tone it back a notch," I yell at the scut-magician. Like he can hear me. Jaysus.

I move, again, and when I say that, crawling, trying to avoid all the sailing debris. The wind is drying the holy water in our clothes. Good luck to the *Slaugh* in Bob's *Sluagh*-begone, no fly weather.

Behind me, and in a lull, like Bob's leg got tired, Mealla springs up, and does a mad rush for the building.

What the hell. Is she off her cake? Blow to the head?

"What are you doing?"

"I cracked the ward."

"Are you joking?"

"No, I'm not joking."

She's closing in on the house when the door opens. Coming out is my old friend, *Luchar*, and his brothers. So *Luchar*, *Brian* and *Lucharba*, the three-peat (repeat). They take what they want or die. Three-peatedly trying. They resembled each other once with their rock-hard, desiccated jaws, and matted, straw-like, long, blonde hair. Big blokes, they're still piss-takers, muscled, keen.

Luchar runs forward, drawing his sword. He is nursing a grudge. The other two follow screaming battle cries.

Mealla.

Every nerve ending of mine screams. I think I actually scream. I forget that she can throw up circles like soap bubbles. The protective covering absorbs his first blow. She's being hammered, strike after strike. Shite. Being forced backwards, she trips. Her concentration shifts.

But then Luchar sees me. Stupid ejit rushes me and leaves her there. Moving weightlessly, he dodges my swing after swing. I'm seething now. I can't see what's happening to Mealla. The arse just won't go down.

Only a slight breeze in the air now. What the hell, Bob?

It feels good to finally plant one hit on Luchar's jaw. In his wobble, I glance over. I expect to see Mealla on the ground, dead. I'm grateful to see the werewolves are there around her, biting and ripping out muscles and tendons.

The three gods won't die again lightly. They never have. The greater the battle, the more energy they have to draw from, the more furiously they fight. I'm cut from Luchar's sword but still upright, barely. Bracing my feet, I swing with all the strength of Ogma. The power of the hand, the power of the *geasa* flow together. "*Luis!* I roar at the bastard. The solid hit resonates up my arm. I watch as Luchar's face twists, and he is gone. Solid that.

I'm panting as I glance across the space. *Lucharba* slashes deep into Liam's thigh. Liam slashes through the muscles in the dead God's arm. Two other werewolves take cuts to their shoulders. It's a scrum.

Two *Pavee* lads punch Celtic knives into the gods; the two

bulls, pierced, and angry, but refusing to die. They are using up our time, and magical energy.

"Bob!" I roar.

I glance around for Mealla. She's near the house steps.

Then the *Sluagh* arrive, like an eclipse of all light, manmade or natural. By the thousands. They fly at us as a fast-moving dark, impenetrable cloud, which close up is skull after skull of rotting teeth and muscle. The bad breath alone could kill me.

The first one takes a direct back-to-hell with my blackthorn club and the word *Luis*. One touches my shoulder, and the holy water there burns it. Wet or dry, the magic works, brilliantly. The *Pavee* are in a water fight. The screech from the *Slaugh* as the holy water drenches them, deafens me. The corrupt vapor from water on *Slaugh* penetrates my ears and nose making them bleed.

My right arm is only moving by the power of Ogma. All I can think of: where is Bob, and what the feck is he doing? The nuns are to my right. I hear a SplatRGun fire. Rose slashes with her sword. My attention diverted, a *Sluagh* lifts me off my feet. This is what they do, carry live bodies until dead, or just get them too high to fall, and then let go.

I know the exact place to find my Ogma knife. I slash at the boney talons that grip me. The *Sluagh* are not used to their prey fighting back. I hit hard on the car park. "You shite- bastards," I call as I take out the water gun. I shoot rapid fire into the cloud. It thins to clear in the shot area. There are still more.

The wolves are fast, tearing with teeth and claw, holding their own. The nuns are using their wands now...out of water. As I watch, one nun is picked up by the arm. She's too much for the *Slaugh*, and she's dropped onto the roof of the crèche. Another is flung onto the spikes of the steel fence.

I'm going to kill Bob.

The lads look comfortable in their determination to slash *Sluagh*. Then I notice the *Pavee* lads are not being attacked but are only attacking.

The whole company is coughing, breathing *Sluagh*. My eyes are streaming. We've got to cut through this. I have to find Mealla.

Wind roars over us. *About time, Bob.*

The souls scatter. Then the barks of dogs. The hellhounds. What took them all so damn long? There *Slaugh* were there before midnight. That's why.

The night clears. Some stars twinkle. Recovery is oxygenated breath by breath.

I stumble as fast as I can to the house. I don't know where else to look. When I see dead *Sluagh* bones on the floor of the entry hall, I'm both stoked and afraid. I can't smell a thing, my nose is bleeding and inflamed, but I can see smoke. Where there's smoke there's fire; and where there's fire, there's Mealla and her salamander.

Water cascades down on me. The rooftop water tank. When I see them in the next world, I'll tell the Godsills their big fire extinguisher works.

I race to the roof. I have no idea what to expect at the top, a hellfire, Black Mass altar, Mealla as the sacrifice? If I get that far. The thought of her dead is sticky in my mind and is making me push my racked and hacking lungs to their limit.

When I see her coming down, relief makes me trip on a riser. "You OK?" I hear myself and think cliché. She answers anyway. "Gotta get out."

And then I think, feck, she's done it. I can't believe it, really. Too easy, like battling thousands of *Sluaghs* is easy, but.... Maybe she has owned up to her sorcerer potential and fried the practitioners with hellfire. Only there isn't a thumbs-up look on her face.

We stumble down the stairs. "It's not the right place," she says pushing out words. "It's not happening here. It's a red herring." Even as the words are choked up, she says them with the full-out passion of hot anger. Like that positive, faithful, strong, considerate-of-others, survivor person, who has been slammed against the wall one million times too many, has had enough. It's taken effort, but she's flat-out pissed.

"The *Sluagh* didn't leave just because of the hellhounds, or Bob," I hazard.

"Can't you feel it? They were magically let go. The practitioners need to consolidate their energies, gather power for the real event that is not here. The *Slaugh* have done what they needed to do. Kill us or instead of that delay us enough to not be of any consequence. Where's Bob?" she asks as we leave the house. And then she sees the nun and gasps. "What happened here? Is Bob dead?"

"Don't think so." I search for the lads. Gone. The nuns are with the dead.

Mealla knows what I'm thinking, and she looks like she could wake the house. "Ok, let's concentrate on if not here, fucking where?" Behind the hedgerow, I hear the werewolves finish off the two brothers. They howl in triumph.

That happy little nugget passes through Mealla and me. We nod an affirmation.

Sister Rose is walking towards us. "I'm so sorry," Mealla says, but Rose nods like she can't draw a breath to speak. She's messed-up looking herself. I saw her annihilating *Slaugh* in a way fables are made from. She indicates with her head to a red glow of magic in the sky.

We hot-foot it to our cars, which are gone. While Rose calls the Clares about the body of the nun, Constance breaks into and hotwires three banger cars. Without delay, I'm in a vehicle that is screaming at top gear up a side street, as we try to find the vibrating source of energy.

"Over the Lee and passed Lady's Well," Rose says as she guesses the prison. "It was Maxwell all along. They call him Sauron in the papers, you know. It was shocking the evil that gripped him. We thought with him in prison, he was one we didn't need to worry about. If anything, we thought, today they might try to break him out before midnight."

My nose pops open in the car. The smell off all of us is violent, and I wish it would close up again. I lay my head back, at the same time holding it steady as Constance drives the last miles to Cork Prison. The pressure of magic is hot, sticky, and pressing in like a well-fitting leather glove on a steaming day. I'm thinking, there's no drink like the next drink, hoping there'll be a next drink.

"It's going to be a mortal, tough fight," I say. "And we have to get in there first. It is a prison."

"Protected from us."

Liam howls.

The race through the streets seems to flip reality into slow motion. Three days ago, I was going to my friend's birthday feast hoping for some good food and wine. I was a bit player in the eyes of the gods, in the game we played.

It concusses the brain when life throws a punch, and you missed the duck. I hear the whine of the cosmos in the car's engine. I feel in the speed of the car as a metamorphic shift. I feel Constance doing her thing, weaving, taking turns and assessing just how much the tires can take. Speeding, slowing, watching for gaps. Her eyes are laser-focused. Her mind calm. Constance. I let that essence find me. Because in this century or another, it really is the same old shite. With the same old shites.

Speaking of old shites, I guess the magician responsible for the kaiju, Bob.

I glance at the faces around me. Frightened but determined. It's a pleasure to know these people. When change is a bitch, and then you die, hell, these are great people to stand beside.

TWENTY-EIGHT

Naomh
Saint

I 've always thought there'd be a sequence of events at the
end of a life. The moment fallibility has consequences. The
wrong choices, or place, or time.

Life has an inbuilt fail button. Same for magic, wrong
choices, place or time have consequences. We are too close. My
mother got too close.

Choices, place, time, the Morrigan's son. She was quick to
see the opportunity there. Opportunity that leads to this last
night run though modern Cork to face the anti-good. She has
always been smarter than I.

I still have the have nightmares of her son slicing off my
hand, the pain, the blood. Fourteen I was. I flex my Ogma hand.
I feel the warmth of the magic there swirling against my wrist.

I also feel, there at my wrist, the energy of Ogma's magic
pressing against the dam of my humanity. I will the barrier
because if I let the magic flood into me, it would bind me. I'm

bound enough. Letting it in, the magic, wouldn't keep me alive. I can still die in this fateful, disastrous sequence of events. I'd just do it with slightly better results.

It's within the last sounding bells of midnight, that we are racing up Patrick's Street in the center of Cork, the tall crane-like streetlamps dripping rain. The wet pavement shines in the flood of light of the prison car park.

There's no wind pushing the rain onto the windscreen of the car. Buckets of it coming down now. It's graveyard quiet except for the flump, flump of the wipers. I feel magic tightening into a great, black cloud above me, pressing down. What I can't feel is the counteracting repel of bones and wood bonfires that used to be on every hillside. I can't smell the burning yarrow to ward against evil when the veil thins. Just because you don't believe in demons, doesn't mean they're not there. Midnight, on Saint John's Eve, charged with magical energy, the energy of the supernatural, has arrived.

And we are locked out of the prison.

As Buttermilk always thought we'd be, we are late for the party.

Mealla stands close to me. Her tense face is highlighted by strong security lamps. "Go to the light," she jokes.

She may be thinking joke, but there's a hard punch to that statement, and it hits me between the eyes. "He's aging. Maxwell, and infirm. He arrived to court in a wheelchair. Why go to all this trouble for a few years of power?"

"I said that," says Mealla.

"You are correct. I agree. I don't think he would. So, not many ways to become immortal. Drink a compound? They don't have one. Deal with the devil? Trading one master for another; they want personal control."

When it comes to me I think it so obvious that I'm kicking my hole that I didn't think of it before. "What is the magic of priests?" I ask my audience. "I'll remind you, transubstantia-tion, the changing of an earthly substance into god. The exterior stays the same; the substance changes. Maxwell isn't calling a demon. He's changing the substance of himself into something or someone else."

"That can't be possible," exclaims Constance. Only I watch her face drain of color. They hadn't realized it either. I only just got there by accident.

Mealla's there. She says, "Whatever he's turning into, it's got to have a built-in get-out-of-jail-free."

The building looks squat, modern, and ordinary. Still, the prison is locked tighter than a walnut around its soft center. In the midnight silence, the magical generation in that walnut is unmistakable.

"Feel it?"

She nods. "Like downed electrical lines in water.

It's stopped raining, or the cloud of energy is acting as an umbrella. Out of the car, my ears pick up the unmistakable chant of the *Imbas Forosnai*. "Shite. Liam. Hear it?"

"The ritual used by the druids to invoke altered states of consciousness," Liam responds. "His fellow practitioners are here."

"How are we going to get in?" That's Rose. The backup, werewolf car has arrived. In the thirty or so minutes to get here, the werewolves are all healed.

"Oh, hell, let's just crack-on, as you say here in Ireland. I can't bear the suspense," Mealla says as the nun's car arrives. "Maybe just knock on the door."

"And say, with just that bit of a laugh, that there's ceremony going on inside we need to get to."

The clouds part and an unexpected moon glares at the earth. I glance at Mealla, and she glances back. It's just the beginning of magical, adrenaline-fueled madness. I'm inhaling the ozone of scorched air, tasting it on my tongue.

Mealla inhales and exhales. "Ok, ok," she blows out, centering for the task at hand. It's all mental. "How *do* we get in? These are twenty-four feet walls that…" she had googled in the car ride over, "…were pre-manufactured and assembled by crane, a feature that won the builder the tender.

"That door doesn't lead directly to the cells, would it? Regular lock maybe?" asks Constance.

We stroll the yards to the front door like it's a normal day. Only the sky is yellow around the floodlights, like before a tornado. "Jaysus, I have a throat on me," I say as if it's a stroll to the pub. I glance at Rose. She's looking flah'ed out like.

All of the sudden here's no worries about getting in, because the door slams open. The security guards are legging it out. Sirens pierce the air to match me own voice screaming in me own head. It's the sound of madness, when all the big lads with badges and guns are running out, and we're walking in. Never better. The werewolves shift.

Inside is a white-bricked reception area and canteen, with a glass atrium overhead, and a play area. "Nice," Mealla says like she's seen worse, another story altogether. The hardness of the blue, cement floor, throughout, is magnifying the cries of the prisoners, left in their cells, even though the heavy walls and thick doors.

It's just that loud.

Staff escaped; the doors are gaping-wide open. No one bothered to close the doors behind them. Mealla is stepping through a door that will take us deeper inside. An ultrasonic boom pushes back on her. The drug dogs bark at us from their kennel down a hall.

I go first this time past some workshops. I stop at the door before the cell area. The hinges are blown, but the lock held.

The shite will be finished by the time we get there.

"We don't know what's on the other side," Mealla says the obvious.

Liam growls like he's back to the days of the *Fianna* and destiny. Then he feckin' tears the locked door off its frame.

It's the escape of heat that hits us first, and then the gale force wind of noise. I feel sweat spring geyser-like from my pores.

All of it, the storied decks and their white tubular-steel railings, the mesh steel paneled courtyards ring with the sound of detritus being thrown by prisoners yelling to get out. The new enamel paint is beginning to peel. The air is suffocating. Fluorescent lights flicker. Mealla hesitates. I'm relieved.

"The place is structurally sound. Concrete, brick cement. The construction could contain a grenade."

She points up. I take in the arching glass roof.

A new breed of hostelry. "Ye give 'em something nice, and there's always some demented fellow to take advantage."

TWENTY-NINE

Ámhghar le teine
Ordeal by fire

It really is a smashing prison, fresh paint...gleaming. The City of Cork is not going to be jacked if it's blown. Me either...at being under a shite-storm of glass. We are moving forward as a tight bunch according to the hot and cold game; hotter approaching the center of magical energy and more danger, cooler, we're inclined to breathe a bit easier.

Closer in, a dynamic pattern of spectrum, magical light, that's shifting from rays, to spirals, is obvious. Transubstantiation magic. Bob did his job. We are too late.

His fairness code of ethics, my arse. I don't know if the *Pavee* are paid mercenaries like, or if they have their own agenda. I'll ask Bob when I'm beating his head into the ground.

Who was it that said, no battle survives contact with the enemy. Well, here it is, the enemy, the beginning of the terrible blending of worlds. The light is not photon particles, but the GrandOther mixing into our world.

We round the corner and gasp to a man, or women as we are blinded by the light. When my retina adjusts, I see one man transubstantiating within a surging of release of magic. The immortal hour. I laugh, a terror-filled, mental reaction. Unleased magic is glowing. The world is realigning, and we have to stop it.

Evil. Hell. Madness. That's what's in front of me. My heart grows icy, no mean feat in this hothouse. Maxwell is controlling who he is becoming. I know, he should know he won't contain who his is becoming, just like all those other burned-out, stone-mad practitioners. It's all hubris.

We watch Maxwell stuff bloodied flesh into his mouth, as part of the ritual to achieve an altered state. The ritual chanting, that was outside, with the doors ajar, is coming inside. From all the moaning that's started up Maxwell's in pain. I'm guessing transubstantiation has never been comfortable.

Perfect time to finish him off; before whatever is next, while he's distracted, and while the supporting practitioners are busy chanting.

A cloud of colored lights, as in tiny hail stones, fall and stick with bug feet to our hair, skin, and clothes. The lightning bugs, are injecting pure fire into my skin. Thousands, and more coming. A swarm of hellfire. As we slap ourselves silly, there's laughter. I know that laugh.

On the floor above us, Laurent has been set free. To frighten us, his spellcasting words are magnified to fill the space. "They are afraid and doomed. Brightness is upon us! Circling left-ward, I curse them! My fire will not falter until the victory is won!"

What victory? Ye punter.

"It's a death curse. He'll start firing when it's up to power." I slap my face and then my neck. "Flank him," I say to the were-wolves. "Round three with this arsehole. Constance points her wand. His attention pivots to her. He smiles.

I feel the power of death the monk has gathered in and

around him. When he gets around to discharging it, when it hits her, within seconds, the wall of her body will explode and aerosol. I've spent my whole life, and all my talents, trying to *not* be in a champion-hero sort of place. Bugger-all champions as tools was my motto. That does flash into my mind, as I shove Constance out of range, and take the hit with my blackthorn.

The discharge is shite-hot with energy. The wood of the club is turning to ash. That sweat stings my eyes, I need to ignore. My human fingers burn. I grip the blackthorn club with my Ogma hand, as I remember why, I...Hate...Magic.

This kind of power might take more than the call-out of a single Ogham letter. While I'm connected to Laurent through magic I shout, "Death goes from me to my foe: Before the One God: Before the people of the *Sídhe*: Before the God Ogma I swear, by the broiling fire inside me. By the power of the Ogham, by the power of *Luis* and the pentagram within the seed of the rowan tree, be ye trapped in the thorn of this this wood."

I have never spellbound my blackthorn club before. I was taught by Scathach, but I wasn't any good. To be honest, I thought it sounded stupid. I include all the Gods because at death's door, why wouldn't you. One of them has to be home. Feck 'em.

In the smallness of a second, as Laurent pauses to draw more energy, a singer in-taking a breath, like, I think to call on the *lunantisidhe* to take care of this thorny problem. A corpse-like scent wafts when a thorn breaks off the club. The thorn charges towards the monk.

All he has to do is duck. His vision might be murky. Or his control of his new, untethered body slow. I'm sure resurrection has its weaknesses. He does move, but too late, and in the wrong direction. His cry sounds as cross as a bag of feral cats. The shape of a pentagram flashes and eats him alive. There's an easy keg at least that I owe the fairies of the blackthorn tree. Maybe a brewery.

In the meantime, Maxwell is reaching an enormous size. He is no longer the short, old, fat priest, with the well sprayed comb-over. He's now a huge, fat, old priest, with a slightly crooked comb-over. He is now decked out in a horned, bull-hide cape, and in a bird mask. Feck it, you almost have to laugh. The plumage is brightly colored of fire, hellfire. He holds a star-speckled, black shield with a silver rim, and is riding in a chariot.

"What the hell?" I hear Mealla exclaim.

"Only the substance changes. Not the exterior."

"He has come with props." She's the only one who would say that, though. The rest of us recognize the *roth rámach*, a chariot that blinds those who look upon it, deafens anyone who hears it, kills anyone who strikes it.

"The Blind Druid," says Rose.

The Blind Druid is engorging on magic, like a big fat leach. His breath causes storms and turns a person to stone.

"From Femoy," I add.

Liam growls.

Maxwell's face is ecstatic, like he's seen a radiant vision. He is a vision, not a bit radiant though.

Eyeballing us, his mouth a smirk of gloating narcissism, he says, "So is the beginning. It begins here, where the passage between worlds is porous. This land marked with thousands of wells, dolmans, passage tombs, and stone circles." His voice is as helium-inflated as he is. It's loud but not booming. It's like a built, muscled man whose voice skipped puberty.

While he's word-bombing us with shite, the chanting practitioners move in. They don't need to chant any more. Rose, Constance, Vianney circle to flank Blind Druid. The werewolves take on the practitioners.

Mealla and I have to hold his attention, and act when necessary. If we're lucky, he's like Mealla, all powerful, but rusty to the Blind Druid thing. I hope to take advantage of his celebratory orations, and his lack of real-time experience. He will want us to know how this happened, how clever he is first, before he kills us. That's how all the movies go. How he is justified. That will buy us time.

Also, how blind is the Blind Druid?

He quits prognosticating. Shite, I whistle to direct his attention towards me. I have a whistle so piercing that dogs will attack me.

"I heard that you were a very good priest. You helped people." Always go for the ego. I dictate to Mealla, "If this goes bad, you and that salamander, burn down the whole place if you have to. Don't let him breath on you. Watch out for the chariot."

The boyo is not biting, he's inhaling. I take a quick gander at Mealla and see the fireball in her hand. She throws. The Druid exhales. The nuns go for his junk. It's a women's thing, and it's all they can reach.

Behind the werewolves are clawing, biting and tearing.

I'm thinking we've beat the odds, as Mealla and I hit the floor, to let his, druid-breath pass over us. The thought barely finishes in my brain before Murphy's Law, what can go wrong will go wrong, enacts.

Maxwell, the vessel for this transubstantiation blows apart. Bits of intestine hit my face. Shite. I wipe my eyes and glance up. Constance and Vianney hit the wall, and then the Blind Druid, the real Blind Druid, breathes on them. Turned to stone. My geasa flares.

Uncontained, the Blind Druid breathes up hurricane wind, rain, and lighting, that whips the interior space breaking the glass roof. Mealla called it.

I split from her side. Can't give him a two for one. She is reciting spells, maybe to put him to sleep. He's watching her.

Rose is there. On an inhale, she runs, leaps, with her sword out ready for his black heart. It's an Ave Maria move. I'm sure she's praying. I'm praying. His peripheral vision picks up the movement. I'm closing in on him now, about to septic his arse with a pitch from a floor below.

Her sword thuds ineffectively on scales. The Druid has shapeshifted into a Scottish *Beithir*, the largest and most deadly of serpents with a venomous sting. The old religion loves their shapeshifting. We are so effin' effed. The only way to cure a bite from a *Beithir* is in water, which already has the head of a serpent in it.

He breathes both fire and stone at Rose. Mealla throws a circle to surround the nun. Mealla screams as the fire burns the circle, and then turns the circle to stone. Rose is entombed.

I wave my blackthorn club over my head, drawing the mouth of the serpent down on me. Buying time, as I watch Liam and Sean peel away from the fight with the practitioners. I distract the creature, playing wack-a-mole with its head, as they close in on the dragon. Too many near misses of hot breath and fangs before they throw themselves onto the mountain of scales, heading for its throat.

The monster writhes and reaches. It blows out breath. Cell doors, walkways, walls, and probably inmates turn to stone. The Beithir twists and strikes its back against the chariot. Liam and Sean smash into it. The chariot that kills anyone who strikes it. The Druid gives them a glance for good measure. Killing, blinding, stoning, done.

"Stop this waste of life," The Beithir declares. "You cannot win. I would have you on my side, the side of Old Ireland and of the old Church." As if to prove his intent, The Blind Druid shifts back into human form, with astericks. He's radiant, god-like. All I'm thinking about is how to get his arse to hell.

The Blind Druid was a student of Simon Magus, Simon the Sorcerer, who taught him his magic skills. Another chancer, Simon, He tried to buy his way into the magical power of the first twelve Apostles.

And now Maxwell, the thick-o, wanting to be a tiny god. Look where it got him.

The Blind Druid relaxes. He knows we can't beat him. He once defeated a coven of druids in an elaborate magical battle.

"I get it, now," I spit at him. The Irish gods don't like uppity druids."

If the Irish Gods are afraid, of this moron, I should be, but the *geasa* is engorging my veins. I've lost track of Mealla, the practitioners, the werewolves, and myself. My geasa only cares about one thing. As I let him talk, I am spellbinding my hawthorn club. I pour the power of the geasa into it. The power of the goddess of death. I invoke the Ogham letter *Tinne*, for holly. As I recite the words, I see the Ogham letter carved into the damaged club glowing. I let that power feed my *geasa* to a height of personal destruction.

Holly is more than a unity of courage, a protection of warriors, it is a conductor. My blackthorn club becomes a lightning rod.

The Druid senses the power I'm gathering. He sees the resolve in the hate in my eyes. He shapeshifts again.

I hurl the magic at the Druid where it will hurt most, in his big ego.

Just as he exhales out.

The clash blows back onto both of us. His roar of pain creates a high velocity wind with electrical energy. The hawthorn Ogham letters absorb the hit. It is reducing the club to ashes. My Ogma's hand burns. I feel like I'm on fire, and my organs boil.

I reach inside for energy, for anything left. I think of Scathach willing me on, making me find my limits. I hear myself say to her that I can't, and she saying back that I can. It's down to rage and a geasa that was always there to see me dead.

I try to straighten through the pain, to take one last probably futile shot. And then some flying thing banks low over my head, upsetting my balance. I glance up to see a blazing giant salamander, going into a sharp turn. It's breathing smoke in its approach. The *Beithir* breathes out, but hasn't time between changing and battle to aim and misses. In one exhalation of deadly magical fire, the salamander fries the shapeshifted druid into ash.

I watch it soar away into the black night. I look for Mealla. She's not here.

THIRTY

Amadán
Fool

There's shock that sets in at the end of these ordeals. Exhaustion as your arms fall to your sides, and there's adrenaline decay. Even worse is when all function is gone and death seems preferable. It's when your brain surveys the mess and thinks what the feck was that all about? When your wits are scattered because malevolence has residue beyond the physical.

How long had it been minutes, a lifetime. Mealla knew…she knew with the nuns entombed she didn't have time to spare for them to live. No time to put anything to sleep or to command a magical creature. She knew this creature had human will so she just reduced it to ash.

The prison is burning. Smoke alarms blare, sprinklers sprinkle. Fresh rain is bucketing through the broken ceiling.

The Druid gone, so goes his magical control. Stone dissolves as if water-washed. Rose, Constance, and Vianney gasp with their first inbreathe. Liam and Sean, the killing magic of the chariot slower than their healing capabilities as werewolves, revive.

I search through the broken ceiling for Mealla. Maybe she's flying back to Canada. I would.

Gathered, but now uncontrolled residual magic expends itself in a final burst of energy as an explosion. The werewolves struggle to protect the nuns they are carrying, as we are all struck by the force. My nose hits the cement floor. I see, but don't hear the inmates at their cell doors. I go for them, but Liam grabs me. "I hear emergency services coming," he says into my face.

Outside, Liam and Sean crush the video cameras, then they shift. All the werewolves are already looking like it was all a very easy number, as their features begin to bloom with health and vigor.

I'm cut, wet, cold, bruised, mentally busted. My Ogma's hand is throbbing, the wrist it's attached to, engorged-veined and bloody, but it could be worse.

The stolen cars are still there in front of the prison. There's a joke in there somewhere.

I keep looking up.

"Sure, you know her. She's well able," Liam says as he starts the engine. The other wolves are tucking nuns into the back. The windscreen wipers flip across the glass, but rain fills in before they can flip back again. You wouldn't put the dog out in it.

$$\cancel{\text{\textbar\textbar\textbar}}$$

"Come in to me," says Buttermilk at the door of the convent. By habit, I am in the dining room. Buttermilk puts glasses, and a bottle of Jameson on the table.

"God, we made a right balls of that."

"It's all sorted." She doesn't believe that, and neither do I.

It's triage here. Painkillers are being washed down by whiskey. Nurses, from the Bon Secours convent, treat our wounds. The smell of disinfectant overrides the smell of whiskey. They put us to bed.

Still no Mealla.

I have come to appreciate the sound of this convent in the morning. The music of prayers, of pots and pans, of table-ware, and of the clinking of lids on teapots. Teapots that's belly are full of hot, black, strong tea. Comforting. Normal. Not alone.

The wolves have beat me to the table. They've probably done a five-k run before breakfast.

"She back?" I ask.

"She is," Liam answers.

The words are life-affirming bubbles floating into my heart. She's always been good with throwing circles.

By lunchtime, Mealla is still sleeping. Liam drops the bottles of beer in his arms onto the table. As I'm reading the label, he says with the certainty of a man who knows his beer, "Beithir Fire is the world's strongest beer. It's medicinal." He twists off a bottle cap and puts the bottle under my nose. "Drink that down for your health." He passes the rest around and drags out a chair and sits. I'm there with the werewolves, Rose, Constance, Vianney, Buttermilk, comfortable.

When Mealla walks in the half-consumed bottles are forgotten, some midway from table to mouth. All eyes are on her. Her stroll from the door to table must have felt an eternity to her, with all our eyes fixed on her, as if she could breathe fire, which she can.

"I'd like one of those if I may," she says as Sean pulls over a chair for her. She tips up the beverage and guzzles down half its contents.

"I always said she could drink off a sore foot," says I.

"I always said where there's fire there's Mealla," adds Buttermilk.

Mealla laughs.

"You almost good?" I ask.

"I have no idea."

"So a flying, fire breathing salamander."

"Amazing, huh?"

"It sounds amazing." Ok, I can't help the smirk.

The nuns in the kitchen, in the halls...the whole convent empties into the dining room.

Sure, Sister Rose calls it then, when she starts the clapping, and then we're all patting ourselves on the back.

Another round of Beithir Fire is opened.

"If a mythical snake is killed, the head must be separated from its body and destroyed. If not, its parts will come together and it will live again," says Liam. "Nothing to worry about there." He toasts Mealla.

"The viper is gone," She agrees.

"How about the *geasa*? Gone?" Asks Liam. "What was it again? I never heard the whole thing."

"Under obligation to let no man put me off my road. Let me not refuse combat to any."

"Desperate. Is it gone then?"

"Burned out...pretty sure."

Glasses raised. "Sláinte."

"The practitioners are going to become more creative." says Liam. "Vampirism, immortality, not a stretch for some of them. Or maybe the exorcists taking control of the demons."

Mealla finishes her second bottle. "I should start a line of apotropaic items. There's a market to vanquish magic now." She reaches for a third, but Liam grabs it out of her reach. "Pretty strong stuff. I'll get you some food."

"Food? Yeah, maybe. I've been sick to my stomach from the glut of magic, or maybe it was the shapeshifting. Have you ever seen a fiery, winged salamander vomit? Have you ever heard a giant, winged salamander vomit? How do you guys do it so seamlessly?"

"Years of practice. Remember your first time, Sean? It was ugly."

She seems good. I relax a bit more.

A few days later, Mealla insists that we visit the Kindred Spirits: Choctaw Native American Monument outside Midleton. "It's the Irish commemorating the donation of money by the Choctaw to Irish famine relief in the eighteen hundreds. Poor giving to the poor. A bonding," she explains.

In a circle, like they are dancing together, are colored, stainless-steel feathers, twenty feet high.

"My dad talks about this," says Mealla. He's not Choctaw, but he's impressed that the tribe gave the Irish people one hundred and seventy dollars in the Famine times in Ireland in the late eighteen hundreds, when the British were starving the population to death. Your enemy is my enemy. It was a lot of money for that time, and for a people in poverty themselves, and just after the Trail of Tears.

The Choctaw weren't the only ones. Many tribes sent money to Ireland, the Cherokee Nation as well, but the Choctaw were first. Do you know that the Lac Court Oreille band of the Ojibwe gave an Irish president a headdress, and he gave them thirty-eight caliber guns? How about that? My dad really likes the Irish, obviously. I think he was hurt by my mother, but she couldn't live on the reservation, and he didn't want to leave."

She smiles. I'm glad she's alive. I still have nightmares.

"Not that the Irish are *that* pure. Edward Doheny made his money as an 'Indian Killer." She laughs. "It's never simple."

"It never is."

And it isn't in this case too. Mealla was too busy shifting and saving us and all that, to notice in the chaos, the torn veil, and in the magical saturation, the veil being breached. She didn't feel him. I did. A moment of insanity. Hard to single out considering the chaos except the split second feeling was heart stopping.

The entity the Irish gods hoped to control as the practitioners were blowing holes in the veil. Not the Blind Druid. That was on me. And anyway, they know how to deal with druids.

It's Himself, their biggest fear, the name they can't say, slipping through the holes and rips of the veil. Of course he did. Where else would he be in all this, the dark fairy, bringer of madness by a single touch. The Amadan.

I was to shut this all down quickly before the veil became too tattered. They made a right bags of that, too late and undermanned. A lack of communication. Even Luchar found his way in three times. Brutal.

The hoor gods and the very bad fairy of dementia on the loose on this side of the veil, there's not enough alcohol in the world to deal with that sort of carry on. What's to happen next? Absolutely no feckin' idea. But I have my *Fianna*, my warrior band, and one of them breathes fire.

Don't miss out on your next favorite book!

Join the Satin Romance mailing list
www.satinromance.com/mail.html

THANK YOU FOR READING

Did you enjoy this book?

We invite you to leave a review at your favorite book site, such as Goodreads, Amazon, Barnes & Noble, etc.

DID YOU KNOW THAT LEAVING A REVIEW...

- Helps other readers find books they may enjoy.
- Gives you a chance to let your voice be heard.
- Gives authors recognition for their hard work.
- Doesn't have to be long. A sentence or two about why you liked the book will do.

ABOUT THE AUTHOR

Julie G Murphy, has a M.A. in Writing Popular Fiction from Seton Hill University and a certificate in short story writing from LongRidgeWritersGroup®.

Her first book, *Flipping Rich Bastards*, was voted 1st place by a judge in the Helen McCloy Mystery Writers of America Scholarship for Mystery Writing; and from four others, it was awarded two thirds and a fourth.

She has two other books, a romance, *Western Knight*, a Melange Books/Satin Romance, and a YA utopic, *As If Something Happened*, published by TouchPoint Books.

She taught English as a second language in Nagasaki, Japan, and has lived in Ireland for two years, with her Irish husband. She went to sea with him on British Petroleum oil tankers. She was born in Idaho, the granddaughter of Spanish Basques, and spent one year with Boise State University in the Basque country in Spain. She now lives in Idaho and Florida.

With her publications and her master's degree in Writing Popular Fiction, she has taught seminars. She is a professional member of Florida Writers Association that connects professional writers with promotional work.

Connect with Julie:

Juliegmurphy@gmail.com
juliegmurphy.wpcomstaging.com

f facebook.com/juliemgaldos
X x.com/Juliemurphy@juliegmurphy1

ALSO BY JULIE G. MURPHY
WITH SATIN ROMANCE

Ogham Magic Series

Wild Hunt

Novels

Flipping Rich Bastards

Western Knight